SENDOFF FOR
A SNITCH

THE JESSE DAMON SERIES

SENDOFF FOR A SNITCH

KM ROCKWOOD

A Jesse Damon Crime Novel

WILDSIDE PRESS

For Aunt Mary,
who always had a mystery novel to read.

Published by Wildside Press LLC
www.wildsidepress.com

CHAPTER 1

Spats of freezing rain pelted me as I hurried home from my overnight shift at Quality Steel Fabrications. I was cold, hungry, tired, and pretty sure that a shower would be a good idea before I got too near to other people. If I hurried, I had time for that, a shave, and a quick nap before the appointment this afternoon with my parole officer.

The late winter sun rose over the horizon and tried to peek through a gap in the lowering clouds, then abandoned the effort as the gap closed. Great. It had rained hard most of the night, and it would probably be raining again when I had to hoof it across town to the parole office.

Rothsburg was an old industrial town on the river that had landed on hard times as most of the factories had moved south, and it didn't spend a lot on infrastructure improvements like drainage, especially in the part of town where I lived. My work boots were already damp from navigating the wet streets.

My apartment—room, really—was in the basement of a dingy building that had originally housed a pizza parlor, and more recently a struggling church, although I hadn't seen any activity there lately. Outdoor steps with an inadequate overhang led down from the sidewalk to my front door. Nobody's idea of luxury housing.

But it would do. And it sure beat the prison cell where I'd been living just a few months ago.

I slowed as I approached the steps that lead from the sidewalk to my front door.

Someone was sitting on them, halfway down.

It was a kid, leaning up against the brick wall of the building. He had on a bright orange fluffy vest with garish purple stars. That was layered over a tan fleece jacket. On his head, he had one of those knit hats with hanging tassels that looked like they'd been made by a Peruvian highlander in the Andes, only with a furry lining. Sitting on that damp concrete had to be cold. The seat of his pants was probably soaked through.

What was a kid doing sitting on my steps?

Stopping at the top and grabbing onto the handrail, I said, "Hey, dude, what're you doing here?"

He looked up at me. I'm not good with kids' ages, but my sometimes girlfriend had a six-year-old and an eight-year-old, and this kid looked bigger than that. At least ten? Maybe older.

His face was blotchy, and his eyes were red and swollen. His nose was running, and he wiped it with the sleeve of his jacket, leaving a slime of snot.

"Are you Jesse, mister?" he asked, his voice catching in his throat. He coughed.

"Yeah,"' I said. "You looking for me for something?"

His shoulders heaved as he took a shuddering breath. "I didn't know where else to go," he said. "And I remembered you lived here."

Interesting. I didn't remember ever having seen this kid before. "Where are you supposed to be?" I asked him. "It's Friday. Don't you have school?"

"I guess," he said, wiping his nose again with the sleeve. "But that's way across town, and I don't know how to get back there."

Hard to make much sense of that answer, so I asked, "How did you get here?"

"My brother brought me. And he told me to wait in the truck. But it's been hours, and he never came back. I remember he talked about you, and he said you lived in this little rathole in the basement. He pointed it out to me once."

He wasn't the first person to use the word "rathole" to refer to my place. "And who," I asked, "is your brother?"

"Aaron Stenski. He works with you. When he goes to work."

Ah. Aaron. I don't know that I knew the last name. But I knew who he was talking about. Not somebody I'd want to trust with a kid. I looked around. The battered blue pickup truck Aaron usually drove didn't seem to be anywhere on the deserted street.

I'm a sucker for kids, especially stranded kids. I remembered what it felt like. Too many times, I'd been the kid waiting while some over-worked social worker tried to find an emergency foster placement. Any emergency foster placement. I'd sit in a hard chair in the social services office, all my belongings stuffed in a plastic garbage bag, wishing I could just fade away and never again have to worry about where I was going to be sent or whether the people there would be kind or cruel. Or even worse, indifferent.

Those people were only in it for the monthly check. Not something I'd wish on any kid.

Pulling my keychain with its single key from my pocket, I said, "We'd best get inside. The rain's getting harder, and it's cold out here."

I went down the stairs, slipping past the kid, and opened the door.

He didn't move.

"You gonna come in?" I asked. "Or stay out here in the weather?"

Looking uncertain, he said, "I'm not sure I'm supposed to go into your place. I mean, Aaron says you're a convicted murderer. Is that true?"

"Yeah." I tried to sound reasonable, as if there's any way to respond reasonably to a statement like that. "But you knew I was a convicted murderer when you came over here, so what's the difference if we talk outside, or go in where at least it's not as cold?" I wasn't going to say where it was warm, because my apartment usually couldn't be called warm. But it was usually dry and not drafty. And as long as I paid the rent, it was mine.

Reluctantly, the kid got to his feet and took a step down toward me. "Ya know, we're not supposed to talk to people we don't know," he said. "At school, they're always telling us we should never get in a car or go into a building or anywhere like that unless we know the people we're with."

"What do they tell you to do?"

"To run away. Find a police officer. Or a lady with kids."

"Sounds like a plan to me. Find a police officer. Or a lady with kids. Run away." If he did either of those things, I could stop worrying about him. "I'm not trying to stop you."

He swiped the sleeve across his nose again. How much snot could one sleeve handle?

"I looked," he said. "I didn't see anybody like that."

"There's a police substation a few blocks down there and two over. To the left." I pointed down the street. "You can prob'ly find a police officer there. And they'll call your mother or somebody to come get you."

"Aaron will be mad if I go to the police."

"I imagine he would be."

Aaron wasn't exactly an upstanding citizen, and he was on very familiar terms with the local police. "Look, kid." I was cold and getting colder. And running out of patience. "I never had no skin charges brought against me, if that's what you're worried about."

He frowned and looked back over his shoulder, up at the sidewalk.

Reminding myself that this was a kid, I tried to think of another way to phrase that. He knew to be careful of strangers, and if he lived with Aaron, he couldn't be totally sheltered. "I'm not a sex offender. That's what they mean by 'stranger danger.' You can check me out on the sex offender registry when you get home if you want. It's on the Internet."

He sat down again and shoved his hands into his pockets.

A few more drops of rain fell. "You can either come in here and tell me what's going on and why you thought finding me might be a good idea, or you can leave." I opened the door wider. "Or even just sit there if that's what you want to do. But I'm going inside."

Standing and taking a big sniff, he came down the last few stairs and followed me into the apartment.

The single room wasn't huge, but it was much bigger than a six-by-eight-foot cell. And I didn't have to share it with anybody. One corner was walled off for a bathroom. In another, under the high window that looked out on an alley, was a standard five-foot-long kitchenette with an under the counter refrigerator, narrow sink, two electric burners, and a few cabinets. It wasn't fancy, but it worked.

I hung up my jacket on a hook and put water in a pan on a burner to heat up. The kid sat in one of the two rickety chairs at my equally rickety kitchen table. It was shoved up against the wall by the kitchenette.

"You know my name," I said, "but I don't know yours."

"Benji." He wiped his nose again with his sleeve.

I took the two steps over to the bathroom, reached in, and pulled out a roll of toilet paper. Putting it on the table, I said, "Use this instead of your sleeve."

He tore off a long strip and held it to his nose, honking away.

"You wanna call your mother or somebody to come get you?" I asked, nodding at the phone on the wall.

The phone didn't get much use. I didn't have anybody much to call, really, but when I'd first been released from prison, I had it installed because I was on home detention. When I was within range, the phone had read signals from the box strapped to my ankle and transmitted them to the parole office, assuring that I had complied with my curfew hours.

Mr. Ramirez, my parole officer, had let me off home detention after a few months, but it had been so expensive to have the phone installed, I just paid the bill every month so I wouldn't have to get it reinstalled if I got put back on home detention. Now that Mr. Ramirez didn't call to check in on me, the phone never rang.

"No, thanks. I got my cell phone," Benji said, patting his pocket.

Cell phone. I didn't have one—who would I call?—and I'd forgotten that most people these days had cell phones. "Then why didn't you call her to come get you a few hours ago?"

"She's in Las Vegas."

"What?"

"She's in Las Vegas. She got some money and she said she felt lucky, so she went out to Las Vegas. She said for a few days. She didn't say for sure when she'd be back." His lower lip trembled.

"When was this?"

"Over a week ago."

"And while she's in Las Vegas, what are you supposed to be doing?" I asked.

"Aaron's supposed to be keeping an eye on me. Mom said she left plenty of money. The first day, we went shopping. Aaron bought me some clothes. Like this." He fingered the orange vest with big purple stars on it. "I wanted one pretty bad, but it's real down, and Mom said it was too expensive. So as soon as she left, Aaron bought me one. He got one for himself, too."

I tried to picture Aaron, who usually sported filthy gray hoodies and grungy jackets, in such a garish garment. "His orange with purple stars, too?"

"Yeah."

From what I knew of Aaron, more than a week was a long time to expect him to hang onto money. I asked, "Does he have any of the money left?"

"There's no food in the house, and we haven't done laundry, and Aaron gets mad if I ask for anything. No beer, either. I think it's all gone."

Probably up Aaron's nose or shot into his arm, if I had to guess. "You hungry?" I asked.

He nodded.

"I don't got a whole lot," I warned him. "But I was gonna fix myself some oatmeal. With brown sugar. You want some?"

"Yes, please." The kid could be surprisingly polite.

Benji didn't need to hear what I thought of a mother who would go off to Las Vegas and leave a child in the care of a known druggie like Aaron. So I didn't say anything as I got out my two bowls, poured some instant oatmeal into the now-boiling water, and put the bag of brown sugar on the table. I got out a box of instant milk powder and poured a little into the bottom of each bowl. Then I divided the oatmeal between the bowls and stuck a spoon in each one.

We both dived right in. I had a feeling that Benji was used to eating pricier food, but I had to eat cheap, and to me, the brown sugar made all the difference. The prison chow hall served oatmeal sometimes, but there was never any brown sugar to put in it. I'd learned about that in one of the foster homes I'd lived in.

When we were done, I rinsed both bowls out and left them in the bottom of the sink.

Benji just sat there.

"Okay," I said, sitting down again. "Where is Aaron, and why did you think coming to see me was a good idea?"

His eyes filled with tears. "Aaron talks about you a lot."

"He does?" That didn't sound good. "What does he say?"

"He says you've got it together."

"What does he mean by that?"

"That you're too smart to get caught."

I laughed. "Did he tell you I spent twenty years in prison?"

"Yeah. He says that's where you learned everything."

"I don't call that 'too smart to get caught.'"

"Well…"

"That's because I did get caught, but good. When I was sixteen. And for something really stupid."

"Aaron says you killed a drug dealer who was cheating you. He says nobody messes with you and gets away with it."

Shaking my head, I said, "It wasn't at all like that. I was just a look-out. For my older brothers. We figured that if anybody got caught, I'd take the heat since I was a juvenile and they were adults. I thought they were just buying drugs. I didn't know they'd killed somebody. And for sure I didn't know you went straight to adult court if you caught a murder charge and you were over the age of fourteen. And then you get sent to adult prison."

"So you weren't guilty?"

"That's not what I said. In this state, if you're involved in a felony and someone dies, you're guilty of murder. Whether you pulled the trigger or were the lookout."

"What was the felony?"

I leaned back in my chair. "Robbing the drug dealer."

"Did you know they were gonna rob the drug dealer?"

"No. I thought they were gonna make a buy. But that would have been a felony anyhow. Possession with intent."

This kid seemed older than I'd thought at first. Not a confused, help-less little guy. So why was he sitting on my doorstep crying?

Still in his jacket and vest, Benji started to wipe his nose with the sleeve again. I shoved the roll of toilet paper closer to him. "You snorted something?" I asked.

He nodded, then took a piece of the toilet paper and blew his nose. Tinges of blood showed.

"You coming down now?"

Again, he nodded. "I guess."

"Meth?"

"What's crystal ice? Is that meth?" he asked.

"Yeah. Where'd you get it?" I was pretty sure I knew.

He stared down at the tabletop, then scratched the side of his neck. "Aaron."

"Aaron gave you meth?" I hoped he was a lot older than he looked.

Benji shrugged. "Not really."

"What do you mean, not really?"

"He had some. I was hungry. He said if I snorted a little, I wouldn't mind so much. The hungry would kind of go away. He didn't give it to me. I took it myself."

But Aaron had provided it. Same difference, as far as I was concerned. "So then what happened?"

"He left me in the truck. Said he'd be right back. And we could go get something to eat. But that was hours ago, and he hasn't come back."

"You try calling him on your cell phone?"

"Yeah. It goes to voice mail."

"Voice mail?" I wasn't sure what that was.

"Yeah. You know, like an answering machine. You leave a message."

The world I'd been released back into was much different from the world I'd left twenty years earlier. A lot had changed, as I'd discovered in the few months since my release. Maybe some people had answering machines before I got locked up. No one I'd known had one. And nobody had "voice mail" or "mailboxes," except for the ones out by the road that the mail carrier put stuff in. I couldn't remember even knowing what a cellphone was back then. If they had them at all.

I asked, "Why'd you come here instead of going home?"

"I was gonna go home. But driving the truck's harder than I thought. And Aaron always said you could get hold of anything you wanted. So I thought maybe you'd have some more crystal ice or something."

Shaking my head, I said, "I don't use. And I sure as hell don't deal, especially to minors. You know how fast I'd be back in prison if they caught me with any type of CDS? And it don't take much meth at all before you're charged with intent to distribute."

"What's CDS?"

"Controlled dangerous substance. Drugs."

He shivered and looked longingly toward the sink where I'd put the bowls.

"You cold?"

"Yeah."

"Your clothes wet?"

"Damp. Especially the jeans. And my socks."

I sighed. Clothes, particularly blue jeans, were expensive. I only had three pair: the ones I was wearing when I was released from prison, and two pair from Goodwill. Even at Goodwill, they were expensive.

"You wanna take a hot shower?" I asked. "If there's hot water. That'll warm you up. And I can fix some more oatmeal if you'd like."

"Yes, please."

I went into the tiny bathroom and turned on the shower. Then I went to put more water on for oatmeal. "Stick your hand under the water and see if it's beginning to warm up." Sometimes it got hot, sometimes it didn't.

Benji looked doubtfully into the bathroom. He'd barely have room to turn around. It was dingy and the porcelain fixtures were stained, but I kept it clean. There's a real incentive in prison to keep the all-in-one plumbing unit clean when it's inches from the bunks. And I kept up with the habit.

He didn't have to step through the door to put his hand under the water. "It's pretty warm," he said.

"I only got two towels," I said. "But you can use them. After you get yourself clean." I'd be heading for the laundromat soon anyhow.

He cast an uncomfortable glance at me. "You gonna stay out here?"

"You mean, am I going to get in the shower with you? No, man. Even if there was room."

He stripped off his clothes and stepped into the shower.

I took his jeans and hung them on the radiator, which was starting to warm up. I hung the socks next to them. Loosening the laces on his shoes and pulling the tongue out, I set them on a chair as close to the warmth as I could. The landlord only had to provide heat between certain hours, and that was all he provided. I kept expecting the pipes, which crisscrossed my ceiling, to freeze one of these cold nights.

When he got out, I handed him a dry pair of socks and my clean pair of jeans. They were too big, but he put them on. He'd have to make do with the underwear he had or go without.

I fixed another bowl of oatmeal. He sat down and gobbled that up.

"Now," I said, pulling up the other chair to the table. "I'm still trying to figure out what's going on here. Your mother is in Las Vegas?"

"Yeah." He licked the spoon. "She got some money. She said she was just going for a few days."

"Do you know exactly how long ago was that?"

He rubbed an eye with the side of his hand. "It'll be two weeks tomorrow."

"And have you heard from her?"

"Yeah. She said she was doing okay. First she won some money, then she lost most of it, but she won some more again. And she met somebody."

"Met somebody?"

"You know. A man." Benji looked at his empty bowl. "She does that, sometimes. Meets a man. Then she thinks she's in love." He swiped at his eyes with the back of his hand.

My mother had been killed in an accident at work when I was a toddler, so I didn't really know what it would feel like to have a mother who was running around with men in casual relationships. But I could imagine. Especially what it would feel like to a boy who was just starting to understand about sex. And it wouldn't feel good.

I asked, "How much money did she have?"

Benji shrugged. "Maybe fifty thousand dollars."

I raised my eyebrows and almost whistled. It could last a good long time in Las Vegas, especially if she were alternating between winning and losing streaks and had any luck at all. "Where'd she get fifty thousand dollars from?"

"From Aaron's dad."

"Say again?"

"Aaron's dad. She was married to him once. Before she met my dad."

I leaned back in my chair. "Why would an ex-husband give her fifty thousand dollars?"

"He didn't exactly give it to her. He died."

"And she inherited it? Was she still married to him?"

"No. They got divorced years ago. Before she married my dad. But she was on a life insurance policy, and I guess he never took her name off it, 'cause she got a check for it."

That was interesting. "Did he have a new wife?"

"Yeah. Suzanne. And I think she was pretty pissed."

Seemed to me she had a right to be. "And did Suzanne get anything?"

"I dunno. But there should have been a lot of money. He had a business he sold about two years ago."

"Did Aaron get any money?"

He shrugged. "Maybe. I don't know much about it. He had two older kids, too. A different mother. And he was married to Suzanne, but I don't think they had any kids together. Mom said he'd promised he'd make sure Aaron was taken care of."

That might have been why the insurance policy was still in her name. If so, she was squandering Aaron's inheritance in Las Vegas.

Of course, Aaron could squander it on his own, and probably would. He'd blow through whatever he got and have nothing to show for it but a bigger addiction problem. He worked the same place I did, the same shift, but he often didn't show up, and he tried to buy drugs from anyone he thought might have them. Including me. The only reasonable explanation for why he still had a job there was that he was a police informant and the company had been asked to leave him on the job for now. A truck terminal, with long haul truckers in and out all the time, could provide a good cover for transporting drugs. Since steel and products made from it were heavy, a maximum weight load left lots of room to tuck something in with the load.

"Aaron says he's supposed to get a lot of money," Benji said. "When the estate get settled."

Maybe the insurance payout hadn't been Aaron's share. "When's the estate gonna get settled?" I asked.

Benji shrugged. "Not for a while, I guess. Mom's money came from an insurance company, separate, so she got it right away. And Suzanne said it'd be a cold day in hell before she let Aaron have any of it, even if she's got to go to court."

If the will said Aaron got some of the money, I didn't know that she'd have any choice, but she could probably mess things up and cause delays. If the courts handling estates were anything like the criminal courts I'd seen, the only ones who'd come out ahead were the lawyers.

This line of conversation wasn't getting us anywhere. "Where do you think Aaron went when he left you?"

Benji stared blankly, then said, "I thought maybe he'd come over here."

"Any idea how long ago it was he left you in the truck?"

"Not really. It was dark. Pretty late. He said just wait for him. I tried to sleep. But after I snorted that crystal ice stuff, I wasn't sleepy."

That wasn't surprising. Meth was a stimulant. I asked, "Where's the truck now?"

Stirring uneasily, Benji looked away from me and didn't answer.

Alarm bells went off in my head. "Did something happen to the truck?"

"Kind of."

"What do you mean 'kind of'?"

"Well, Aaron left it on the street by the park down by the railroad tracks. By the underpass. You know it?"

I did. The railroad ran along with the river and looped through town, left over from a time when every factory had an active siding. Now only a few trains came through. Underpasses carried street traffic under the main line, but in the industrial section of town, street level sidings branched off all over.

In the late afternoon and evening, the park Benji was talking about was an open air drug market. And lots of hookers met their johns there. For a cheap quickie, they'd take the johns into the underpass.

It was not a good place to leave a kid. Or a truck, for that matter.

But then if Aaron—or his mother—had any concern at all about what was good for a kid, Benji wouldn't be in this predicament now.

"Is the truck still where he left it?" I asked.

"Not really."

I sighed. Benji was a master at not stating things directly. "What's not really?"

He started to wipe his nose on his sleeve, but reached for the roll of toilet paper instead. "Well, Aaron took the key. But I knew he had another one in the glove compartment. So when I got tired of waiting, I found it and started the truck up. At first, I was just gonna turn on the heater for a little while."

"And?"

"And then I thought maybe he wasn't coming back any time soon, and maybe I could drive it and go home. You know. Driving doesn't look all that hard. You just turn the key to start the engine, put it in gear, press down on the accelerator, and steer. Step on the brake when you want to stop."

I sized him up. He was probably tall enough to reach the pedals and the steering wheel at the same time. "So you tried to drive it?"

"Yep. I figured I could go home."

He wasn't home. "But what happened?" I asked.

He sniffed. "I got it started okay. And got out into the middle of the street. But when I tried to drive it across the railroad tracks, the front wheels got caught and turned sideways. I couldn't get it unstuck."

"So where is it now?"

Benji shrugged. "I guess still stuck in the railroad tracks."

I looked at him in alarm. "You mean, like the truck is still on the tracks?"

"Kind of."

"There's no 'kind of' for that. It's either on the tracks or not. Which is it?"

"Still on the tracks."

That line wasn't used that much anymore. No passenger service. But it did run past Quality Steel Fabrications where I worked and a few other industrial sites. And sometimes we'd get a shipment of steel or drums of chemicals by rail. The other places might get shipments, too. That meant a train could come by at any time. It wouldn't be moving fast, but one characteristic of trains is that even if it was moving slowly and the engineer saw something on the tracks, it took forever to stop.

I got up and grabbed my jacket. "See if your pants are dry enough to wear. If they are, take off those too-big ones and put them on. And get your shoes."

"Where are we going?"

"We're going to go see if we can get Aaron's truck off the tracks. Before a train comes along."

Benji's eyes opened wide. "A train?"

"Yeah. What do you think runs on those tracks?"

"I didn't think trains came here anymore."

"Well, there's not a lot of them. But there are a few. And all it would take is one to both crush the truck and maybe hurt some people on the train. You still got the key?"

He finished zipping his pants and tied his shoes. Then he reached into his pocket and pulled out a key.

A scattering of rain drops splattered on the sidewalk as we hurried toward the park. It was too early for either the dealers or the hookers to be looking for business yet. Two lone figures sat on benches on opposite sides of the park, both nodding in time to their own thoughts. Or, I reminded myself, music coming through earbuds so small, they weren't visible to passersby. People had things like that now. Neither one of them paid any attention to us.

We rounded a corner, and there it was—Aaron's blue pickup. Its front wheels were wedged at an odd angle between the crossties and the asphalt at the edge of the railroad bed. I bent down and studied them. If I backed up slowly and turned them, I might be able to get enough room to straighten them out enough to ease the truck off the tracks. Or drive forward over them.

I didn't really have a lot of experience driving. I'd been locked up before I'd ever had a chance to get a driver's license, and it didn't look like I'd have the opportunity to get one for a while now. Or the money—licenses weren't free. Or the money to buy a vehicle. So that project was on a back burner for now.

But this wouldn't be driving, really. Just easing the truck off the tracks and parking it on the street beyond.

I climbed into the driver's seat, and Benji got in the other side. I started the engine. Despite never having a license, I'd driven home a few times when my brothers had been too wasted to get us there. They'd had an old car for a while. I'd been stopped a few times and gotten traffic tickets, mostly for driving without a license, but it had never been in the nicer cars they came up with sometimes, which I now realized were probably stolen.

Turning the wheels, I backed up a bit. Sure enough, the wheels felt like they were coming free. I straightened them out, switched gears, and gently pressed on the accelerator. The truck didn't move at first, but then it lurched forward at an angle across the tracks. I reversed again and felt the wheels bump up over the asphalt edge. Pulling carefully onto the street, I headed for a long expanse of curb up the hill, away from the underpass, where I wouldn't have to worry about maneuvering into a tight parking space. The truck glided to the side of the street and bumped the curb. I relaxed and leaned back.

A flashing blue light swept over the truck's cab.

I looked in the rearview mirror.

Cops.

CHAPTER 2

My throat went dry, and all my muscles tightened, freezing my hands on the steering wheel.

At least that left them in plain sight, which was a good thing.

Panic swelled in my throat. I tried to choke it down and think.

Benji turned around and scrambled to his knees to look out the back window. "There's two of them," he said. "A man and a woman. They got something in their hands."

"Guns?" I asked.

"Nope. Looks more like flashlights."

Not a whole lot better. The flashlights were heavy and would do a good job clunking someone over the head. In this case, that someone would be me.

The cops approached, one on each side of the truck.

"Roll down the window and shut off the engine," the male cop on my side said.

First, I had to shift the truck out of drive. I pried my right hand off the wheel, grabbed the gear lever, and put it in park. With the other hand, I fumbled with the buttons on the door, trying to open the window. With a loud "click," the doors locked.

The cop's hand that wasn't holding the flashlight went down to his holster.

Stabbing frantically at the buttons, I managed to get the window next to Benji rolled down. Finally, the window next to me. Fumbling with the ignition, I turned the key the wrong way in the ignition, making the starter whine, then the other way, shutting off the engine. I pulled the key out and laid it on the dashboard. And put my hands back on the steering wheel.

The cop raised his eyebrows and waited to see what I would do or say. I just sat there, staring straight ahead.

Flicking on the light and bringing it up to the window, he shined the beam around the inside of the cab. His fingers gripped the flared front of the heavy flashlight from below, positioned so he could pivot it effectively. I sat still, knowing he could just flip it up across my face with a quick motion of his wrist.

"Anything in here I should know about?" he asked.

Heaven only knew what drugs or paraphernalia Aaron had left lying around. Or even worse, what weapons. "Not that I'm aware of, sir."

He looked like he didn't believe me. And why should he? "Not that you're aware of? If you're driving a vehicle, you're in control of it. And you're responsible for anything that's in it. You know that?"

"Yes, sir."

"So let me ask again. Anything I should know about? Guns, knives, rocket propelled grenades, bombs?"

I licked my dry lips. "I sure hope not."

"Drugs?"

"No." What else could I say?

"Let me see your driver's license."

I closed my eyes. "I don't have a license."

"Revoked?"

"No, sir. I never had one."

"At your age? Got any ID on you?"

Fortunately I had my wallet, which held my work ID. And my old prison ID tucked in the back. I wasn't going to pull that out if I could help it.

"I have to reach into my pocket to get my wallet," I told him. I didn't want him to think I might be going for a weapon.

"Go ahead."

Reaching into my pocket, I pulled out the wallet and handed it over to him.

He held onto it, but didn't open it.

The light drizzle picked up. Drops of moisture puddled on his hat.

"Now." He turned back to me. "I don't suppose you have any registration for the vehicle?"

I glanced at Benji. "Does Aaron keep the registration and insurance and stuff in the glove compartment?"

Shrugging, he said, "I dunno." He started to reach over to open the door.

"Don't touch it!" I told him. "Just sit still."

His hand sprang back, and he looked at me, his eyes clouded.

I closed my eyes and leaned my head back, careful to keep my hands motionless. "Might be in the glove compartment," I said to the cop. Along with who knows what else. I didn't say that part.

"Richards?" he said to the female cop, who was standing next to the open window by Benji. "You wanna take a peak in the glove compartment?"

"Okay, Cunningham." She reached in and tried to open it. The door stuck.

I hoped it wasn't locked. And that the registration would be right on top.

"Who owns the truck?" the cop asked.

"Guy by the name of Aaron," I said.

"No last name?"

"No. Well, yeah. But I don't remember what it is."

"Does he know you're driving his truck?"

"No, sir."

"And how do you know this Aaron?"

"We work together. At Quality Steel Fabrications."

"And why aren't you at work now?"

"We work the night shift. Midnight to eight."

"Uh-huh. And where is this Aaron person now?"

"I dunno. He wasn't at work last night."

I looked over at Officer Richards. She had managed to get the glove compartment door open and was rummaging around. I expected something illegal to fall out any minute. A joint, a little baggie of white powder, a bottle of pills, a Saturday night special, a stick of dynamite. Nothing would surprise me.

But nothing fell out. She came up with a rectangle of cardstock. "Here it is."

"What does it say?" Officer Cunningham asked.

"The truck's registered to Gina Michaels." She looked at me. "Who's Gina Michaels?"

I shrugged and glanced at Benji again.

"That's my mom," he said.

Richards said, "Your mom? Does your mom know this guy has her truck?"

"No. She's in Las Vegas."

"And aren't you supposed to be in school?"

"I guess. But I didn't go home last night. So I couldn't get the school bus."

"Oh? And why is that?"

"Because my brother was supposed to be taking care of me, but he left me in the truck and didn't come back." Benji let out a sob.

The cop nodded toward me. "This isn't your brother?"

"No. That's Jesse. He's a friend of my brother."

While I wasn't pleased to be characterized as a friend of Aaron's, at least he didn't say, "My brother's dealer" or something like that.

"And your brother is who?"

"Aaron Stenski."

Cunningham glanced at me. "This the Aaron you told me owns the truck?"

"Yes, sir. I didn't realize it wasn't registered to him."

Looking thoughtful, he said, "So if this Gina Michaels is owner of the truck, and she's in Las Vegas and doesn't know you have it, would it be safe to say it's stolen?"

Swallowing hard, I said, "No, sir."

He shook his head. "Let me get this straight. Who, again, is this Gina Michaels?"

I shrugged.

"That's my mom," Benji repeated. "But it's Aaron's truck. She never drives it."

Cunningham peered at me. "Can you tell me why you, who don't have a license, are driving a truck that belongs to a lady who's in Las Vegas? And why you have her son, a minor who should be in school, in the truck with you?"

He was never going to believe me, but I had to try. "The truck was stuck on the railroad tracks. I wasn't really driving. I just moved it. And I was going to park it here."

"And how did it end up 'stuck' on the railroad tracks?"

"That was my fault," Benji said. "I thought maybe I could drive it home. But the wheels turned in by the track, and it wouldn't move."

Cunningham cast a knowing look at his partner, who nodded back at him. I wondered if it was a report of the truck on the tracks that brought them out here.

"Here," he said. He tossed my wallet over the hood of the truck. "Why don't you run the ID?"

Richards snatched it out of the air and went to the patrol car.

Gloomily, I thought about what was going to pop up when she punched in my name. Convicted felon for sure. Violent convicted felon. Which would turn this into a felony traffic stop.

We waited.

"Cunningham!" Richards had climbed out of the patrol car again and was striding toward us, her hand on the butt of her service gun. The holster flap was unsnapped.

"What?" the other cop said.

"Get that kid out of the truck and step back. I got backup coming."

"What?"

"The driver. I ran him. He's right, he doesn't have a license. But he does have quite a record, and he comes up 'armed and dangerous.'"

Of course I would.

Cunningham backed up away from the truck. Both cops now had their guns in their hands. He said, "Let the kid out."

My chest tight, I said to Benji, "Get out of the truck slowly and go back to the patrol car. Do what they tell you to do."

"What are you gonna do?" he asked me, not moving.

Probably go to jail, I thought. But all I said was, "Just sit here until they tell me to do something else. You'd be smart to always do what the police tell you to."

"The kid's getting out of the truck," I called out the window. My knuckles were white from the grip I had on the steering wheel. I knew better than to move my hands without an order from them.

Benji gave me one last puzzled look and opened the door. He slid out and slammed the door behind him. I didn't turn around to watch, but I kept an eye on him in the rearview mirror. He walked back to the patrol car. Richards put him in the back seat. The other cop backed farther away from the truck.

The scream of sirens filled the air. Another patrol car skidded around the corner and almost hit the truck, but managed to stop in time.

Yet another one raced toward us from the other side of the railroad tracks. He was coming too fast, I thought. He should slow down before he actually hit the tracks.

He didn't. The car bounced in the air and bottomed out with a sickening thud. Couldn't be good for the oil pan. Or his nerves.

Great. They were all going to be pissed off, and they were going to blame me. There was nothing I could do about any of it.

Or much I could do about anything else, either. I sat there trying not to move, but still breathe.

The truck was surrounded by a sea of blue uniforms, all of them keeping their distance. Maybe there were only six or so, but it sure felt like a lot more. Most of them had their guns drawn and pointing at me.

One of them had a bullhorn. "Driver."

That was me. No point trying to explain I hadn't really been driving.

"Throw the keys out the window."

I scraped it off the dashboard and tossed it out gently. I didn't want it to look like I was trying to throw them at anybody. It hit the asphalt with a metallic clink.

"Reach out the window and open the truck door. From the outside."

I reached through the open window and felt around for the door handle. I finally found it and fumbled with it, trying to figure out how to make it open.

"Do it. Now."

Couldn't they see I was trying?

Apparently not.

At last, I gripped the handle the right way, squeezed it with my awkward fingers, and the door mechanism clicked. I shoved the door open with my knee and waited for further instructions.

"Get out of the cab. Face away from my voice. Put your hands on your head and interlace your fingers."

Hard to do all at once. I eased off the seat, planted my feet on the ground, turned toward the truck, and put my hands on the back of my head, fingers interlaced.

Then I braced myself for what I was afraid was coming.

Sure enough, I was tackled and thrown to the ground face down. Since I'd been anticipating it, I was able to fall away from the truck and avoid crashing my head into the open door. But my nose and chin had hit the pavement pretty hard. And I bit my tongue.

Someone slammed a knee down on my neck, and my legs were pinned to the ground. My hands were pulled roughly behind my back. I felt the familiar clamp of too-tight handcuffs on my wrists. I tried to relax my muscles and let them be manipulated, but they wouldn't loosen up. Something warm and wet mingled with the damp gravel around my face. I stuck the tip of my tongue out and tasted it. Blood.

Strong hands encased in plastic gloves hauled me to my feet. Someone frisked me, feeling my pockets, under my jacket, between my legs. All they found was my keychain. They already had my wallet.

I blinked, trying to get the dirt out of my eyes. Everything was blurry.

"Should we put him in a car?" someone asked.

I couldn't see well enough to know who was talking. Not that it mattered.

"Here comes the sergeant," someone else answered. "Let's ask him what he wants to do."

I could feel my tongue, swollen and sticky from blood. I leaned my head forward so the blood would drip down my chin instead of filling my mouth. I knew how sick swallowing blood could make a person.

My arms would have bruises where I was being held. Out of the corner of my eye, I saw a new pair of boots approaching.

"What do we have here?" the person attached to the boots asked.

I kept my gaze on the ground and couldn't see who was talking. "Stolen truck, Sarge. Driven by a felon on parole. He don't have no license."

"When was it stolen?"

No one answered.

"You had to have run it. Does it come back stolen?" the sergeant asked.

"Well, no."

"Okay. So maybe it's stolen, maybe it's not. Who's it registered to?"

"This lady, Gina Michaels. But she's in Las Vegas."

"How do we know she's in Las Vegas?"

"Her son told us."

The sergeant sighed. "If this is her son, the truck's probably not stolen. She might have told him he could drive it."

Cunningham pointed toward the patrol car where they'd put Benji. "No. Her son's in the back of that car."

"Bring him over here."

Richards brought Benji over. He was sobbing.

The sergeant looked at him in dismay. "A kid. Is he hurt?"

"I don't think so," the woman said and turned to Benji. "Are you hurt?"

"No," he choked out between sobs.

"Then why are you crying?" the sergeant asked.

"I'm scared."

"Scared of what?"

"That you're gonna do something to me."

The sergeant looked at Richards. "Like what?"

"Something to hurt me."

"Why would we want to do something to hurt you?"

"I dunno." His shoulders shook.

The sergeant looked helplessly toward Richards. "Then why would you think that?" he asked.

"Look at what you did to Jesse," he said. "You hurt him. He's bleeding."

The sergeant lifted his hat and ran his fingers through his hair. "This man—Jesse—we didn't really mean to hurt him. Just restrain him. He's a dangerous criminal."

Benji sobbed again. "He was helping me."

The light rain picked up, sweeping across the cracked asphalt.

One of the other cops came up, something in his hands. "Here," he said to Benji. "You want a teddy bear? I got some in my trunk. We give them to kids."

Turning my head, I watched.

Benji hugged himself and shook his head. "I'm too big for a teddy bear."

I licked my lips and said, "Benji, you're never too big for a teddy bear." My tongue was thick and the words were slurred. "Go ahead and take it."

As soon as I spoke, the grip on my arms tightened. The sergeant turned toward me. "What were you doing with this kid?"

I shrugged. "He came over my place 'cause his brother left him in the truck. I was just trying to help him get it off the tracks."

"And then what were you going to do?"

"See if I could find someplace for him to go."

"Like Social Services?"

I didn't like the sound of that, but they were the right people to find Benji's mother, in Las Vegas or wherever. And take care of him until she got back. "I guess," I said.

Still looking uncertain, Benji took the teddy bear. Hugging it tight to his chest, he buried his face in it.

Richards steered him back to her car, out of the rain.

The sergeant took out a notepad and a pen. "So," he said. "We're gonna call Social Services for the kid. And a tow for the truck." He glanced at me. "You okay with that?"

It certainly wasn't up to me. "Sure," I said.

"And do we have this guy on any charges?" he asked, looking at the assembled cops.

"Stolen vehicle," Cunningham said.

The sergeant shook his head. "Maybe unauthorized use. But we don't even know that for sure now."

"Kidnapping," Richards suggested.

"Maybe interference with custody. But again, we don't know that for sure." The sergeant's pen poised over his notepad.

Cunningham tried again. "Driving without a license?"

The sergeant nodded. "Technically, I suppose. Did you see him driving?"

"Just a few yards. He pulled over and parked before I got my lights turned on."

"No resisting arrest, assault of an officer, giving false information?"

"Not really. Except he gave the wrong name of the person who owned the truck."

"How's that?"

"He said this guy Aaron something owned it," Cunningham said.

"Where's this Aaron?"

"I dunno. The kid says that's his brother, who was supposed to taking care of him."

"So the person the truck is registered to is Aaron's mother, as well as the kid's mother?" The sergeant scribbled on his notepad. "So the kid and this Aaron are brothers? But this guy isn't related to them?"

Cunningham shrugged.

"So." The sergeant brought the tip of the pen to his lip. "It seems to me it could be a logical error, if the truck in fact is registered to the mother of the person he thought owned it."

The cop raised his eyebrows. "I guess."

The sergeant turned to me. "Your face is bleeding. Do you need medical attention?"

"No, sir." If they got me medical attention, they'd have to write reports. And if they wrote reports, they'd have to justify the injury. I'd be much better off if the whole incident could be forgotten.

"So if we take off the cuffs and cut you loose, what would you do?"

Letting me go without charges was the best possible outcome I could think of, and more than I'd dared to hope for. "Go home."

"And stay there?"

"Until my appointment with my parole officer this afternoon."

"Who's your PO?"

"Mr. Ramirez."

"And are you going to tell him about this little incident this morning?"

I debated. It was always better for a PO to hear about things from a parolee than from a cop, or anyone else, but I wasn't sure that's the answer the sergeant wanted. I finally said, "If you think I should, I will."

The sergeant nodded. "I think you should. There'll be a report."

"Okay."

"Turn around, and let's get those cuffs off."

I turned around and stood still while the cuffs were unlocked and removed. My wrists tingled. I resisted the urge to rub them and restore the circulation.

"But Sarge—" Cunningham started to say.

The sergeant looked at him. "You at roll call this morning?"

"Of course."

They had turned away and were ignoring me, like I wasn't there. I looked at the ground, but I was listening closely.

"Then you remember what they told us about detention center?"

Cunningham took his handcuffs and snapped them back on his belt. "Yeah. It's overcrowded as it is, and they're worried about it if this storm gets as bad as they say it might."

"Right. They're trying to get the population down where they can."

"So we're not going to bring in somebody we don't have a very good reason to hold."

The sergeant turned to me. "You still here?"

"My wallet and keychain."

Someone handed me my wallet and keychain. And a wad of tissues.

I held the tissues up to my mouth and nose.

"You can go now," the sergeant said, "if you're sure you don't need medical attention."

I didn't need to be told twice. I glanced back at the car where Benji sat. He had the teddy bear pressed up against the side of his face, but he lifted a hand and waved to me. I waved back and turned to leave.

The shortest way home was back the way I'd come, but a patrol car and cops blocked the sidewalk. I didn't really feel like winding my way through them. Instead, I turned down the road beside the tracks, which ran down through the underpass. There was no sidewalk there, and I'd have to go a few extra blocks before I could cross back and head for home, but I'd much rather do that.

Not quite believing that they weren't holding me, I walked away as quickly as I dared, careful to keep my hands in full sight. I had to fight the urge to break into a run. I kept expecting any second for someone to shout an order for me to stop, or worse, to grab me. The rain was beginning to pelt down.

The underpass was dark and dingy, lit only by the red and blue flashers on the patrol cars. There were lights set in the concrete supports, but they were broken out. Probably knocked out by the cheap hookers who took an occasional john down there for a five dollar quickie. I shivered and kept going. Water ran down the pavement and rushed toward the storm drains at the bottom of the underpass, puddling around the grates.

The cascade was too heavy for the storm drains to handle. That wasn't a good sign. It had rained most of the night, and it was picking up again, but if everybody was right, the storm was just starting. This was a low-lying area, possibly the lowest in the city, aside from the actual river banks. If the drains were overwhelmed already, we might be in for some serious flooding.

As the road rose on the other side, I glanced back and could no longer see the cops, although the eerie flashing lights still shone in the shiny wet dimness of the underpass. I pulled the tissues away from my face and looked at them. They were a soggy, bloody lump. I debated about tossing them into the street, but in the end, I put them in my pocket, flipped up the hood of my jacket, and shoved my hands deep in my pockets.

They'd make sure Benji made out all right. Probably call Social Services. I doubted anyone would concern themselves with Aaron's whereabouts. He had only been gone for a few hours, and he was a junkie, known to be unreliable. Somebody—maybe his mother—would have to report him as missing before they'd even consider looking for him. If an emergency was declared because of the rain and the flooding, and it looked like we were headed in that direction, police priorities would change to ensuring public safety. A missing druggie would be way down on the priority list.

Benji was probably headed for an emergency foster home until his mother showed up. I'd been in a number of them when I was a kid. Usually, they weren't too bad. The social workers would go for the cheapest solution, but even if Aaron surfaced, no caseworker in his right mind would hand Benji over to him. Not after he'd abandoned the kid in a truck at night. Until his mother showed up, Benji would be physically well cared for. But there wasn't much anyone could do for the hollow ache I was sure was growing in his gut.

Sloshing back to my place, I realized I wouldn't have time for a nap after all. I could fit in the shave and shower, though. Just as well. I could feel my muscles stiffening up, and a couple hours sleep might make it worse. I did need to wash the blood off my face and out of my hair, though, before I met with Mr. Ramirez. Even if I stuck pretty much to the truth, the story I was going to tell him would be pretty hard to swallow. POs are suspicious by nature. With my face bruised up, I must look like I'd been in a fight. No need to look and smell like I hadn't bothered to clean myself up in recent memory.

CHAPTER 3

The waiting room to the parole office was in the basement of a building in the county complex, with the main police station and the county lockup upstairs. The courthouse was right next door. Made it convenient if they decided to lock one of us criminals up for a parole violation.

The room was crowded. I preferred morning appointments, when not so many people would be ahead of me, but then, nobody ever asked what I preferred. The radiators on the walls hissed and steamed, throwing off excessive heat, and condensation dripped down the grimy glass of the windows set high in the walls. An overwhelming odor of unwashed bodies and urine filled the air. A woman in a ragged overcoat held a dirty rag to her mouth and coughed unceasingly.

I signed in on the clipboard left on a ledge by the window to the receptionist's desk, which was unoccupied. Then I looked over the uneasy crowd. The only empty seats were in the middle of the room. After all the years in prison, I would feel too exposed and vulnerable in them, so I took a place standing against a wall, keeping as far away from the radiators as I could. Stripping off my jacket and folding it over my arm, I settled in to wait.

Every once in a while, a stocky woman with big red fingernails and bigger, redder hair appeared from within the depths of the inner offices, checked the clipboard, snapped her gum, and then called out a name. She would then open the door and let the person she'd called precede her down the hallway.

More people entered the waiting room, signed in, sized up the seating, and either chose a seat or leaned against the wall. No one spoke.

Anyone done with their appointment left the back offices, fled through the cramped waiting room, and dashed out the door, avoiding all eye contact. Their faces showed their relief. Without counting or paying really close attention, there was no way to tell if anyone had been whisked away up the interior stairs to a holding cell in the police station above.

Eventually, the woman picked up the clipboard, ran her sharp red nail down the list, and looked up. "Jesse Damon?" she called.

I stepped up to the window. "Yes, ma'am."

She ran her gaze over me disdainfully, as if wondering if another, more suitable Jesse Damon could be found if only she looked further. Finally, she opened the door and stood back, her gum cracking. "You know where you're going?"

"I know where Mr. Ramirez's office is, if that's where I'm supposed to be going."

"Where else do you think you'd be going?"

No point answering that. I stepped up to his open office door.

Mr. Ramirez's head, topped with a dark thatch of curly hair, was bent over the paperwork on his desk. His beefy forearm moved as he made notes on a form. I stood, waiting for him to invite me in. From her post by the door, the lady glared at me like it was my fault I was still in the hallway.

He looked up and frowned. "Come in and sit down."

I eased into the office and lowered myself into the worn wooden chair in front of his desk.

He leaned back in his desk chair and eyed me. "You been fighting again?"

Not a good start. "No, sir."

"How come every time you come in here, you look like you've gotten the worse end of a fight?"

I touched my swollen lip. "Not every time," I protested.

"Often enough." He sat up straighter. "And somehow, I get the impression you really don't get the worst of it in most of your fights." Shaking his head, he said, "You gonna tell me about how you ended up with a busted lip this time?"

I'd tried to figure out how to tell him about this morning, but I hadn't come up with a way to say it that didn't sound like I was whining. I said, "I got stopped."

He shook his head again. "By the cops, I take it?"

"Yes, sir."

"Doing what?"

No matter how I said this, it was going to strain credibility. "I was moving this pickup truck off the railroad tracks."

"I didn't know you had a driver's license."

"I don't."

"So is that what you got stopped for?"

"Sort of." It occurred to me that I probably sounded just about as evasive as Benji had. If I'd found that annoying, I could just imagine how Mr. Ramirez felt. But I was struggling with how to explain it.

"What the hell do you mean by 'sort of?'"

"Well, there was this truck, see, and it was caught on the railroad tracks."

Mr. Ramirez closed his eyes and sighed. "And how did it get caught on the railroad tracks?"

"This kid—he's maybe ten or so—he was trying to get home. When he tried to drive across the tracks, the tires got stuck between the ties and the edge of the road."

"I suppose this kid couldn't have had a license, either?"

One thing at least I could say that was believable. "No, sir."

"So what was he doing driving a pickup truck?"

"His brother had left him in it. Told him he'd be right back."

"How do you come into this?"

"Well, the kid, Benji's his name, came to my apartment, looking for help."

"And this Benji knows you how?"

"He don't, really. But I work with his brother."

"The brother who told him to wait in the truck?"

"Yes, sir."

The desk chair squeaked as Mr. Ramirez stirred his impressive bulk. "Even if I took all that as gospel—which I don't necessarily, by the way—how did it end up with you getting all beaten up?"

"Not really beaten up. Just hitting the ground hard."

"When you were stopped by the police?"

"Yeah."

"Did you resist or something?"

"No. They'd run my ID." I didn't think it needed much more explanation than that.

"So they handled it as a felony traffic stop?"

"Seems like it."

"And you didn't get down on the ground when they told you to?"

"They didn't say to. They just took me down."

He nodded. "But they didn't hold you."

"No, sir."

"You get a ticket for driving without a license?"

"Nope."

"Where's the truck?"

"I dunno. I left it parked by the side of the street."

"What happened to the kid?"

I shrugged. "They kept him."

Mr. Ramirez grinned. "Didn't think you were a good candidate for custody of a kid, huh?"

"I guess not."

"I can't imagine why." He pushed his chair back from his desk and stood up. "There gonna be a report filed?"

I remained in the chair. At just about six feet, I would tower over Mr. Ramirez's five foot one or two inches. But he still outweighed me by fifty pounds. I said, "The sergeant said there would be."

"Then I'll request a copy. For the file." He shuffled some papers on his desk. "Did you give your fee to the receptionist when you came in?"

"There was nobody at the desk."

"You got the money?"

"Yes, sir."

The expenses of parole ate into my income fairly considerably. Thank goodness I'd landed a pretty good job. Quality Steel Fabrications participated in a program that gave them tax breaks for hiring convicts about to be paroled. They'd hired me right out of prison, and I was determined not to blow this one chance I had at a decent job. I'd started as a laborer and machine operator, and now I drove a forklift. Kind of a funny job for someone who didn't have a driver's license, but the company provided its own industrial truck certification training program.

He escorted me to the front desk, which was now occupied by the woman with big hair and nails. I peeled off a few bills and handed them over to her. She snapped her gum and punched something in on her keyboard. A printer whirred to life.

She leaned back and, ignoring me, smiled up at Mr. Ramirez. "You set for the wet weather?"

He nodded. "The road might flood, but my house is up on a hill. Should be okay. We got enough food and water to last for a few days if we lose power and can't get out. The road does flood sometimes, but ever since the Army Corps of Engineers did that flood control project on the river—what was it, twenty-five years ago?—it hasn't been bad."

She snapped her gum. "Wouldn't surprise me if we did lose power for a while. The electric companies haven't been very good about fixing things when the lines go down lately."

"They certainly haven't. Even in the big cities, D.C. and Baltimore, they've had outages that lasted days. Weeks, sometimes."

"I hope they get their act together better than that. But it does sound like we're in for some flooding. There's a lot of snowpack up in the mountains, and if we get all the rain we're supposed to, it'll melt a lot of that. On top of the rain."

They weren't talking to me, but I listened. If the power went out, I wouldn't be working. I couldn't afford that. Like I had any control over it.

The woman handed me my receipt.

"You can go," Mr. Ramirez said to me. "Next week. Same time."

"Yes, sir." Clutching my receipt, I slipped into my jacket and waited for Mr. Ramirez to open the door so I could leave.

He did so, and I slunk through the waiting room, avoiding looking at anyone, out the door, and up onto the street.

Rain, harder than ever, soaked through the shoulders of my jacket in minutes.

Maybe I'd better check the weather forecast for the next few days. I didn't have a TV or radio at home. A TV was probably out of the question until I had a lot more money, but one day soon, I'd buy a radio. Meanwhile, I headed for the public library, where I could read the newspapers and, if I could figure out how to use it, check one of the computers for the latest weather news.

I used the public library a lot. Mrs. Coleman, who had been my foster mother for a couple of years in my early teens, had introduced me to it. "It's taxpayer supported. Which means it doesn't cost you anything to use it. And it's for everybody who lives in the area. All they ask is that you follow the rules and take care of the materials you use so they can be available for the next person."

Except for the computers and such, it hadn't changed all that much in the years I was locked away.

The prison library had been a real lifeline for me over the twenty years I was locked up. I signed up for it every week and got the three books I was allowed. I worked most days in the prison laundry for the princely sum of a dollar a day and the privilege of getting out of my cell for those hours, then came back to the housing unit, locked in, and read. I couldn't afford a TV then either, and the one in the dayroom was a constant source of argument over what to watch. Unless there was a sporting event most of the guys wanted to watch, cartoons usually won out. I wasn't particularly interested.

When I was released, I was on home detention with a black plastic monitoring box strapped to my ankle. I was allowed out for work and a very limited time to run errands. I made it a point to squeeze in a visit to the public library as soon as I could.

I'd been a bit afraid they'd refuse to issue me a card. The circulation clerk, Mandy Radman, had unquestioningly accepted my prison ID for identification and my month-to-month lease for proof of residency. For that, I was eternally grateful to her.

Taking the steps up to the front door two at a time, I stopped in the entry to take off my jacket and hat. They were soaked. I shivered. Both of them were wool, and while wet wool did retain heat, it wasn't exactly cozy or comfortable.

Mandy was at the front desk, sorting through a stack of books. She and I had struck up a strange kind of casual friendship. When she'd realized that her marriage had turned sour—actually, it had not been a good idea from the get-go since her husband liked her inherited money, not her—she'd started off the deep end, but I'd been able to get her to see her lawyer for a divorce instead of taking more drastic measures. Like asking me to kill her husband.

I stopped by the front desk to say hello.

"Looking for something to read, in case the power goes out and you can't watch TV or anything?" she asked.

I just shook my head. "Here to read newspapers."

She probably couldn't get her mind around somebody who couldn't afford a TV, and I wasn't about to tell her that. She'd feel sorry for me. She might even offer me an old cast-off TV. I didn't want that.

She lived in a big old house in the old part of town. A mansion, really. Her parents had died in an accident when she was in college, and as an only child, everything they'd owned was left to her.

I was pretty sure she worked at the library for many of the same reasons I'd worked at the prison laundry all those years. It gave structure to her life and got her out on a regular basis. Although I was sure it paid a hell of a lot more than a dollar a day, I knew she didn't need the money.

Someone came up to check out some books, so I headed for the reading room. Careful to put my wet jacket over the back of a non-upholstered chair, I slid into a seat and grabbed the latest edition of the *Rothsburg Register*, the local paper.

The front page had a big weather map and a few articles about the storm. I found it hard to sort out the hype from the factual reporting, but it did emphasize that we were in for a lot of weather in the next few days.

As if we didn't usually have weather of some sort.

I didn't know how much rain we'd be getting, but I kept reading. If it was bad enough that the staff at the parole office was concerned, it had to be a lot.

A late winter storm was swirling in from the Atlantic, carrying a lot of moisture. It was poised to meet a cold weather pattern, also carrying moisture, that was surging over the mountains. They should be encountering each other any time now, and whether we got socked with rain or snow or a mix would be dependent upon the temperature. People should be prepared for whatever came, from several feet of ice and snow, to heavy rains and flooding.

The reports didn't really tell me anything I couldn't have figured on my own. We had bad weather and more was coming. So what else was new? With a sigh, I folded the newspaper, put it back on the table, and got to my feet.

Mandy smiled at me as I went past the desk. I smiled back and stopped.

She was the first person after I was released who'd treated me with normal social courtesies. As a prison inmate, most of my interaction with other people over the last twenty years had been me obeying barked orders given by correctional officers, or trying to keep to myself to avoid trouble from other inmates. I think we were both a little socially awkward. And lonesome. I had a pretty good idea about why I was like that, but except for being shy and uncertain of herself, I saw no reason why she would feel that way.

She frowned as she looked at the wet jacket in my hands. "If you're going to be out walking in that—" she nodded to the streams of water cascading down the window "—shouldn't you be wearing a raincoat?"

It would be nice, I thought, but I said, "All I got's the jacket. No raincoat."

Raising her eyebrows, she said, "You need a raincoat."

I shrugged. She might be right, but that didn't get me a raincoat.

"Wait," she said, reaching under the counter. She pulled up a roll of black plastic trash bags.

"I know it's not elegant," she said as she pulled one off the roll and reached for a pair of scissors, "but it should help." She cut down the back seam of the bag, then cut a hole in each side near the bottom. "If you put this over your shirt, but under the jacket, it'll keep the water off your shirt and help keep the warmth in."

She flipped it upside down and handed it to me. I slipped one arm through each hole and pulled the cut seam together in the front. Then I put the jacket on. It was chilly, but she was right—the wetness didn't reach my already damp shirt.

"My dad used to take me camping when I was a kid," she said, "and he always said there was no point in hauling along a raincoat as long as we had plastic trash bags."

She took another bag and cut a bottom corner off diagonally. "Here," she said. "You tuck this inside your hat, and it'll make a waterproof lining."

She certainly had a point. The slick plastic wasn't particularly comfortable, but it would keep my head dry.

"Nothing I know of to do for your feet," she said, frowning down at my wet work boots.

I didn't know of anything, either.

"You'll just have to change into something else when you get home."

Change into what? I didn't own another pair of boots. Or shoes. Once again, I wasn't going to let her know how poverty-stricken I was.

She glanced around, then pulled a few more bags off the roll. Bundling them with the one she'd cut the corner off, she handed them to me. "Here. These might come in handy. Stick them in your pocket."

Gratefully, I took them. Maybe I could carry this concept a little further and figure out a way to keep my feet dry, too. I did have some clean, dry socks.

Opening the door, I headed out into gale-force winds. Rain pelted me from every direction. I ducked my head close to my chest. Mandy's makeshift waterproof linings were working, though. My blue jeans clung to my legs. I wasn't sure I could feel my feet, and my arms were getting soaked, but my head and torso were not getting any wetter, and the wool jacket and watch cap were actually holding in body heat. Assuming my body was producing any heat.

I hurried home. I'd only have time for a few hours sleep before I was supposed to report to work at midnight for a welcome Saturday shift. I took overtime shifts whenever they were offered. The time and a half pay came in handy. And if the power did go off and we couldn't work for a few days, it would be even more important.

Water careened down the outdoor stairs that led to my apartment and gurgled down the drain set in the concrete. Thank goodness that drain was working better than the ones in the underpass by the railroad tracks.

Once inside, I striped off all my wet clothes. Even my underwear was damp. The unpredictable radiator was cranking out heat, so I hung the blue jeans and shirt over that. Moving one of my kitchen chairs close to it, I pulled out the tongues from my boots and propped them on the seat of the chair so the insides were facing the radiator. The jacket I turned inside out and hung over the back.

Shivering, I pulled on dry clothes and dumped a can of chili into my frying pan. It was either that or ramen noodles, and I was hungry enough that I wanted a filling meal. While that was heating, I made two peanut butter sandwiches for work and stuck them in my lunchbox. I filled the thermos with instant coffee and stowed it next to sandwiches. Not exactly an appetizing lunch, but come four a.m., I would be very glad I had it.

When the chili was hot, I scarfed it down, swallowed a scalding cup of instant coffee, rinsed out the pan and the bowl, set my alarm clock, and tumbled into bed. I didn't like to go to work tired—it was too easy to do something stupid or dangerous.

* * * *

The shrilling of the alarm pulled me out of a deep sleep. Tough to get going, but I didn't mind. I'd never been able to sleep solidly like that in a prison cell, surrounded by the nighttime noises made by the mass of miserable, incarcerated humanity.

Worst was the frequent "scrape, scrape, scrape" of someone sharpening a scrap of metal on the concrete into a shank. If a CO unlocked the grid and came on the tier, that sound would cease immediately and be replaced by boot steps and jangling keys. It would begin again when the grid slammed shut behind the departing guard.

And there was always the scents—too many people in too small a space without adequate access to showers and clean clothes—that was never quite masked by the industrial strength disinfectant.

I shut the alarm off and lay there for a few seconds, appreciating my solitude and gathering my courage to get up into the cold. Of course the heat was off.

If I fell back asleep, I risked being late for work. I swung my feet out from under the pile of blankets and onto the floor.

Into several inches of icy water.

CHAPTER 4

The water soaked right through my socks, and it was freezing.

I reached over and hit the light switch. The overhead light flickered, but came on. Just as I touched the switch, it occurred to me what a dumb thing that was to do. This was an older, poorly maintained building. In the best of circumstances, the wiring was questionable. By no means could this be considered "best of circumstances."

The apartment had only two electric outlets, and both of them were situated low on the wall near the floor.

And here I was, standing in a few inches of water while I fooled around with an electric switch. Was I trying to electrocute myself?

The light steadied, and I was still alive. Water was seeping in from under the front door. Maybe the drain outside was blocked. I sloshed over and opened it to take a look. A higher wall of water surged in.

More water cascaded down the steps. Shivering, I reached through the murky, foul-smelling mess and felt for the drain covering. It not only wasn't blocked, but water seemed to be rising out of it. I shut the door, and the surge became a seep once again.

I went to my single window and peered out. The window was only inches above ground level, and it looked out into an alley that ran beside the building. The security light over the dumpster revealed a flowing stream of water headed toward the street. If it got any deeper, it would start leaking in around the window, too.

Looking around in despair, I wondered if I was going to lose everything I owned. The apartment had come furnished, so I really didn't have that much of my own stuff to lose, but I couldn't afford to replace what I did own.

And if the apartment was flooded, where was I going to stay?

First things first. I went to the wobbly dresser along one wall and pulled out all the clothes I owned. I also took my small stash of cash—it was just about $100 now—and shoved that in my pocket. I also grabbed an unopened package of four tiny flashlights attached to flimsy key rings. I'd seen them at the dollar store and gotten two packages. The power in the apartment was not one hundred percent reliable. The flashlights only gave a pinprick of light, but it was a bright light and a whole lot better than total darkness.

No question I would be going to work. An overtime shift like tonight paid time and a half. No point in staying here and missing out on that. So the question was, what could I do with my stuff?

The socks I was wearing were completely soaked, and I knew working all night with wet feet would be a nightmare. I took a rolled-up pair of dry woolen socks and put them in my lunch box, next to my sandwiches. I added a clean, dry set of underwear, then folded a pair of blue jeans on top. The lunch box wouldn't close. I set it aside for now.

Taking the rest of my clothes, I put them in one of the plastic trash bags Mandy had given me. I put the trash bag in my laundry basket and looked around at what else I had. I added some of my limited supply of food, the things that would spoil if they got wet—bread, ramen noodles, oatmeal, and the open jar of peanut butter.

The whole thing wasn't too heavy. I stood on one of my chairs. Its seat sagged under my feet, and the whole thing swayed, but it held. I hefted the laundry basket as close to the overhead pipes as I could. Using torn bits of plastic trash bag, I tied it to the sturdiest-looking pipes. That ought to keep everything dry, even if the water rose to street level.

Unless the pipes broke.

I looked mournfully at my bed. It was lumpy and drooped, but when I snuggled down into the valley in the middle, it was much more comfortable than a prison bunk. I rolled the sheets, blankets, and pillow up into a sausage roll and tied it with more torn strips of plastic. Then I secured the whole roll to some other pipes.

I couldn't think of any way to secure the mattress. My strips of plastic were pretty much used up. And I didn't think they'd be strong enough to hold the mattress anyhow, even if the pipes could take the load.

When I stepped off the chair, I realized the water was creeping up my shins.

The dishes, pans, and cutlery might get dirty and need a good scrubbing, but they shouldn't be ruined by the floodwaters. I left them in the sink.

Thank goodness I'd left the boots up on the seat of the other chair. They were damp, but they weren't soaked. Although, they might be by the time I got to work. I got dressed, putting my warm sweater over my flannel shirt. The jeans and socks I was wearing were thoroughly wet, but there wasn't much I could do about that. I slipped into the jacket with its plastic lining and grabbed the lunchbox.

I'd forgotten that I couldn't get it closed, so it wasn't latched. The contents fell out on the table and toward the edge. I caught everything just before it tumbled into the water.

Putting everything but the jeans back in, I secured the latch on the lunchbox and folded the jeans, which I tucked inside the sweater I was wearing. I picked up my boots and opened the door.

Another wall of water, higher than last time, surged through the door. It came up to my knees. In my wet sock feet, I waded out the door and into the waterfall that tumbled down the stairs toward my apartment.

When I got to the sidewalk, it was covered with an inch or so of flowing water. Glumly, I realized most of it was headed toward my stairwell.

No matter how wet it was, I couldn't walk all the way to work without the boots on, so I stepped into the shelter of the entry to the storefront church upstairs to put on my boots. The interior was dark and silent. I debated about putting on the dry socks, too, but decided I'd be better off if I waited until I got to work to put them on. At least they wouldn't get drenched immediately.

The steel plant was uphill from my apartment. In the streets, a few inches of water flowed relentlessly down toward the river.

I was so wet by the time I got to work that I left a stream of water behind me. The crowd gathering for the overtime shift was smaller than usual. A few other people looked damp and bedraggled, but no one else was as soaked as I was.

Of course, no one else on the shift walked to work, at least in weather like this.

A puddle formed around my feet as I punched in, and the trail of water followed me as I walked across the shop floor.

The workers on the shift that was about to end finished up their work. Sparks and the smell of hot steel and oil filled the air as they hurried to turn out a few more pieces and then double checked their quotas. The midnight shift was smaller than the other two. The operators who were shutting down their equipment put it in safety mode, while those who would be relieved momentarily made sure everything was ready for the next workers.

Everyone eyed the damp floor behind me and glanced toward the high windows, but it was dark and no one could see the rain. The pounding of the machinery masked the sound of the driving rain on the metal roof and made conversation below a shout impossible.

I went into the men's room to change my pants and socks. It was an expansive place, all aged porcelain sinks and dented steel urinals, added when indoor plumbing for factory workers came into vogue. During WWII, when the plant ran at full capacity—three shifts, seven days a week—producing bomb casings, the restrooms underwent a huge expansion. Now, with smaller shifts, it was much bigger than we needed, and only the front section was lighted. A long bench ran under a window set high on the wall. The hexagonal white tiles had long ago turned dingy gray.

A row of hooks lined one section of the wall. I took off my jacket, turned it inside out, and hung it, hoping it would have a better chance to dry off some than if I left it on the crowded hooks next to the time clock. I sat on a bench under the hooks and pulled off my boots. Of course they were wet, but that couldn't be helped right now. I changed to the dry jeans and socks, then hung the wet ones up on other hooks. I hoped nobody would mess with them.

Grabbing my lunchbox, I went back out to the tables sandwiched between the time clock and a row of battered vending machines that, when they were in the mood, dispensed a variety of stale snacks and a dark liquid that purported to be coffee. By some trick of technology, the coffee dispenser sometimes failed to provide a paper cup. It then became a fully automatic machine, not only dispensing the coffee, but also managing to consume it by sending it down a drain, which then overflowed onto the floor from beneath the machine.

I adjusted my hard hat and glanced around at the people assembled for the shift. Over half the shift hadn't shown up. Since it was the sixth shift this week, overtime, no one would get written up for missing it.

Aaron was nowhere to be seen. No surprise, but I was pretty curious about where he was. Probably up to no good.

But Kelly had come. Kelly was the other forklift driver on the shift and my sometimes-girlfriend. She'd be a lot more than sometimes, if it was up to me, but she insisted on keeping it what she called "non-committed." We both had issues, and I respected her decision not to make our relationship more permanent. Besides, what could I really offer any woman in terms of a relationship? I was on parole, with twenty years backup time if the parole was ever violated. Not exactly a stable foundation for any type of long-term arrangement.

Kelly usually worked out in shipping, loading and unloading trucks, while I handled the work in the shop and warehouse, bringing parts, removing pallets of completed products, and generally moving anything that needed to be moved. We kept an eye on the workload and helped each other out. Kelly had a problem with reading—couldn't read at all, really, although she had learned to recognize certain words and knew what they meant—and the paperwork had recently changed. She needed help with packing lists, bills of lading, and the like.

It gave me a chance to spend some time with her at work. It wouldn't be long, though, before she got it mostly figured out on her own.

I was willing to bet that the management staff, who stayed shut in their offices most of the time and didn't know any of the laborers, had no idea what a problem it could be for some of us when they changed the paperwork around.

If more people didn't show up for work, though, John, our foreman, would assign me to a production job and have Kelly handle all the forklift work. Kelly had seniority over me, so that was fair enough. But it would mean I would be tied to whatever machine I was assigned to all night and not have a chance to talk to her. And she'd be on her own with anything that needed to be read. If John realized she couldn't read, he would likely take her off the forklift and assign someone else to "her" job.

I tried to catch her eye, but John was talking to her, giving her instructions for the shift, and she was listening intently. As soon as he dismissed her, she hurried off to the charging stations, where the electric forklifts would be plugged in to recharge their batteries. I turned to watch her go, her long dark hair pulled into a ponytail under her hard hat, the end of it brushing her ample rear.

Frowning, John came up to the rest of us and looked over the little knot of workers gathered. He then stared at his clipboard, tapping his teeth with a worn pencil stub.

"Jesse." He gestured toward me.

I got up and made my way over next to him, where I could hear what he said if he raised his voice enough.

"Go get your lift. They've changed the assignments, and we have to assemble a lot of loads tonight. Get back to the dispatcher's office and see what you need to get from the warehouse."

"Okay." I debated asking why we were preparing to ship so much out on a Saturday, but decided John might see that as me challenging the instructions. Workers at my level don't ask questions. They do what they're told.

He said, "There's a lot of floating ice on the river. Looks like most of the bridges might have to be closed, including the new one on the interstate. A couple of the shippers dispatched extra trucks this weekend, trying to get ahead of that."

"You want me and Kelly to work out who does what on that?" I asked.

John nodded, not particularly concerned as long as the work got done and we didn't create any problems squabbling about who took what task. He knew we got along pretty well.

I went back to the charging stations, passing Kelly as she drove by. She waved to me and smiled. I nodded and grinned foolishly back.

A row of forklifts were plugged in to charge their batteries. Beyond that were a pair of tug mules, which are enormously strong industrial tractors designed to pull loads, and a few assorted hand lifts. I went to one of the forklifts and pulled down the clipboard with the pre-shift checklist from its nail.

Bert, one of the drivers from the four to midnight shift, eased his lift into an empty charging dock and clambered down. He plugged it in and grabbed the clipboard that hung next to it. Patting his pockets, he shook his head and turned toward me.

"Left my pencil somewhere. Can I borrow yours?"

Surprised, I made one last notation on my list and handed my pencil over to him. Most of the workers on that shift didn't talk to me. Everyone in the factory knew I was on parole for murder. Because of some unsavory rumors that had drifted around, a fair number of them thought erroneously that I was a convicted child molester, on the sex offender registry. They figured I got off easy and didn't deserve to be back on the street. Ever.

Not a whole lot I could do about people who were too stupid or lazy to look it up on the registry, which was online, before they would believe that about anybody.

So most of them gave me a wide berth. That was okay with me, as long as they didn't give me grief. In the last few years, Quality Steel Fabrications had made no secret of the fact that it was taking full advantage of tax breaks available for giving jobs to convicts on parole. And with a large state prison complex just outside town, they never had a problem finding parolees to hire.

It was a huge break for me. I'd been locked up for twenty years, and I didn't have any family or friends to help me out. This was a decent job, with good benefits, and I did my best to make sure the company never regretted having hired me. What coworkers on another shift thought about me shouldn't matter, I tried to convince myself. I would hate to admit that it hurt."How's the weather out there?" Bert asked.

I shrugged. "Wet. Just as glad it's not colder. It'd be one hell of a snow storm, Or worse, an ice storm."

He made a last mark on the clipboard, stepped behind the lifts, and started to slip the pencil into his shirt pocket. "I hear we're in for some flooding. They might even close the bridges."

I hung up my clipboard and held out my hand to take the pencil back. I'd need it throughout the shift, especially if I ended up loading and unloading trucks. "True, that," I said, thinking of the water in my basement apartment. How deep would it be when I got off work?

Holding out the pencil, he said, "You run into any impassible roads on your way in tonight?"

"I walk," I said. "A lot of water in the streets. But not so's you couldn't drive through it."

He nodded. "Got to be careful, though. Sometimes it looks like it's just a few inches on the road, near a stream or a culvert or something, but you try to drive through it, and it don't take all that much to float you right off the road and downstream a bit."

"Dangerous," I agreed, wondering why he was carrying on this conversation with me. He usually ignored me.

"Yeah," he continued. "And the underpasses can get flooded, too."

When I'd moved the truck the morning before, the drains in the underpass were already sluggish. It had rained all day. I wondered what it was like now.

The other lift driver on that shift, Diffy, came careening around the corner. Because the electric lifts run silently, we hadn't heard it approach. Bert and I both jumped back to avoid being hit.

Diffy slid his forklift into the docking bay, bumping the wall with a resounding thud. Several of the clipboards tumbled from their nails.

"Hey, dude," Bert said. "Watch it there. You almost nailed us."

I went over, picked up one of the fallen clipboards, and put it back on its nail.

Diffy leapt off his lift and came back, drawing himself up to his full height in front of Bert. "What're you doing standing in the aisle?" he asked. "That's asking to be hit."

"No, it's not," Bert protested. "You got to be in the aisle sometimes."

"Yeah? What're you doing jawing with this jailbird?"

I straightened up and looked toward him. "I don't want no trouble," I said.

Diffy turned toward me and spit on the floor. "Wasn't talking to you," he said. "Probably do the world a favor, though, if I ran into you and put you out of commission. Save a couple of kids. You can bet I wouldn't talk to you."

Last thing I needed was getting in trouble over something stupid at work. But I was in the union now, so I couldn't be fired for just anything. And Bert was a witness to this. So I raised my eyebrows and said, "No? Who you talking to now?"

A mulish expression came over Diffy's face. "You, punk."

"Oh. I must have been mistaken. I thought I just heard you say you wasn't going to talk to me."

Bert snickered.

Diffy's face turned red, and he turned to Bert. "You think you're so smart. You think you're gonna run the forklift on overtime tomorrow? I'll see you don't. I'll get the shift."

Bert just grinned. "Go for it. I turned it down, anyhow. They're not running our shift tomorrow, so it'd have to be day shift. I'm not going home just to be back in less than eight hours."

Fists clenched, Diffy turned on his boot heel and stomped away.

"What's the matter with him?" I asked.

Bert shrugged. "He got caught smoking back by the exhaust fan. Thinks I turned him in."

"Did you?"

"Nope. Foreman was looking for him, and I told him which way Diffy was headed last I saw him. What else could I do? But I didn't know what he was doing back there."

"What was he smoking?"

"I dunno. Cigarette, I suppose. But could have been a blunt or something."

I picked up another fallen clipboard and hung it up. "You'd think that'd mellow him out some."

"Yeah. But it doesn't seem to have." Bert climbed on Diffy's abandoned forklift and straightened it out.

I pulled the plug out from the wall, attached it, and made sure it was charging.

"Thanks, man." Bert picked up that clipboard from the floor. "Can I borrow the pencil again? He didn't fill this out, and if there's any grief about drivers not taking care of the paperwork on this shift, I'll get caught up in it."

I handed it over. "You gonna put his name down?"

"Uh-huh. Sure ain't gonna put mine down, the way he was driving that thing. If he tore anything up, I don't want to get blamed."

The factory whistle signaled the shift change. I took my pencil back and stuck it in my pocket again. Then I swung up on the forklift and eased it out into the aisle.

"Thanks, man," Bert said again and waved as I pulled off.

I waved back.

John would keep an eye on things on the shop floor. It was a light shift. He'd move what he could with a hand lift and come get me if he needed me to move anything.

But before I headed to the shipping room, I swung by the plating room. Four operators worked in a continual thunderous rhythm, removing shiny finished products from the moving hooks in front of them and replacing them with dull, unfinished shelves. The hooks then rose to a series of steaming tanks of chemicals which would clean them and electroplate a shiny finish. The operators would no sooner have loaded one set of hooks than the next set, carrying its finished parts, would be in front of them. Two pallets stood in front of each work station, one for the finished parts and one with the parts that needed to be plated.

Those pallets were too heavy for John to move with a hand lift. The platers took almost a whole shift to set up and another to tear down, so regardless of how few workers showed up for the shift, they would run the whole time.

Hank, the plating room group leader, waved me over to his office and shut the heavy door. The din from the platers still rattled the window in the door and meant we had to shout, but at least we could carry on a conversation.

"What the hell's going on tonight?" he asked, gesturing at a messy pile of paperwork on his desk.

When I was new here, Hank had taken me under his wing and taught me how to run the platers. I owed him. He'd worked at Quality Steel for several decades, most of them in the plating room. He couldn't read worth anything, but he had compensated over the years by developing a phenomenal memory for information given orally. Now that almost everything was in writing, though, he struggled with deciphering his instructions. Like Kelly, he worried that he'd lose his job if any supervisors realized he couldn't read. Loyalty, hard work, and common sense meant nothing to the young suits who ran around rearranging the work.

"I know they've rescheduled things a bit. Some extra trucks are coming in, trying to get some product out before they shut down the bridges. If they do."

"Wouldn't surprise me at all if they do," Hank said. "You seen them big chunks of ice floating in the river?"

I picked up the paperwork. "Nah. I didn't get over that way." I sorted through it quickly, grabbed the stapler on his desk, and stapled each multi-sheet set of specs and directions. He could read numbers all right, so I took my pencil stub and started numbering them.

"First, these wire baskets. Five thousand of them." I circled the stock number and the quantity and put a big "1" in the corner of the paper.

He nodded and took those papers.

"Then these big shelves. You know, the ones that are almost five-foot long. Thirty-five hundred of them." Once again, I circled the relevant numbers and wrote a big "2" on the front of the first page. "They want nine hundred forty of those bins with the hooks on the back. You know, the ones that like to get caught on the edges of the plating tanks." I wrote a big "3" on that.

He grimaced. When something got caught, the plater would have to be shut down and the operator would have to climb up to the catwalk surrounding the tall tanks to fish it out. They would take a lot longer than the timekeeper thought they should, and the entire operation would fall behind schedule. Happened every time we ran those shelves, but there was never any allowance made for it, so Hank would be left trying to explain why his crew hadn't reached their quota.

"Thanks," Hank said gloomily, putting the papers in a careful pile back on the desk.

I left the office and climbed back on the lift, driving down the aisle in front of the platers. Two of the operators nodded a greeting, but the noise level was too high to say anything. The other two operators were not accustomed to running the platers and were struggling to keep up with the never-ending parade of plated parts and empty hooks. They had to concentrate on their work and couldn't spare even a few seconds for a glance in my direction.

Assuring myself that all the platers were stocked with parts, I drove out to the shipping room to see what Kelly and I needed to do. Truckers liked to be out on the road early, before traffic out on the roads picked up for the day. If anyone else was out in this weather.

Semis were backed into several of the truck bays. Kelly was picking up loaded pallets from a row and loading them into a trailer. The driver, his cowboy hat pushed back on his head, was checking his paperwork against the load.

When I got closer, I could hear the rain drilling down on the truck bay overhang and the roof of the trailer. I shivered, thankful that I had brought the dry socks and jeans to change into. The socks were damp and getting damper by the minute, but damp was a far cry from squishy wet.

I wasn't looking forward to this shift.

CHAPTER 5

John was talking to a small knot of truck drivers, and he gestured me over.

"We need to finish loading them," John said. "They've got to get over the river, and at the rate the rain is coming down, they might close the bridge any time. Check the packing lists and see what you have to get from the warehouse."

I nodded. "Are we expecting shipments tonight?"

"We were," John said, glancing down at his clipboard, "but it's anybody's guess whether they'll be able to get here."

I drove over to the dispatcher's office, darkened and locked on this shift. Outside the door, a computer sat on a shelf, ready to spit out the multi-page packing lists. I climbed down, punched in a code and the date and shift, and stepped back while it spit out a huge volume of paperwork. I held my hand out to catch the sheets as they came out.

When I'd first come to work here, just a few months ago, the packing lists had been hand-generated, one-page affairs with a straightforward list of what the shipment should consist of and the quantity. Some genius in the front office had redone the system so that a computer program took care of assembling the packing lists and bills of lading. It also was supposed to track inventory and make all kinds of information available at a glance. And of course, it created the complicated work orders for Hank in the plating room.

It may have worked well for the office staff. As far as we were concerned, the computer didn't tell us jack shit. All we were authorized to do was punch in a set of numbers and watch the reams of paper flood out. If we weren't careful to catch all of it as it spewed forth, a cross-current in the drafty shipping area would catch some sheets of paper and blow them around. Even if we could gather them all—and I think there were still a few caught high in the rafters from before we'd all realized this—we'd have to try to reassemble them. Since they didn't have headings or page numbers, that could be quite a chore.

Now, instead of one handwritten page, we got a whole stack of paperwork we had to decipher. I didn't mind so much, since I could read pretty fast, but some people, like Hank and Kelly, had trouble shifting through all that stuff to find the information they needed. But what did the office staff care if those of us who actually did the work had a harder time of it?

We had two clipboards available, but management didn't deign to provide staplers or paperclips here, and the clipboards held only so much.

I folded down the corner of each set of papers and tore a narrow strip in the folded corner, then twisted it. It was an effective system that held the sheets together, the system we used in prison to keep voluminous stacks of legal paperwork organized. Staplers were kept locked in desk drawers accessible only to staff. Paper clips, which in practiced fingers made great handcuff keys, were completely forbidden.

Since I knew Kelly would have trouble with the packing lists, I tried to catch up with her a couple of times a shift to help her with the paperwork. She got mad sometimes, since she didn't like to admit she couldn't do it on her own.

Kelly finished loading the truck. The driver checked his load, signed a receipt, and handed it to Kelly. She glanced at it and folded it, then slipped it down the neck of her sweatshirt, tucking it on top of her large bosom.

The driver closed and locked the back doors and climbed into his cab. His lights came on as he pulled away.

A blast of driving rain blew through the open door. Kelly hurried over to hit the button that brought the overhead door down.

I thought about my apartment. How high would the water get? Where was I going to go if staying there wasn't possible? I could ask Kelly if I could camp out at her place for a while, but I was a bit afraid of what it would do to our volatile up-and-down relationship.

As it was, Kelly treated me like a regular person, not a paroled convict. An equal. I was eternally grateful to her. Would all that change if she knew I didn't have a place to stay? She might see me as super-needy. I didn't think I could stand having her feel sorry for me.

Not only that, but she was the only woman I'd ever slept with.

I didn't want to jeopardize a budding relationship, either with pity or too much togetherness.

The apartment would either be okay or it would not. Nothing I could do about it now, though, other than to hope the water stopped rising before it ruined the furniture, not to mention the heating, plumbing, and electrical systems in the building. If the sanitary sewers backed up in addition to the storm drains, the whole place would be completely uninhabitable for a considerable length of time, even if the landlord decided to spend the money to get it cleaned up. I had to stop obsessing about it.

What I could do, when I got off from work, was go buy some tarps, bungie cords, and rope, and I'd be able to get some more of the stuff, like the mattress, hung up high enough that it stayed dry. Maybe.

We worked through the night. I pulled stock and assembled loads, lining up the pallets and crates in the order we expected to load trucks. When Kelly got swamped with work, I switched to loading trucks.

As we got nearer to eight a.m., one last truck backed into a bay. The driver came in, shaking rain off his hat. "Done closed the bridge, right after me," he said. "Almost didn't make it. Water's high, and you can hear them damn chunks of ice crashing into the bridge supports."

"You want me to load you, even if you can't get back across the bridge?"

"Hell, yeah. I'm going east, then south. I don't need to go back over it again." He chewed and looked around for someplace to spit. "Make sure you get it right this time. Last time, somebody here made a mistake."

I hoped it wasn't on our shift. We hadn't heard anything about it. "You got the wrong stuff?" I asked. "Or you were short?"

He laughed. "That's just it. I was over by one crate. So I just let it be. Made me a few bucks. But it's likely that where there's one mistake made, others will be, too. And not always in my favor."

The missing crate might not show up until the warehouse was inventoried, and by then, no one would be able to figure out what had happened to a single missing crate. I wondered why he hadn't just kept his mouth shut.

"That guy Aaron, who works here. You seen him tonight?"

I looked warily at the driver. "Didn't show up for work tonight. But it's overtime. He don't want to, he don't have to work it."

Aaron had been missing a lot of work lately. Anybody else would have been fired. Anybody who wasn't a police informant.

"Damn," the guy said. "He told me he'd be here tonight."

Kelly was busy loading root baskets at the other end of the dock, so I found his shipment, which I'd assembled earlier, and swung the lift around to pick up the first pallet.

The driver pulled out his log book and a pen and sat down at a rough-hewn table the packing crew used for breaks. "Gonna write me some fiction here," he said.

When I looked over, he was slumped over the table asleep. I wondered if he was looking to buy some crystal meth from Aaron so he could keep awake. And how safe he would be out on the road. Either with the meth or without it.

I finished putting the last bit on the truck and went over to shake his shoulder and wake him up.

"You can't be done yet," he said. "I just sat down here." He insisted on taking the packing list and scrambled over the load, checking every pallet. I called John over to okay it.

That part wasn't totally necessary, but John was right there, and if it made the driver happy and meant he was less likely to complain later, it seemed like a smart move.

John initialed the packing list and stepped over to straighten out the top row of a crate by the packing line. The crew was working a man short and had to hustle to keep up with the conveyor belt delivering the finished parts.

The driver slammed the doors to the trailer shut. "You tell Aaron I'll be back here one night next week, hear? And that Denver wants to see him. That's me. Nick sent me. We got business to finish up." He rubbed his red eyes with the back of his hands. "He can't hide forever, and there's a lot of people looking for him."

I nodded, even though I had no intention of conveying the message. I wondered what kind of trouble Aaron had managed to get himself into now. He sure had a knack for it.

Tearing off the sheets that the dispatcher would need in the morning, I slipped them through the slot in the door of the locked office. John watched the semi's taillights disappear through the gate and then walked to the edge of the loading dock and peered down. "Oh, my Lord."

I went over and looked down with him. At least a foot of dark, foul-smelling water was pooled against the building at the foot of the bay.

John shook his head. "Them storm drains must be completely backed up. It's been years since we've had flooding anything like this. I just hope they don't overflow into the regular sewers. That'd be a real mess."

Remembering the water on my apartment floor, I had to agree with that assessment. I fervently hoped the same thing.

Near time for us to punch out. Day-shift workers were milling around the time clock, gloomy at the prospect of spending an entire Saturday at work, even if it was time and a half. But they'd be glad they'd done it next Friday when the paychecks came.

Everything was running as smoothly as it could. I made a round to make sure all the work stations had what the machine operators needed to start the new shift and cleared a few pallets of finished goods back to the warehouse. There were a few wet spots on the floor, and as I watched, big drops splashed from the ceiling at least thirty feet overhead and plunked onto the worn wooden floor. The roof was leaking. I'd never seen it do that before.

Satisfied that everything was taken care of for the minute, I parked the lift, leaving it running, and made a quick stop in the men's room.

The jacket that I'd left hanging on a hook was bunched up on the floor under the bench. Who would do that? Maybe it had fallen off the hook and someone had just kicked it out of the way.

Swearing under my breath, I picked it up and shook it out. It was still pretty wet, but at least it no longer dripped. I hung it back up. I knew I'd have to be wearing it in less than an hour.

The blue jeans were also kicked under the bench. I hauled them out, too, and hung them back up. The socks were nowhere in sight. I looked around, then checked the stalls. Sure enough, there they were, floating in one of the toilets. That had to be a deliberate move.

Shaking my head, I fished them out. They were good wool socks, expensive and almost new. I rinsed them out in the sink and then hung them back on hooks.

Messing with my stuff was just stupid, senseless vandalism. It was probably some of the idiot kids on the day shift, who might think it was a great joke. I knew a few people on my own shift, like Aaron, who had the same moronic sense of humor, but they weren't working tonight. Most of the shift were serious, somewhat older people who appreciated the jobs. I debated about taking the clothes with me, but they might get in the way. Instead, I took everything off the hooks, bundled them together, and stuck them way back in a corner under the bench where someone would have to really look to see them.

I'd taken a longer break than I'd intended or was entitled to, so I headed back out to the shop floor.

No more trucks showed up. If anyone had phoned in, the calls would have gone to the dispatcher's office and been recorded. With the offices closed on our shift, no one answered the company phones.

The day foreman, Bucky, came in and started his pre-shift rounds. When he got to the shipping room, he stood and watched me. I was removing a filled pallet from the packing line. I pulled it out, moved it across the floor, and dropped it.

Usually, the line boss from the packing crew would go to the stack of empty pallets against the wall and put one in place when they needed it, but they were running short-handed. John—and common sense—had told me to help out where I could.

Swinging the forklift around, I took a small stack of pallets and moved it closer to the end of the packing line. Then I got down, grabbed one off the pile, and put it in place so the packers didn't have to stop their work.

"Thanks, man," the line boss shouted over the clanking of the overhead conveyor.

I got back on the lift and headed back to the filled pallet I'd dropped. Bucky was standing next to it, tapping a pencil on his clipboard.

"Where the hell's Kelly?" he asked.

I looked around. "Loading that truck, down there," I said, pointing to the last bay all the way down the dock.

"Then what the hell are you doing moving stuff around here?"

I blinked. "John told me to help out here."

"You call this helping?" He gestured at the lines of pallets and crates waiting to be loaded on the trucks that hadn't come in. "You're just letting the work pile up here like this? Kelly would never do that."

He might be a foreman, and by definition always right, but it didn't seem to me like Kelly would disassemble the carefully arranged lines of picked stock, each grouped according to its scheduled pick up time, each with its packing slip folded neatly into a plastic envelope clipped to the front pallet. Although the trucks might not arrive like they were scheduled, sooner or later, they'd show up. Taking everything back to the warehouse, putting it back in its place, and then reassembling the shipments made no sense to me.

"You'll have to ask John," I said. "He sets the priorities. I just do what he tells me to do."

Bucky wrinkled his forehead and frowned down at his clipboard. I sat on the idling lift, wondering if I should go get some more work done, or stay and listen to what he had to say. Technically, as a foreman, he was my supervisor, even if he was from another shift. For sure I didn't want to get written up for insubordination for either driving off or contradicting him.

John ambled up, rubbing his tired eyes. The papers on his clipboard were rumpled and smudged.

Bucky gestured toward the pallet I'd come to pick up. "What the hell is all this crap? He's just been piling up the pallets from the packing line instead of taking them back to the warehouse."

John raised his bushy white eyebrows at me. "Aren't you taking the finished pallets to the warehouse?" he asked me.

I was puzzled by the question. "Yes, sir."

Bucky snorted. "Don't lie, you lazy bum. It won't save your ass."

Even more confused, I leaned back on my seat, but I kept my mouth shut.

"What makes you think he's been doing that?" John asked.

He shook his head. "I saw him. He picked up a pallet from the end of the packing line and, instead of taking it back to the warehouse, he just dumped it there." He pointed at the pallet I'd come to pick up. "And look at all the other crap he's left lying around." He waved at the lines waiting for trucks.

"Why did you put the pallet there instead of putting it away, Jesse?" John asked.

"I was getting some more pallets to stack over here, by the line," I said. "And since they're working a man short, I got down and put one in place for them."

"And then what?" John asked.

"Then I was gonna take the finished one back to the warehouse."

"Yeah, right," Bucky said. "What about all this other stuff you were too lazy to move?"

John turned to look at the lines of pallets and crates. "Those are assembled shipments. The trucks didn't come in."

"What?" Bucky's face turned red, and his nose wrinkled up.

"The trucks didn't come in," John repeated. "I hear the bridge over the river's closed. Might not be any more trucks until the storm's past. Maybe not even for a while after that, if the river's too high."

Not particularly anxious to be around to see the dayshift foreman's reaction to being corrected, I eased the forks under the pallet in front of us and lifted it, raising the front of my forks so the load settled back snuggly. "Should I put these away?" I shouted over the packing room noise.

John glanced at me. "Yeah, go ahead. Then make sure the platers are supplied for the next shift."

"Yes, sir." I was glad to be away from the dispute.

Only a few workers had shown up. Usually, the day shift was the biggest by far, but there were barely enough people there to keep the continuous operation lines going. Of course, if the bridge was really closed, anyone who lived on the far side of the river wasn't going to be able to make it in to work. I wondered how many of those on my shift lived over there, too, and wouldn't be able to make it home.

If the homes weren't flooded out.

I picked up a pallet of finished parts from the plating room.

Now Bucky had Hank backed into the wall outside the office. He was stabbing his pencil at the clipboard he had clutched in his hand. Hank, who towered over him, was frowning and shaking his head mulishly. I'd be willing to bet that the plating room group leader hadn't shown, and he was trying to convince Hank to stay for another shift. Or at least until they could tear the platers down for the shortened weekend.

Even if he didn't want to, I knew Hank would do it rather than leave them in a lurch. And as soon as the new shift started, it would pay him double time.

I headed back to the shipping docks for one last check, but everything seemed to be more or less caught up. Kelly was off her lift, attaching big blue tags to a row of crates. I glanced around to make sure Bucky hadn't magically shown up, then eased to a stop next to her.

"You coming over?" She smiled at me, her snapping dark eyes bright in her dusky face. Her long dark hair, tied back in a ponytail, tumbled from under her hard hat and brushed her plump behind. I had to fight down an urge to reach over and stroke her hair.

I grinned back. I could think of no better way to spend a rainy Saturday than at her place, fixing dinner for her kids, playing games with them, and reading stories to them. Then, after they were asleep, joining Kelly in her big warm bed, nestled up against her expansive bosom.

"I'd love to. But I got to check on my apartment first."

She made a face. "Then come on over when you can," she said. "But make it late afternoon. I got an appointment with my lawyer about the divorce settlement. The kids are with their dad. He's supposed to drop them off at nine tonight." She raised one eyebrow and grinned.

"Don't give my spot in the bed away," I said, a wave of giddy warmth washing over me. "I'll be over if I can make it."

She nodded and swung back up on her lift.

I parked outside the men's room so I could go in and get my wet clothes.

No one had messed with them this time. I folded them more neatly and tucked them back in the plastic bag. I went out to get the lift. I had to return it to the charging bay to run the end of shift checklist and plug it back in.

It was gone.

I stood there, clutching my bag and staring stupidly at the place where I'd left the lift. I blinked and rubbed my eyes, but it still wasn't there.

Finally, I roused myself and looked around. I could see the packing line, where the next shift workers were pulling on their gloves and adjusting their hard hats, waiting to take over when the whistle blew. A truck driver checked the row of crates that would be loaded as soon as the lift driver for this shift showed up. He should already have been there.

Down at the end of the dock near me, a truck bay stood open with no truck pulled in. Rain and wind howled in.

I stepped over to it and looked down. There was the lift. It had run off the dock and was sitting upright a few feet away from the wall, water pooling over its wheels.

John came around the corner. "Close that damn door, Jesse," he called. "We don't need more rain in here."

Turning to face him, I said, "I got a problem here, sir."

After one glance at my face, he hurried over to the bay and looked down. "How the hell did you manage to do that, Jesse?"

I shrugged. "I didn't, really. I left the lift parked for a few minutes while I went in the john."

Immediately, I winced. Couldn't I have used another term for the restroom?

John shook his head. "You left it running?"

"Yeah. We always leave them running if it's just going to be a few minutes."

He nodded. He knew that was true. "So what do you think happened?"

"I dunno. I didn't leave it facing the dock, so it couldn't have just started itself and rolled out. Besides, when I went into the men's room, the door must have been shut. I would have noticed if it was open like that." I gestured toward the open bay.

"So you think somebody did this on purpose?"

"Maybe. Or maybe somebody was trying to play a trick on me and hide it and didn't know how to drive it."

"They're not all that hard to drive," John said. "The tricky part is handling the forks. And somebody had to open the door."

I sighed. "True, that." I looked out at the rain pounding down. "I guess I ought to go down there and see if I can get it going and bring it in."

"No. It's sitting in water. It's electric. Even if you could get it started, it would be dangerous. We'll have to get a tug mule or something to haul it out. And let it dry out completely before we try to start it. Or report it so a mechanic can check it out."

That made sense to me. "Should I go get a mule?"

Waving the clipboard in his hand, Bucky stomped up to us. He gestured toward me. "This fool drive the lift off the dock?"

He hadn't looked. How did he know it was down there?

John didn't answer directly. "We're figuring out how to get it out of the water and back in here."

Bucky snorted. "What, and have him on the clock for another few hours? I don't think so. He shouldn't make money because of his stupid accident. Unless it wasn't an accident."

"What do you mean?" John asked.

Bucky glowered at me. "Maybe he did it on purpose."

"I'll punch out," I offered, "and come back to get it out. Off the clock."

"What, and not be covered by workman's comp? So you can sue the company? I don't think so. You get the hell out of here." He took a menacing step toward me.

John moved closer to me. "Jesse, you punch out and go. We'll take care of this."

The whole thing didn't make sense to me. Although I had no idea how this could be my fault, I felt responsible for trying to fix it. I started to say something, but the look on John's face stopped me. I nodded and turned away, heading down the long hallway toward the time clock.

A forklift came rushing toward me, swerving in my direction even as I backed up against the wall.

Diffy was driving. Although the rest of his clothes were dry, his pants were soaking wet to the knees.

CHAPTER 6

The rain was coming down harder than it had been when I'd gone into work. Sheets of water swept across the pavement, and the street itself was a broadening river.

If I was going to have any chance to get the rest of my stuff up out of harm's way, I had to do it now. That was assuming, of course, that the water in my apartment wasn't going to rise above street level.

I stopped at the Best Deals for Your Dollar store on the way home. It was crowded with people buying flashlights and batteries, bottles of water, and plastic tablecloths. Plastic tablecloths. That puzzled me for a minute until I realized the shelves that had held tarps were empty.

After I picked up a couple of packages of bungee cords, I looked for rope. I had to settle for a few plastic clotheslines, but they looked pretty strong and wouldn't stretch. I got in the long checkout line.

Tugging an end of one of the clotheslines free from the packaging, I tested its flexibility and strength. It felt strong enough, but the flexibility wasn't good. It would have to do. I knew how to tie knots.

Back when I was first locked up, I had a cell buddy called Skipper who was not entirely sane—the first in a long series of randomly assigned people who shared that unfortunate characteristic. He looked like a stereotype of a sailor, skinny and permanently burnt by the sun and salt water, and he had a long history of convictions for stealing sailboats. But it never seemed to slow him down. As soon as Skipper was released, he'd sneak into a marina, choose a likely boat, and sail it away all by himself, which was not an easy feat. He'd sail it around for a few days, then eventually he'd try to sell it, which was usually when he got caught.

When we were sharing a cell, he was obsessed with collecting dental floss, most of it used, and braiding it into ever-thickening ropes. I had nothing better to do, so I worked on it with him. He taught me how to tie all kind of different knots.

Eventually, he used the dental floss ropes to rappel down the outside of the cellblock and then made a try for the outer perimeter. He got caught on the razor wire.

I ended up being drilled for hours about what I knew, which wasn't much, but I had to concede that I knew about the dental floss. I told them I knew he was making rope—contraband in and of itself—but that I thought he was planning to sell it to other inmates to use as clotheslines in their cells. And maybe fishing lines to pass notes and commissary items from one cell to another.

Likely story, but they couldn't disprove it. And I was still there. I picked up ninety days in disciplinary segregation. I have never spent a longer ninety days. That daunting experience convinced me the best way to handle doing time was to be as cooperative as I could be with the institution staff and procedure. Basically avoid trouble whenever I could.

I liked to think of Skipper out there, beyond the bay and well into the ocean, sailing on a probably stolen boat into the sunset.

A boat, stolen or otherwise, might come in handy now if the flooding got much worse.

If a single clothesline wasn't strong enough to hold my stuff up, I could braid three of them together. I had six of them.

As the line of customers inched forward, I ended up standing next to the grocery section of the store. I looked hungrily at the packages of food. The bread and milk were all gone, and as I watched a lady snatched up the last few boxes of cold cereal. What little food I had was in the laundry basket hung from the pipes, but most of it needed to be heated, and I was pretty sure I wasn't going to tempt the electrical gods again by using any appliances or lights in my apartment until things dried out considerably. Which might be quite a while. I added a bag of generic trail mix to my purchases and promised myself I wouldn't open it until I was really hungry.

The lights flickered and went out. The electronic cash register died. The checkout line ceased its glacial forward movement. At least it was dry in here.

We all looked out the big front window. The buildings across the street still had lights.

The manager came rushing out of the tiny office, a calculator in his hand. "You'll have to add up the purchases with this." He gave it to the cashier.

"The display won't work," she said. "It needs more light than we've got."

Nodding, the manager went back into his office and came back with a flashlight. He shined it onto the calculator. "This work?"

"Yeah," the cashier said. "But I can't hold it and use the calculator at the same time."

With a sigh, the manager took a box of candy on the counter and dumped the contents into a bin. Then he tried to set the flashlight on the box, but it kept rolling over.

He reached below the counter and came up with a stack of plastic bags, placed them on top of the box and nestled the flashlight on top. "How's that?" he asked.

"Okay, I guess," the cashier said, "but I got no change."

"What'd you mean, you got no change?"

"The cash register won't open. All the change is in there."

The manager looked at the darkened cash register. He tried pushing a few buttons, but of course, it wouldn't open. "I got some cash in the office," he said and hurried away.

He brought out a cash drawer and placed it the on the counter. "You know how to add everything up on the calculator?" he asked.

"If it's got a price on it," she said. "If it don't, I can't scan it, can I?"

"Of course not." The manager picked up the first item on the counter—a box of crackers. "This has a sticker. It's two twenty-nine. Punch it in."

"Okay."

He picked up the next item, a jar of peanut butter. "Three twenty-nine. Punch that in."

The cashier stared at the calculator. "Now it's this big long number."

"Did you hit the plus sign?"

"No. You didn't say to hit the plus sign."

The manager's thin lips got thinner. "Hit the plus sign. Do that every time you add a new item."

"So how do I get this big long number off?"

"Hit the 'clear' button."

"Okay."

"Now punch in two twenty-nine. Got that?"

"Yeah."

"Now the plus sign. Now the three twenty-nine."

"Okay."

"What do you have now?"

"Five fifty-eight."

The manager picked up the next item, a can of chili. "This says one seventy-nine. Punch that it."

"It's on sale two for three dollars," the customer grumbled.

The manager closed his eyes. "Punch in a dollar fifty instead."

The cashier stared at the calculator. "I already put in the one seventy-nine. How do I get that out?"

"Hit the 'clear' button."

"That took everything off."

The man in front of me shifted his shopping basket from one hand to the other. "This is gonna take forever."

I nodded in agreement.

"And they haven't even gotten to the sales tax. Or making change."

Again, I nodded.

"I don't think I need this stuff that badly," the guy said. He put his basket on an empty shelf beside us and left.

I glanced in his basket. Toothpaste, a package of socks, and some plastic flowers. Nothing I really wanted to buy.

If there's one thing being locked up for years teaches a person, it's how to wait patiently. And I wanted the stuff I'd picked out badly enough to wait.

My turn finally came. The manager announced the prices, the cashier punched them into the calculator, and they came up with a total. They seemed to have abandoned the idea of sales tax.

I fished the money out of my pocket, counting out exact change. The bills were wet and limp. The cashier, a bemused expression on her face, smoothed them out and put them under the counter. "Maybe they'll dry," she said.

I tucked my purchases in the same bag as my wet clothes and went back out in the cold and wet, heading for home.

Once I was past the back of the courthouse complex going in the direction of my apartment, the neighborhood deteriorated block by block. Every day when I walked by, more and more of the storefronts were vacant, a few with windows cracked or boarded up. Broken fences surrounded weedy patches of yard in front of ill-kept row houses. Even the water cascading next to the curbs looked dirtier and carried more trash.

And the water was definitely getting deeper in the streets. It no longer paused to make large, lazy circles over the storm drains, but just continued rushing on its way, as if there was no room in the storm sewers for any more. There probably wasn't.

The streetlights overhead flickered a few times and went out. It couldn't be an automatic turn off because it was daytime; it had been daytime for a few hours now. If they were on light sensors, not timers, they had stayed on because the day was so dark. But why would they have gone out now?

I glanced at the buildings. None of them showed lights. The power must have gone out there, too.

Turning a corner a few blocks from my place, I was confronted by a line of sawhorses mounted with blinking, battery-operated caution lights. Several utility trucks and fire trucks stood in the flooded streets, their lights flashing. I felt like I had stepped onto the garish stage of some surrealistic underwater show.

As I hesitated, a firefighter in bright yellow turnout gear stepped up. "Can't go any further, Mac," he said. "Lines are down all over the place. The electric company's trying to get the power all shut down."

"How long's it gonna be?"

He shrugged. "Your guess is as good as mine. But a while."

Standing there looking stupidly through the gloom toward my apartment, I realized I couldn't go home. I'd have to find someplace else.

The firefighter glanced in the same direction. "You live down there?"

"Yeah."

"Well, there's a mandatory evacuation. I don't know how long it's gonna be. But everything past here down to the river is flooding anyhow. You got things you need to get?"

"Kind of. I was hoping to get some of my stuff out so it might not get ruined."

He shook his head. "Tough. You live on the ground floor?"

"Basement."

He winced. "Don't know there's much you could do, anyhow. But I can't let you past until the electric company says it's safe. You got someplace to go?"

I shrugged.

"They're setting up an emergency shelter at the high school," he said. "At least it'd be a place to get in out of the rain. And they'd feed you. Probably have a cot, too. Maybe dry clothes."

Great. I could just imagine how welcome I'd be at an emergency shelter. It'd be okay if no one recognized me, but I couldn't see them not having a couple of cops stationed there. One of them was bound to know who I was.

Kelly had invited me over, but she wouldn't be home for a while yet. I could stop at the library. If they still had power and the computers were working, I could maybe even find out how much longer they expected it to rain.

I retraced my steps back toward the center of town.

Some lights were on at the library, but it had a big sign on the door that just said, "Closed." No sanctuary there.

Sanctuary. I thought about churches. Surely a church would let people in who had nowhere else to go in out of the rain.

Two big churches were across from one another a block down from where I was. I turned in that direction.

The first of them had a big hand-lettered sign on it that said, "Closed due to power outage." How could a church close? But it had. Maybe churches weren't open all the time like they used to be. Or maybe I was wrong and they never had been.

I went up the steps to the other one and pulled on the huge bronze handle. It didn't budge. Peering around, I saw a sign that said, "Please use side entrance," and an arrow pointing down the alley to the side of the building.

The church offices were around there. Through the glass doors, I could see the waiting area was crowded with dripping people, most of them wearing fashionable raincoats and other protection against the weather.

The church must have had an emergency generator. The whole interior was lit, but dimly.

I opened the door and stepped in.

A man with a clipboard approached me. His lip curled back as his eyes traveled over me, from wet boots to soaked watch cap, still lined with the corner of plastic trash bag that Mandy had given me. He drew himself up straighter and sighed. "Are you a member of our congregation?"

When I was a kid, I'd lived mostly in foster homes. In the best one, Mrs. Coleman, the foster mother, had insisted that all the children in her home dress up and attend church with her every Sunday morning for as long as they lived there. I figured I was more in the category of sinner than church-goer now, and since I had no intention of reforming and being saved, at least right now, I hadn't gone into any churches in the couple of months since my release. But I remembered how peaceful those Sunday mornings had felt, sitting with Mrs. Coleman and listening to the choir. Since I'd gotten off of home detention, I liked to walk downtown when church services were held, listening to the choirs.

I gave the only answer I could. "No."

"I'm afraid," the man said, shaking his head, "that we will probably not have enough space or supplies to give shelter to all members of our own congregation who may need it. The church board made a decision that we need to reserve our resources for our own members."

Take care of their own. Hard to argue with that. It did seem like a surprisingly unchristian attitude. Practical, though.

I turned to go.

"The Red Cross is setting up an emergency shelter at the high school," the man said. "You could go there."

He was the second person to suggest that. The high school was all the way across town. The accommodations would be dormitory style, with row after row of cots. I had a pretty good idea of how uncomfortable I would be in that setting, probably never be able to sleep, but it might be a good place to go get something to eat. Maybe even some dry clothes. I could go check it out, at least.

The flooding in the streets was getting worse. The town was hilly, with some fairly high places and some really low. The low ones would probably be underwater. If I picked my route carefully and got to the other side of the railroad tracks on a bridge instead of an underpass, I should be able to make it there.

The aptly named High Street was a good place to start. It did have an underpass for the railroad, but a block or two farther on was a bridge.

I pulled the jacket closer around me and my things and turned into the driving rain.

An occasional car passed, throwing up a wake behind it.

The direction I was heading was away from the river, on higher ground. In my neighborhood, steep streets led down to the water. Downtown, with the county complex and the churches, was fairly flat, and then the town rose gently through neighborhoods with nice houses and a view of the river. The new high school was beyond that.

As I approached one of the railroad underpasses, a couple of cars were stopped at the edge of a big body of water. Someone driving a big 4WD SUV had driven into the flooded area and stalled. People think because they're 4WD, they can go anywhere. But they're just machines, with limitations like any machine. Big, expensive machines.

I stopped next to a bus shelter, where another gawker had tried to get out of the rain. The bench inside it looked just as wet as the bench outside.

Water continued to surge into the flooded underpass, swirled lazily around, and continued into a dark tunnel under the embankment beyond. Trash can lids, a lawn chair, tree limbs, and other debris bobbed on the surface.

In the little bit of time I stood staring, the water rose to the window level of the SUV. I hoped the occupants had gotten out and waded to safety.

No such luck. The front window on the passenger side rolled down, and a woman's head and shoulders emerged. She inched herself up so she was sitting on the door, her legs still inside.

Was she going to climb out and try to wade out of the water?

A few cars had stopped at the edge of the water. The driver of one got out and shouted something to the woman, but I couldn't pick up what he said, and I doubted she could, either, over the sound of the pounding rain and the rushing water.

I stepped over to the man. He had on an expensive overcoat. It was probably as soaked through as my grungy jacket, but had cost a lot more. He had to have a cell phone.

I leaned close and raised my voice. "She needs help. You gonna call 9-1-1?"

He looked stricken. "I tried. It's busy."

"9-1-1 is busy?" That shouldn't happen.

The man shook his head. "I've tried a few times. I just can't get a call through." He looked toward the stalled vehicle. His voice rose even louder. "Oh my God! She's got a kid in there."

Sure enough, the woman was wrestling to shift something from inside the SUV and through the window. It was a toddler. She finally got him—or her—free of the window and hefted the child onto the roof. We couldn't hear much, but he was struggling and crying. When the woman got him deposited up there, she ducked back inside and came up again, this time shoving an unwieldy car seat through the window and upward.

She finally got it heaved up on top and struggled herself to a half-standing position on the door frame.

The water was still rising, coming precariously close to the window opening.

Scrambling up on top of the SUV herself, she gathered the child and the car seat to her and looked pleadingly at us, panic in her eyes. The thin fabric of her shirt was plastered to her shoulders and breasts. Her hair hung in strands to her shoulders. She must be freezing.

Somebody had to do something to help the little family. Surely a first responder of some sort—police or fire rescue—would arrive any minute.

If one happened by. Or someone managed to get through to dispatch.

I glanced around, but aside from the apparently futile fumbling with a cell phone, no one was inclined to try to do anything to help.

There would be assistance just a few blocks away, where I'd been turned back. It shouldn't take me more than five or ten minutes to hurry back there, and less for them to get here, since they'd be driving.

A big tree branch hurtled down the street, carried on the torrents of water, and slammed into the side of the vehicle, moving it a foot or so.

Ten minutes might be too long.

CHAPTER 7

I tossed most of the stuff I was carrying onto a bench by the bus shelter and fished out the clotheslines I'd just bought. Maybe I could stretch a line from the side of the street to the SUV.

Stuffing the other clotheslines into my jacket's voluminous patch pockets, I tied one of the clotheslines to the trunk of a sturdy tree by the side of the road, using a clove hitch, and tugged on it. The knot held, but the rope didn't feel very sturdy at all.

Tying two others around the trunk of the tree, I backed away, braiding as I went.

It was only a couple of hundred feet from the sidewalk to the SUV, but it felt like a mile.

As I worked on the rope, the man put his cell phone in his pocket and stepped into the swirling water.

He stumbled, arms flailing, and almost went down. Stepping back up on the curb, he shrugged and shook his head. Then he looked toward me and the rope.

Another car pulled up. A big BMW, a luxury car. The window rolled down. "Shall I call 9-1-1?" a shrill female voice called.

"If you can get through," the man shouted back.

She busied herself with her cell phone. "I'm getting a busy signal!"

The bystander nodded.

I'd backed to the edge of the water, holding my line tight as I braided it. I turned around and glanced at the woman and her children on top of the SUV. She sat on the roof, watching me intently as she clutched her toddler close to her with one hand and gripped the car seat with the other.

I reached the end of the first set of clotheslines and pulled the second three out of my jacket pocket. I tried to tie one of the new lengths onto the old one, but the rope slackened and my fingers slipped on the wet plastic.

The man stepped to the curb, but didn't step off again. "Can I do anything to help?" he shouted.

Taking a few steps back toward the edge of the road and handing him the braided rope, I yelled, "Hold this taut so I can try to tie the ends."

He took the rope, but looked at me doubtfully. "Will the knots hold?" he asked.

"I hope so."

Skipper had taught me different kinds of knots, including the grapevine bend, which should work here. I closed my eyes and said a quick prayer to Skipper, if such an appeal could be called a prayer. I practically heard him saying, "You want to be real careful with your knots. If you tie them right, any weight you put on the whole thing will tighten them. But if you get them wrong, they can slip. You don't want a knot to slip when you're halfway down a wall or something."

I didn't want a knot that would slip now, either.

The man watched as my frozen fingers worked on the slippery ends. I could hardly feel the stiff plastic, but I forced my numb fingers to maneuver the ends into the correct formation.

When I'd gotten all three new ropes tied to the old ones, I pulled the whole thing as tight as I could, praying that this slippery line would hold.

It did.

The man raised his eyebrows. "That's good," he shouted. "Where'd you learn to tie knots like that. Boy Scout camp?"

In spite of the situation, I had to grin at the contrast of a Boy Scout camp vs. the prison cell where I had really learned to tie knots. I shook my head and yelled, "Nope," as I gave the whole assembly a final hard tug.

"Then you must have been a sailor," the man persisted.

Ever since Skipper, that idea had appealed to me. But the fact that I was facing close to another twenty years on parole, when I wasn't supposed to leave the state, might put a crimp in any plans for that career.

I just shook my head and kept backing into the water, manipulating the clotheslines.

The water rose over my knees. If I'd thought I couldn't get any wetter, I was wrong.

"Take off your jacket and boots," the man called. "They'll weigh you down. And if you fall…" He didn't complete that uncomfortable thought.

He was right.

But I couldn't see walking out there without the protection the boots gave my feet. I stripped off the jacket and tossed it over to him.

He put it on the bench with the rest of my stuff.

I backed toward the SUV. After the swirling water got over my hips, I had trouble staying on my feet. When it got to my waist, it was all I could do to stand upright. The water was now circling in a large swirling, surprisingly powerful current as torrents flowed down the streets and into the underpass.

Taking what line I had left, I passed the rope through the open windows and tried to make a clove hitch around doorframes. I didn't have quite enough rope, and my hands were so cold I wasn't sure I was getting the ends of the rope where I needed them to be.

When I let go, the line wasn't as taut as I would have liked. But when I pulled hard on it, it held.

I turned to face the frightened face of the woman on top of the SUV.

"You wanna give me one of the kids?" I hollered.

"Will the rope hold?" she asked.

I shrugged. "I sure hope so."

As she hesitated, the vehicle lurched a few inches in the water, tightening the line.

I didn't blame her for not trusting me. I wasn't sure I trusted myself. I said, "Or I can stay here with one kid while you take the other one."

That didn't seem like as good an idea. She was tiny. I wasn't huge— a little over six foot and a hundred and eighty pounds—but I'd been doing physical work, and those were pretty solid pounds.

She closed her eyes for a minute, then handed down the struggling toddler.

I turned him so he was facing me and clutched him to my chest with one hand, while I hung onto the rope with the other. "Put your legs around my waist and your arms around my neck," I told him.

He was frightened and sobbing, but he did what I told him.

"Now hang on tight." I began the trip through the water back to the sidewalk.

With the rope to hang onto, it was easier to make it to the sidewalk than it had been to get out to the SUV, even with the extra weight of the kid hanging on to me.

A floating plastic recycling bin swept toward us. I turned my back to shield the kid and braced myself. It bounced off my back and continued on its way. It didn't knock me over, but I'd have a nasty bruise there.

The man held his arms out for the kid as soon as I got close enough for him to reach. The kid didn't want to let go of me, but I moved in next to the curb and let the man grab him. I had to pry his arms from around my neck.

I turned around and made my way out to the SUV again without waiting to see what they were going to do with the kid. I hoped someone had a dry blanket and enough sense to take his wet clothes off, wrap him in it, and put him in a car out of the rain.

The woman was kneeling on the edge of the SUV's roof when I got back out. She handed me the car seat. A tiny figure in a pink hooded outfit wailed, arms thrashing. "Try to keep her out of the water," the woman said.

What did she think I was going to do? Dunk the car seat in the water to see if it floated? I hefted it onto my shoulder. The baby continued to scream. I didn't blame her in the least. I felt like screaming myself.

"You need to climb down and come along behind me," I shouted to the woman over the noise of the baby and the rushing water.

She looked frightened and shook her head. "The rope might not hold!"

She had a point.

"Okay," I shouted back. "As soon I get to the edge, you get down and follow."

"I can't," she wailed.

Jeez. I was making two trips with the kids, and she wouldn't even try to get herself over there? The water was getting deeper, lapping at the roof of the SUV. But we didn't have time to argue about it now. I turned and waded toward the sidewalk.

When I got to the sidewalk again, the man stepped out and reached for the car seat. I couldn't see who had the toddler, but I wasn't about to waste time worrying about it.

Another car, a little green one, pulled up to the edge of the water. I hoped it was someone who could help. I was getting awfully tired, and I just wanted to close my eyes for a minute and take a rest. I was just coherent enough to realize what a mistake that would be.

As I looked toward the new arrival, the line jerked in my hand and I heard a noise behind me. The man, baby and car seat still in his hands, gasped and stared.

The SUV had lurched again, this time moving noticeably. It was listing slightly to one side.

The mother, still stranded, threw herself down flat on the roof. She made no effort to climb down to the rope and make her way to where we stood.

The hell with her. She was the one who'd driven into the flood, she could get herself out. I was so cold. Besides, I might not be able to make a third trip without falling from exhaustion.

The man looked at me doubtfully. "You gonna go get her, too?"

I just looked at him.

"She doesn't look like she can make it," he said. "She's crying."

Forcing myself to look at the SUV again, I had to admit he was right. She was just lying there, crying.

The vehicle slipped a few feet sideways and tilted further.

With a resentful glance at the small crowd gathered, I plunged back into the flood. I made my way back to the SUV. She got to her knees at the edge of the roof, still crying.

"Come on," I said as she slipped into the water toward me. "Hang onto me the way the kid did. Arms around my neck and legs around my waist."

She clung to me, trembling. Under ordinary circumstances, I'd have been pretty uncomfortable with a woman clinging to me like that, but this wasn't an ordinary situation. With one hand, I kept my grip on the rope and put the other hand under her bottom. She had enough sense to lean into me.

The line slackened, then pulled taut again. I looked over my shoulder at the SUV. It was starting to float. A big branch crashed into it. It lurched and practically yanked the rope from my hand.

Turning back to face the group watching, I clung to the rope and headed toward the sidewalk.

When we were almost there, the rope slacked in my hand, then sagged and began to twist around my leg. I tried to shake it off, but almost lost my footing.

I let go of the rope and shoved it away from me as best I could. I changed my course to a diagonal toward the sidewalk and away from the now-useless rope.

The woman clung to me, and I could feel her shudder as she sobbed.

A flash of light almost blinded me, followed by another and another.

Anxious hands reached for the woman, pulling her up onto the wet concrete of the sidewalk.

I tried to keep going, but my knees sagged and my feet refused to move. I looked up at the source of the light flashes.

A reporter for the *Rothsburg Register*, the local newspaper. Carissa something. She'd written articles about me before, none of them flattering. With pictures that made me look like a deranged, violent fool. I couldn't worry about what she'd come up with this time. At least, not now.

As I swayed on my feet, my boots feeling too heavy to lift enough to clear the curb, the thought occurred to me that she could have held out a hand to help me up onto the sidewalk, but she was too intent on taking pictures. And she stood in the way of anyone else helping.

Finally, the man shoved her aside. He grabbed my shirt and pulled me forward.

I stumbled on the curb and went to my knees. I was so cold. And tired. If I could just lie down for a little while and rest, even in this rain, maybe in a little while, I would feel well enough to get up and see if I could find someplace out of the weather.

Before I could act on that thought and collapse, someone grabbed my arm. "Can you stand up?"

Dumbly, I nodded and struggled to my feet, trying to keep upright by leaning heavily on the person's shoulder.

"How're the kids?' I mumbled. If for some reason they weren't all right, this whole thing would have been a waste.

The person—a woman—said, "They should be fine. Howard is taking them to the hospital. Calling 9-1-1 still doesn't work. It's a good thing you got everyone when you did. Look at the SUV."

My head was heavy and wanted to fall to my chest, but I lifted my head to look. The vehicle had rolled over on its side and seemed to be floating in the swirling water.

"I think we should get you to the hospital, too."

"No! I'll be fine." I struggled to take my weight off the woman's shoulder and stand up straight. I managed, but I could tell I was teetering uncertainly.

"Why not?" she asked.

I searched my foggy brain for the reasons it seemed like such a bad idea. Partly the cost—I had insurance through my job, but the co-pay would be hefty. I hated hospitals. And if anyone, like the cops, were looking for me, I'd be easy to find.

Why would the cops be looking me? I seemed to think they might be looking for me, but I couldn't remember why. Had I done something recently? My mind was blanking.

But I wasn't about to say that to the woman who was helping me. I shook my head, trying to clear my thoughts. Mistake. I would have fallen over if she hadn't caught me.

"Why not?" she repeated. "You're freezing, and you might be hurt."

I found words surprisingly hard to form and harder to say loud enough so she could hear me over the rush of the water. "I'm not really hurt. But I am cold. And tired. I just need to find someplace to warm up and rest."

"You're slurring your words. You probably have hypothermia. I'll drive you to the hospital."

"No. Too expensive."

She made a tsking sound. "It's a bargain next to dying or getting really sick and having to stay in the hospital instead of just going to the emergency room."

I knew she was right about that. But the last thing I wanted was anybody asking questions while I was this confused and vulnerable. I said, "They're probably overwhelmed by more serious cases. And what would they do anyhow besides give me someplace warm and dry to get some sleep?"

"You might be right," she conceded. "Come on. I'll take you to my house."

"Your house?" Why would someone I didn't know want to take me to her house? And did I have an obligation to tell her I was on parole? For murder? "I think there's a shelter at the high school. You could give me a ride there."

She steered me toward her car, the BMW. "The shelter is probably just as overcrowded as the hospital. And they wouldn't take you in this shape. They'd send you to the hospital. It's either my house or the hospital. Come on."

I took a few steps in the direction she had aimed me. What was I forgetting? I stopped. My jacket and other clothes. "I need to get my jacket and stuff."

"It's right over there on the bench. You get in the car, and I'll go get that."

I was too tired to argue with her. She opened the car door, and I eased myself into the passenger seat. I ran my hand over the soft leather of the seat.

"I'm all wet. I'm gonna ruin your seats," I said.

"Nonsense," she answered.

The inside of the car was warmer, and it wasn't raining in there. I leaned my head back against the headrest. I wondered what time Kelly would be home and if I could make it over to her place. Still too early. I didn't really want her to arrive home and find me passed out on her front porch.

Maybe the shelter in the high school would take me. They'd have dry clothes and blankets. Probably a place I could lie down. I was just cold. And tired.

My hands were shaking violently. All of me was shivering uncontrollably. Maybe I should be going to the hospital.

Maybe I just didn't care that much what happened to me. My eyes closed.

The car shook as someone yanked open a back door and then slammed it shut. The driver's side door opened, and the woman climbed in.

"I really ought to try the shelter at the high school," I said. My teeth were chattering, and the words came out weird.

The woman started the car. Warmth flowed out of the heating vents. I thought about moving my hands nearer to them, but I didn't have the strength.

She put the car in gear. "I don't want to hear any more about a shelter."

Belatedly, it occurred to me that I recognized the voice. I tried to turn my head to get a look at her face, but my neck didn't seem to work right.

"Mandy?" I asked.

CHAPTER 8

"Yes?"

I shook my head. "Sorry. Just confused."

She made that tsking sound again. "Typical hypothermia symptom. You really should go to the hospital."

"No!" My shivering became more violent, if that was possible. I tried to sound reasonable. "I mean, I'd probably end up just sitting in the emergency waiting room for hours. In my wet clothes." My tongue felt thick and clumsy, and my chattering teeth closed on it. Hard. It hurt.

"I doubt it," she said. But she turned the car toward her house, away from the hospital. I knew where she lived, and I'd been to her house once before.

She had a garage door opener so no one had to get out of the car to open the door. The garage wasn't attached, though, so we would have to walk across an open area to get to the house. The rain continued to pelt down.

Mandy got out of the car. "You stay here while I go open the back door." She opened the car door and took my pile of soggy belongings.

I leaned my head back again and closed my eyes. The air in the car was warm. Despite the shivering, I could just drift off to sleep here and worry about where I was going to go when I woke up. It even seemed like a good idea.

Mandy was back, holding the car door open and tugging on my arm. "If you can't get out, I'll have to take you to the emergency room."

"Sorry." I stirred myself. "Just fell asleep."

"Or passed out."

I moved my reluctant right foot over the doorframe and to the ground. My boot squished in the wet gravel.

Mandy steadied me, and I managed to stand. With a hitching gait, we moved toward the back door of the house. The stairs up to it looked too steep for anyone to climb, but with her supporting me, I made it up them and through the door.

We were in a long hallway with a washer and dryer lined up against the wall. A big washtub stood next to them. I made it that far and put my hands on the edge, leaning on it.

My stuff was in the tub. Wet as it all was, that was probably a good place for it. I touched the wool of the jacket. It was soaked. A musty, wet wool smell tickled my nose.

What did I expect? Roses?

"There's a small bathroom there," she said, indicating a door by the end of the hall. "Can you stay down here while I see what I can find in terms of warm clothes?"

I could stay all right. But I wasn't sure it would be on my feet. I said, "Yeah."

"Good. I'll be right back. Meanwhile, see if you can get your wet clothes off."

Then I'd be naked, I wanted to say. But she must have known that. Maybe that's why she pointed out the bathroom. So I just said, "Okay."

She went through the inner door into the main part of the house, and I peered stupidly down at my boots. They were thoroughly wet and should come off. And probably join my other things in the washtub so they didn't drip on the floor.

I tried to take a step toward the bathroom, but my legs didn't seem to be working right. Seeing no good place to sit down, I finally just sank to the floor and tried to make my numb and shivering fingers work on the laces. They refused to come undone. I leaned my head forward and rested it on my knees. It had been years since I'd felt like crying out of frustration, but I could see myself doing it now.

The door opened again. "Are you awake?" Mandy asked.

"Yes, ma'am." I lifted my head. "I'm just trying to untie my bootlaces."

She knelt down next to me and made quick work of the double-tied bows. Then she loosened the laces, yanked out the tongues, and pulled the boots off.

I tried to protest, but the words wouldn't come.

She worked the soaked socks off my feet and stood up. "You need to get those clothes off."

With her help, I got up and leaned on the washtub again, staring at the boots and socks that now lay on top of everything else.

I started to fumble with the buttons on my flannel shirt. She brushed my hands aside and undid them. Then she removed one of my hands from the edge of the tub and tugged on the sleeve of the shirt. It slid off my arm.

She put that hand back on the edge of the tub and did the same with the other sleeve.

"Now your T-shirt and pants," she said.

I gathered what strength I could muster. "I can manage them." Determined to prove I could, I let go of the wash tub and pulled the T-shirt over my head. Without falling over.

"Do you need me to undo your zipper?" she asked.

"I can get it," I said with more assurance than I felt. My hands were warming up a bit. They hurt like hell, but my fingers were beginning to follow the instructions my mind gave them. I demonstrated to her that I could grasp the zipper and pull it down.

She nodded. "I put some clothes on top of the washing machine. Do you want me to help you get them on?"

"No, ma'am. I can manage."

"Okay. I'm going to put the teakettle on. And then I'm going upstairs to put some dry clothes on myself."

I didn't usually drink tea, but I wasn't going to turn down anything warm.

She went back through the door into the kitchen.

I pulled the pants off and dumped them on top of the other stuff. I knew the air wasn't freezing, but it felt that way when it hit my bare skin. I looked at the clothes she had left. I wasn't sure I could manage to pull the T-shirt or the rugby shirt over my head, but there was a sweater that buttoned up the front. It might be itchy against my skin, but at this point, I didn't care. I struggled to shove my arms into the sleeves, finally managed, and then I pulled it closed in front of my chest, fumbling a few of the buttons closed.

It was soft and warm, not itchy at all.

The pants were more of a challenge. I didn't want to go without underwear if I could help it, so I pulled on the boxers, balancing against the tub. Then I put on the pants she'd brought. They were some kind of flannel-lined khakis. A little big, but they didn't threaten to fall off. And they felt wonderful.

The socks were an impossibility. I left them and went into the kitchen.

A woman stood there, taking the teakettle off the burner. She wasn't Mandy.

I just stood and blinked, swaying lightly.

"You must be Jesse," she said, gesturing at one of the chairs surrounding a table. "Why don't you sit down?"

I practically collapsed into the chair.

She looked at my bare feet and frowned. "Didn't Mandy bring you a pair of slippers?"

I hadn't noticed any slippers, but I was beyond noticing much.

She went into the hallway and came back with the clothes I hadn't been able to manage and the slippers, dropping them next to me. True to their name, I could just slip my feet into them. They were lined with something soft and furry.

"I'm Nicole," she said. "Would you like some tea? Or something stronger?"

I would have preferred coffee, but she wasn't offering that. "Tea's fine."

"We've got some brandy. That might be better for you." She went over to a cupboard and opened it.

I agonized over what to tell her. Better to get the ugly truth out. "I'm on parole. I'm not supposed to have any alcohol."

"Really?" Nicole raised her eyebrows. "I didn't realize that. I mean, Mandy told me a little bit, like that you were on parole, but…"

"Yeah, well. I'm not gonna take a chance of getting in trouble over something stupid like that. Until I'm off supervision, they could send me back to prison for that."

"How long will it be until you're off supervision?"

I smiled grimly. "Another twenty years or so."

Her eyes opened wide. "And how long were you in prison?"

"Close to twenty years."

She shook her head. "Do you mind me asking what it was you did?"

I shifted uncomfortably. I hated it when people asked things like that. "I was convicted of murder." I usually just let the conviction stand on its own.

"Who did you kill?"

I tried to avoid this conversation whenever I could, and this was the second time in two days I'd be having it, but if I was going to be spending some time here, she deserved an honest answer.

"I didn't really kill anyone myself. I was the lookout while my older brothers tried to rob a drug dealer. I thought they were just going in to make a buy. The dealer ended up shot. I was outside, so I really can't tell you exactly what happened."

"And you were convicted of murder? That doesn't seem fair."

"Fair doesn't enter into it. In this state, anyone involved in the commission of a felony that results in a death is guilty of murder. You don't have to be the one who pulled the trigger."

"Or even know a felony was being committed?"

I stared at the tabletop. I'd been over this hundreds of times in my mind. "No one would have believed me. They thought I was inside the apartment, and I didn't deny it when they first questioned me. I look a lot like my brothers, and I don't think they ever caught up with them on this one. Besides, the drug deal itself was a felony, so it really isn't a matter of not knowing a felony was being committed. I just didn't know about the robbery. Or the shooting."

"Still…" She put the mug of tea on the table in front of me. "How old were you?"

I wrapped my trembling hands around the mug. "Thank you," I said. "I was sixteen."

"Sixteen? Weren't you a juvenile?"

"Murder and rape charges automatically go to adult court if the defendant is fourteen or older in this state."

"I didn't know that."

The heat from the mug felt good on my hands. "I didn't, either. But I found out fast enough."

Nicole sighed and changed the subject. "Mandy said you were quite a hero. That you saved a woman and her two children. They all might have drowned. You, too."

I tried to grin, but my face felt stiff and unmoving. I needed a shave. "I don't know about drown. But I think we might have frozen."

"Mandy said you tied a rope around a tree and waded out to the car. And after you got everyone to dry ground, the car rolled over."

"There wasn't any dry ground," I said. "Everywhere was pretty… darn wet." I'd almost dropped the f-bomb. On a woman I didn't know. In someone else's house. Jeez, was my respect meter turned off today? My brain certainly felt that way.

"Well, out of the water, at any rate."

"True, that."

She peered at me critically as I held onto the mug but didn't try to drink any of it. I could hold my hands pretty steady as long as they were clutching the mug.

"Can I heat you up a can of soup? That'd be warming. And more filling than just tea."

I hadn't realized I was hungry, but soup sounded good. "Yes, ma'am. I'd appreciate that." I thought for a minute. "You still got electric power."

She went back to a cupboard and got down a red and white can. "Mandy has an emergency generator. It doesn't run everything, but it keeps a few things going." She looked at the can in her hand. "Chicken noodle okay?"

"Yes, ma'am."

I tried a sip of the tea. My hand shook as I raised the mug, and I almost spilled it, so I put it down. I didn't need to make a mess. Or get the front of the sweater wet.

"This is a nice soft sweater," I said, rubbing my cheek against the shoulder.

"It should be." Nicole poured the soup into a bowl and stuck it in the microwave. Handy things, microwaves. Kelly had one.

"It's one hundred percent cashmere," she continued. "Only the best for Mandy's ex, Sterling. Did you know Sterling?"

"Yeah." I knew Sterling Radman. He'd been an executive at Quality Steel Fabrications, where I worked. And involved in nefarious get-rich-quick schemes, most of them involving fake IDs and drugs, shipped out packaged in products manufactured by Quality Steel. He'd tried to frame me for the murder of a forklift driver who'd gotten so into crystal meth that he was no longer a reliable accomplice to Radman's schemes.

I hadn't really followed up on how the case was progressing, but I imagined that, instead of sending me back to prison as he'd planned, Radman was either there now himself or well on his way. He'd cop some kind of plea and, in the way of white collar criminals, be sent to one of the low security, "country club" prisons for a few years.

Unless they managed to make the murder charges stick. He'd have a good lawyer; I imagined they'd negotiate a deal that dropped them. I didn't think they had really solid evidence, although there was very little doubt he was guilty.

Sterling had also tried to strip Mandy of her inherited wealth. She was in her late thirties and naïve when she married him, and she'd let him manipulate her for a while. Then at one point, she'd been looking for a way out and maybe some revenge, but thank goodness she'd talked it out with me before she did anything rash. I'd managed to get her to go to see her lawyer, who of course helped her file for divorce.

Nicole smiled. "I've been encouraging Mandy to get rid of Sterling's things. But those clothes have certainly come in handy, haven't they?"

"Yes, ma'am." I flexed my shoulders in the soft warmth of the sweater.

When the soup was hot, Nicole took the bowl out of the microwave and placed it in front of me with a spoon.

Concentrating on keeping my right hand as steady as possible, I raised a spoonful to my mouth.

It tasted wonderful.

Nicole brought over some crackers.

Before I knew it, the soup and crackers were gone.

"Thank you," I said, taking a sip of the tea. My hands were only shaking a little now. I yawned. I was having trouble keeping my eyes open.

Nicole frowned. "Wanting to sleep is a symptom of hypothermia. It's only early afternoon. You shouldn't be so tired. Are you still feeling so cold?"

"Not nearly as cold I was a little while ago. And I worked all night—I got off at eight this morning. This is when I'd usually be sleeping. But they've blocked off the streets around my apartment, which is probably flooded anyhow."

"No wonder you're so tired." She approached me and held up her hand. "Let me feel your forehead—see if you feel too cold. Or too hot."

With an effort, I didn't flinch away from her. I caught a whiff of flowery perfume. Her hand was soft and smooth.

"You feel warm enough. I'd say you could go sleep in the carriage house out back—it's furnished and all—but the heat was turned off and the pipes drained."

"Nobody lives there?"

Nicole blushed. "Well, technically I do. I rent it. But I started spending most of my time here in the main house with Mandy, and eventually, I just moved in with her. So we figured no sense spending money heating an unused apartment."

Why would she feel a need to explain her living arrangements to me, of all people?

"Maybe it'd be better if you took a nap on the sofa in the back parlor," she said. "I could get you a pillow and a blanket."

That sounded like a great idea to me. "If you don't mind."

"No, I think it would be fine. Let me run upstairs and check with Mandy."

Nicole came down carrying a pile of blankets and pillows. "She's pretty tired herself and is lying down, but she says that would work. Let's go make up the sofa for you."

I got unsteadily to my feet and followed her.

The house was a huge old Victorian mansion. Its downstairs consisted of a confusing maze of smallish rooms, some of whose original purpose I could only guess at. We passed through a dining room off the kitchen, through a long hall with a staircase leading up, and into a series of rooms along the other side of the house.

Nicole led me to the last one, a room with large windows overlooking the back garden, barren and brown at this time of year, but with a hope of approaching spring. Rain lashed at the glass.

She indicated a long, fragile-looking couch along one wall and tossed a pillow on one end.

I stood there dumbly, feeling clumsy and out of place with the spindly furniture, delicately patterned rugs, and dusty rose curtains.

"Lie down," she directed, "and I'll cover you up."

The pillowcase was white, with lace and little pink flowers embroidered on it. I'd lost my hair tie somewhere along the line. I was sure my hair was filthy. Not to mention I usually worked up a good sweat at work. It didn't seem right to put my head on that pillow.

"Lie down," she repeated.

I eased myself onto the couch and lay down with my head on the pillow. It had a smell that reminded me of spring at the Colemans, the foster home where I'd spent the happiest years of my life. My mind searched for a word for it. Lilacs. That was it. The Colemans' yard had a row of lilacs along the property line in back.

Nicole settled a soft blanket over me and smoothed it, followed by a heavier quilt. My eyes closed.

"Think you'll be warm enough?" she asked.

"Yes, ma'am," I mumbled, but I was already almost asleep.

* * * *

When I woke up, I had no idea how much time had passed. Dim light shone through the expansive windows. Rain drummed at the panes, but without its previous ferocity. Lying there for a moment, I mindlessly savored the soft warmth of my makeshift bed.

Then my brain started to kick into gear. Where the hell was I?

I ached all over. Had I been in a fight? I tried to clear my head.

The mental image of the woman and children on top of the SUV in the flooded underpass came back to me.

Running my hand over the soft fabric against my chest, I remembered. I was in Mandy's back parlor, with all its delicate furnishings. I'd better move carefully.

What time was it? Did I have to go to work tonight? I couldn't afford to miss a shift. And I certainly didn't want to be let go for not showing up and not calling in.

What day was it? I'd gotten off work on Saturday morning. An overtime shift. My workweek started at midnight Sunday—really Monday morning. So I should have at least a whole day to worry about that. I hoped.

Lying here forever was not an option. I had a feeling my battered body was going to protest any movement at all. I rolled over.

I was right.

Heaving myself to a sitting position, I flexed my shoulder muscles and ran my hand over a tender spot on my back. Was that where I'd been rammed by a big floating branch or something?

The shirts and socks I hadn't been able to manage before lay on a chair nearby. I reached over and grabbed the socks, pulling them on. This time, my fingers obeyed me, although reluctantly, and I didn't feel like I was going to keel over on my face any minute. A decided improvement.

The air was chilly. Could Mandy's emergency generator start the furnace? Shivering, I peeled off the sweater, put on the other shirts, and then put the sweater on again over them.

Shuffling my feet around on the floor, I found the warm slippers and stuck my feet in them. Light outlined a door. I opened it and stepped into the hallway.

Voices came from beyond the hallway, toward the kitchen. I went in there.

An enticing aroma of fried onions and sausage tickled my nose.

Nicole and Mandy were sitting at the kitchen table, wrapped in fluffy pink robes.

Mandy jumped up and gave me a hug. "Jesse! How are you feeling?"

I returned the hug awkwardly. My mouth was dry, and I wasn't sure I'd be able to form words. I licked my lips. "Okay," I managed to croak out.

She pulled a chair out for me. I slipped into it.

Nicole got up and poured tea for all of us. She took a loaf of something from a breadbox on the counter and cut off a few slices, which she put on a plate.

"Thanks for bringing me here and letting me stay. I was really tired. And cold." I grinned. "And confused."

Mandy nodded. "It was the least I could do, after you were so brave, rescuing those kids and their mother."

I shrugged. "Couldn't just let them stay there."

"Nobody else seemed to have a real problem with that."

I remembered the man who'd stepped into the water and then retreated. "They just didn't know what to do about it."

"But you did it."

"Had to try something." I sniffed the enticing aromas.

Nicole put the plate on the table. "Banana bread," she said, getting another mug and filling it with tea. "It's a little old, but it's still good."

I took a piece and bit into it. "My foster mother used to make this," I said, "when the bananas started to turn black."

Nicole laughed. "That's when I make it, too."

"It's still raining pretty hard," Mandy said. "Do you want me to give you a ride over to your place? You can see if it's really flooded. The power's off all over town, though. Thank goodness I decided to get that generator."

I had no desire to go back to my apartment while it was still raining so hard. If I could get near it. It would be depressing.

"I don't think I'll be able to get in it," I said. "It's a basement apartment. The whole area was pretty flooded when I went by this morning.

A friend from work said I could go stay at her place. She wasn't going to be home till late. But that was last night, I guess."

"I can give you a ride over there, then," she said. "After breakfast. Until then, you can stay here. Is that okay with you, Nicci?" She smiled fondly at the other woman.

Nicole nodded. "Of course."

Mandy cast an intense look at her that I couldn't read. "This is your home now, too. And I wouldn't want to do anything that made you uncomfortable."

Nicole reached over and patted her hand. "If you're comfortable with him staying here, then I am, too."

I didn't want to put them in an awkward position. "Look, I wouldn't blame you if you didn't want me here," I said. "I mean, I'm on parole and all. I can go stay someplace else."

"Nonsense." Nicole's hand closed over Mandy's. "Mandy told me all about how you talked her out of doing anything outrageous when Sterling was driving her crazy."

With an effort, I kept a straight face. Mandy had tried to hire me to kill Sterling so she could get away from him. I'd pointed out that that was what divorce was for and taken her to her lawyer's office. He'd made sure she had a safe house in which to stay while he plowed through the legal tangles.

Mandy nodded in agreement. "I owe you. So just stay here for a little while. We have a breakfast strata in the toaster oven. It should be done in about a half hour. Then I can drive you over to your friend's."

I had no idea what a breakfast strata was, but if it was the source of those wonderful scents, I'd love to have some. Gratefully, I nodded.

"Let's go check out the news and weather," Nicole said, getting up. "The TV's in the middle parlor. We didn't want to make any noise and wake you up. One outlet in there is hooked into the generator."

I drained my mug of tea and followed them.

The middle parlor was furnished in spindly chairs and fringed lampshades with another patterned rug on the floor. Gingerly, I eased myself into one of the chairs, afraid it would collapse beneath my bulk. But it held.

Mandy picked up something that looked like a TV remote control, pointed it toward the fireplace, and clicked it.

A fully built fire sprang to life. I stared at it.

Seeing my puzzlement, Mandy laughed. "Gas," she said. "It doesn't need any electricity. And it throws off some nice heat."

Nicole nodded. "We might as well eat in here, too, when the strata's done."

Sounded like a plan to me.

Mandy switched on the TV. I stared at that, too. It wasn't like any TV I'd seen before. It was about four feet long and really thin. How could everything needed to get a TV show be in that huge wafer? But it worked fine.

She flipped through the channels until she came to a local all-news broadcast.

The flooding was the main item being covered. Pictures of the river overflowing its banks, an electrical substation sitting in the middle of a water-covered lot on fire. An SUV on its side floated lazily in a flooded underpass at the mouth of a tunnel.

Mandy shivered. "That's where we were."

"Good thing Jesse got the people out of it before it tipped over," Nicole said.

Next was a scene of emergency service workers with chain saws, bathed in flashing red lights, cutting huge downed trees into manageable pieces and heaving them into piles next to the road.

They flashed to pictures of the exterior of the prison outside town. A place with which I was very familiar, but from an entirely different perspective. I couldn't remember ever seeing it from the outside, at least in the daylight. Prison transports ran at night.

The sight of it made me wince. Instead of the usual spotlights sweeping the area between the inner and outer perimeter fences, the dimmer emergency lights were on. That meant the entire complex had no power. And that meant the only light the cells were getting would be from the generator-operated backup lights in the centers of the tiers. The heat was probably off. And the kitchen wouldn't be operational, meaning no hot meals. Once a day, employees would bring around an entire day's food in paper sacks while the inmates remained locked in their cells. I knew a lot of people would wolf everything down right away and then have nothing until the next day.

I wondered if the plumbing was working, or if the sewers had backed up. Not a pleasant thought.

The picture on the screen switched to a weather map. The rain would continue through the night, with more flooding. The announcer went into how this mega-storm had formed, a moisture-laden front swirling in from the Atlantic and merging with a system coming over the mountains. It seemed to be stuck now, right over us. The last time a storm of this magnitude had stalled over the area had been in 1972, when Hurricane Agnes had hovered over the area for days, dumping rain and flooding rivers.

That had been in June, though, not early spring like this, so they hadn't had to contend with snowmelt in the mountains or ice on the river.

A state of emergency had been declared in Rothsburg. Most places of business, including the factories, were closed until further notice. So I didn't have to worry about getting to work.

And my paycheck would be missing those hours.

Nicole set up fancy little tables next to the chairs in the parlor for us to eat breakfast. She brought in plates with large rectangles of casserole. The plates were delicate china with dainty painted flowers and a gold rim. I reached for the plate she'd put next to me, but it felt so fragile in my work-roughened hand that I put it back down and pushed it to the center of the little table. It might be valuable, and I was terrified it would crumble in my grasp.

Apparently, strata was some kind of baked egg dish with sausage and onions and cheese and slices of apple. It was really good. I wondered if it was hard to make. The ingredients were pretty affordable, and I bet Kelly and her kids would love it.

"Your clothes are still wet," Mandy said as she collected the plates. "And even if they'd dried, I'm afraid they're not very clean."

That was an understatement. I'd worn them to work, where I sweated a lot, then into the dirty floodwaters. Not to mention the "extra" clothes that had been thrown around the restroom floor. And the socks dunked in the toilet.

I knew I could wear some of them, if I had to—I had a very limited wardrobe, and one of the major chores in my life was trying to have enough clean and dry clothing for work. I didn't seem to have much success in that area.

Since I couldn't exactly go around naked, I'd have to wear them regardless of their condition if Mandy wanted the things she'd lent me back.

But I'd really hoped she'd let me keep the things she'd lent me, at least until I could get my stuff to the laundromat.

"So," she said, "I've got all of Sterling's things. I suppose I can get rid of them, but I haven't yet. You can have some if you can use any of it. Mostly he wore suits to work, but when he moved here, he got a lot of things from some of those outfitter catalogs. He said he might want to get a deer license and hunt, but he never did. Want to see if you want any?"

I was in no position to be choosy. And if any of them were like the cashmere sweater, I'd thoroughly enjoy them for as long as I could. "Yes, ma'am. I'd appreciate anything you can lend me. I'll make sure it's clean when I bring it back."

"Oh, you can have it. I don't want any of it back. I put some of it in the morning room."

A mourning room? I'd never heard of such a thing. Maybe where the ashes of departed family members were kept? Or mementos? Surely it wouldn't be caskets with actual bodies. But I didn't want to appear totally ignorant, so I didn't ask.

I followed her to a little room off the dining room. Gathering light, although still muted by the storm, shone through the large windows. The room faced east, and on a sunny day, it would be flooded with morning sunlight.

There was no urn with ashes that I saw, and no photographs or certificates or such. Definitely no caskets.

But there was a huge pile of warm clothes, some of it with the tags still on. Chamois cloth shirts. Rugged flannel-lined pants. Long underwear and thermal socks. An unfashionable, but very serviceable waterproof poncho. Best of all, an almost-new, down-filled jacket and a pair of high-topped leather boots.

My hungry eyes went to the boots. I picked them up. They weren't steel-toed, so I couldn't wear them to work, and they were a half a size too big, but I bet if I wore two pairs of socks, they'd fit just fine. And I could save my steel-toed boots for work.

"I wish I could offer you a shower," Mandy said. "The generator won't run the hot water tank. But you could change into whatever you want."

It was hard to figure out what to say. "Thank you," seemed appropriate, if inadequate, so I said that.

"We can hang onto anything else you want but can't carry now, and you can pick it up when you come back for your other things," Nicole said. "I'll wash them when we get the laundry equipment going again. And you can get them when you get settled back in your apartment. Or where ever."

I wondered when that would be. And where.

"Speaking of that…" Mandy reached over and took Nicole's hand. "I was wondering if you were interested in house-sitting for two weeks or so after this all clears up? I don't want to leave the house completely unwatched, and I'm not sure I trust the security firms around here."

The hired security firms were probably okay, or they wouldn't be in business for long, but I didn't voice that thought. "Sure," I said. "If you'd like me to."

"You could stay in the carriage house out back," she went on, "and check on the house every day."

"Sounds like a deal."

"I could pay you."

"No!"

Her face twisted in concern.

"I mean," I said, "after all you've done for me? And if I was staying in the carriage house, you certainly don't need to pay me. I wouldn't take money from you anyhow. When is this?" If it was coming up soon, I could maybe stay there until I figured out the fate of my apartment.

She smiled and looked at Nicole. "As soon as we can arrange it. Now that same-sex marriage is recognized in this state, we're getting married and going on a honeymoon."

CHAPTER 9

I set out for Kelly's place better dressed than I'd ever been in my life. Long johns, lined chinos, a soft chamois shirt, a heavy wool sweater, a warm down outdoorsman's jacket that didn't have garish red and black checks. And on my feet, a sturdy pair of boots lined with two heavy pairs of socks. I clutched the folded poncho. Unless the rain stopped, which it showed no signs of doing, it would be very useful.

Mandy pulled the car out of the garage to give me a ride.

The streets were eerily quiet in these early Sunday morning hours, and the traffic signals non-functional. The buildings we passed were dark. Water gushed across sidewalks and swirled lazily around clogged storm drains. Mandy kept to the center of the streets and avoided low-lying areas.

Occasionally, we encountered another private car, but where were the emergency responders and the utility crews?

Kelly's kids would be up, so I didn't worry that it would be too early to go over to her house. Their dad was supposed to return them at nine last night, and they'd have gotten to bed late, but they were always a little unsettled when they came back from visitations with him. And what kid would sleep in anyhow?

Mandy dropped me off in front of the house. Kelly had gotten the big brick house in the divorce settlement. Making the mortgage payments ate up a lot of her salary, but she loved it, and it was in a good neighborhood with a solid school for the kids.

It was dark like everyplace else. I dashed from the car to the front porch, trying to minimize getting the down jacket wet.

The drapes on the front windows were drawn. While that blocked out the light, it also blocked out some of the cold, and with no power, I was sure the heat in Kelly's house wasn't working.

I punched the doorbell.

No one answered.

Distressed, I went to the window to see if I could peer through a slight gap between the drape and the edge of the window.

All I could see was darkness.

Could the kids still be asleep? Especially if it was cold in the house, maybe they just stayed in their beds. That would at least be fairly warm.

I went back to the door and tried the knob. Locked. Just as well, I supposed. If it had been unlocked, I would have had to decide whether to go in without an invitation or not. Technically, that would be breaking and entering, even if Kelly had told me to come over.

As I reached to try the doorbell again, a thought stuck me. The doorbell ran on electric current. The power was out. So the bell wouldn't sound. How dumb could I be?

I raised my hand and rapped my knuckles on the door.

A few seconds later, it creaked open. Chris stood in the doorway, wearing his jacket, his dark curly hair going in all directions and his nose red and running.

"Jesse!" He threw the door open.

"Yep." I grinned at him. "How's my man doing?"

He stepped back and looked up at me, a sob catching in his throat.

"What's the matter?" I asked, stepping in and closing the door against the weather.

He pulled his jacket a bit closer. "It's cold in here," he said, "and we're hungry. And Mom hasn't gotten up yet."

I frowned. "Did you try to get Mom up?"

"Yeah. She told me to go fix breakfast for me and Brianna. But there isn't much food. And I don't know what to fix. There's no cereal or bread. I can't find anything."

Too much responsibility for a little kid. Chris was eight years old. Brianna was only six. She was nowhere in sight.

"Where's your sister?" I asked.

He hung his head. "She's hiding in her closet. She wet her bed, and she's afraid she's gonna get in trouble. And her jammies are all wet. She won't let me help her find her dry clothes."

"Get in trouble for wetting the bed?" I cast my mind back to Mrs. Coleman, my foster mother. Most of the kids she cared for were in emergency foster care. Lots of them wet the bed. She said that was only to be expected of children who were traumatized, so she handled it with understanding and patience. And waterproof mattress pads.

I took off the jacket and draped it on a chair, then I headed for the stairs. "First, let's go get Brianna. Nobody's gonna get her in trouble for wetting her bed."

Chris followed me. "Dad would," he said, his voice catching in his throat. "Sometimes, he'll spank her for wetting the bed. And Mom might yell. If she's been drinking."

Turning to face him, I said, "Has she been drinking?"

He shrugged. "Maybe. A little. She was okay when we first got home, but then she got upset. There were no lights. She told us to go to bed, but she stayed up."

I knew Kelly did drink sometimes. More than was good for either her or the kids. She'd cut way back for a while, and I thought things were going pretty good for her. For us.

But then Old Buckles, her father, had come to stay with her. He'd used her address for his home plan when he'd been released from prison, the same one where I'd spent so much time. Only, he was doing life on the installment plan, while mine was straight time.

Maybe that was why she wasn't freaked out by my background like most people were.

He was a biker, pretty high up in the ranks of a local club called the Predators. Kelly knew he'd spend most of his time with his buddies, but she thought he'd do it up at the clubhouse in the hills. Instead, he hung around her place, and some of his buddies did, too.

One of them, accustomed to the acquiescent women who rode with the bikers, made a pass at her when Old Buckles wasn't around. She turned him down. Enraged, and probably drunk or high, he beat her up and raped her.

That could drive anyone to want to drink to drown out the feelings. But not everyone would follow through. In Kelly's case, though, it looked like it may have triggered a return to heavy drinking.

"Anything special she was upset about?" I asked.

Chris twisted the end of his sleeve. "She said you said you was gonna come over last night, but you didn't. That you'd stood her up."

I caught my breath. Although I'd told her I'd try to get over yesterday, I didn't think I'd actually promised. Just said I'd try. There had been too many uncertainties to promise anything yesterday. But she'd felt I let her down.

We climbed the stairs and went into Brianna's room. Sure enough, the blankets and top sheet were thrown on the floor, and the bottom sheet was wet. There was a waterproof mattress pad on the bed.

The closet door was firmly closed. I went over and knocked on it. "Brianna. Please come out."

"Go away!" she said in a strangled voice.

"Brianna. I can't go away. We need to find you some dry clothes. And wash out the wet sheets and things. At least open the door."

"No!"

I wasn't sure what to do. "I'm gonna wash out the wet stuff," I told her. "How about giving me the wet pajamas, too?"

Chris pulled on my sleeve. "The washing machine won't work," he pointed out. "Or the dryer. I think it's the electricity being out."

"Yeah," I agreed. "But I can at least rinse stuff out in the bathtub all right. And hang it up to dry. Where can we find some dry clothes for Brianna?"

He gestured across the room. "Laundry basket," he said. "Mom did some wash, but didn't get the clothes put away yet."

Rummaging through the contents of the laundry basket released a pleasant, flowery smell. Fabric softener. I pulled out some heavy corduroy pants, a turtleneck shirt, and a warm sweater. "Any undies?" I asked Chris.

"Probably in the dresser."

I opened the top drawer and found panties, undershirts, and socks.

"Brianna," I said, standing next to the door. "I'm gonna open the door and toss these clean clothes inside. Please put them on and toss your pajamas out to me."

"No!"

"You have to. It's cold. You're gonna get sick, staying in wet pajamas." I yanked the door open a few inches, reached in, and dropped the clothes on the floor. "I'm also gonna throw in a tiny little flashlight," I told her, "so you can see a little. But I'm taking the wet stuff into the bathroom, so I won't be right here."

I took a package of the flashlight out of my pocket and dropped it through the gap in the closet door.

Chris looked with interest at the flashlights. "Can I see one?" he asked.

I handed him one. "You can have one. I got a couple. But I don't know how long they're gonna last, so don't waste it when you don't need it."

He took it and turned it over in his hand, pushing the little button that turned on the light. "Neat!" he said. "Thanks!"

I gathered up the sheets and the mattress pad. Underneath, the mattress itself was dry.

"Can you go downstairs and get me some laundry detergent?" I asked him.

Kelly's house was on the municipal water system, so she should continue to have water despite the power outage. Unless the pumping station got overwhelmed by flood water. That was not a comforting thought.

Water gushed out of the spigot. I turned on the hot water, hoping she had a gas water heater, which might still work. No such luck. All the water was frigid. But it did continue to flow.

When I went back into Brianna's room, her pajamas lay on the floor outside the closet door. A big step in the right direction. I picked them up and dumped them in the bathtub, too, along with a big glug of detergent from the bottle Chris brought me and stirred it all with the handle of a plumber's helper I found next to the toilet.

"We're gonna let that soak a while," I said.

I ought to go see if Kelly was all right. She probably was, but totally hung over. I was postponing discovering whether my fears were true. And cold as the house was, getting Brianna into dry clothes was a priority.

The door to Kelly's room was open a few inches. I pushed it open a few more.

Kelly lay on her back, tangled in sheets and blankets. An almost-empty bottle of Southern Comfort lay on the floor next to the bed. The whole room had a sour whiskey smell to it. And like everywhere else in the house, it was cold.

I stepped into the room to make sure she was still breathing. I held a hand down next to her mouth and nose and felt damp warmth as she exhaled. I had no idea what I would have done had she not been breathing.

Her waist-length hair had been done up in a braid, but the braid was twisted across her neck, and big strands of hair were working their way loose. Her nightgown was unbuttoned, and the blankets didn't cover her magnificent breasts. One bare foot stuck out off the side of the bed.

I shivered. How far out of it did she have to be to not wake up enough to pull the bedding up over herself?

I eased the blankets out from under her and pushed her foot back onto the mattress. Then I covered her up to her neck with the blankets and tucked them around her.

She stirred and rolled over without opening her eyes. "Go away!"

Like mother, like daughter, I thought. But Brianna was a kid. She didn't have much choice in what happened in her life. Kelly, on the other hand, was an adult. And she had control.

I backed into the hallway and shut the door again.

Chris stood by the top of the stairs, his eyes clouded and his fist pressed up against his mouth. "Is she okay?"

"I think so. Or she will be," I said. "When she gets some more sleep."

He nodded wisely. "Needs to sleep it off."

Not something an eight-year-old should have to be concerned about.

"Are you warm enough?" I asked, eyeing his clothes.

He shrugged. "I guess. I mean, I could put on my warmer jacket if I got really cold."

I headed toward Brianna's room.

"She went downstairs," he said.

"Good. Let's get the stuff rinsed out and hung up as best we can," I said.

I let the water out of the tub, refilled it with fresh water, and tried to rinse the detergent from the fabric. Waterlogged, it was heavy, and I could hardly lift it. I finally knelt next to the tub, let that water out, and rinsed everything under running water, then squeezed out what water I could.

Good enough, I decided. When the power came on, the stuff could be washed again. Meanwhile, I hung one sheet over the shower curtain rod and the pajamas over a towel bar. They dripped on the floor, but I didn't see what I could do about that. The mattress pad, soaking wet and very heavy, I left in the bottom of the tub. Maybe some of the water would drain out.

We went downstairs. Brianna was sitting on the sofa, staring wistfully at the TV.

"Not gonna work, honey," I told her. "Not till the power comes on."

"I'm hungry," she said.

Chris and I went to the kitchen. I opened the cupboards. Not a whole lot of food to begin with, and most of it, like the packages of macaroni and cheese, needed to be cooked.

"Any peanut butter?" I asked Chris. "Or bread?"

He shook his head. "Mom said she had to go to the store."

The pickings were slim indeed. I took down a container of hot chocolate mix and a pouch of powdered milk. We wouldn't be able to heat it up, but it would be filling. And reasonably nutritious.

"Any ice cream in the freezer?"

Chris shrugged. "I dunno."

I debated. Unopened, the freezer would hold food for a few days. If I opened it, I'd severely shorten that time. But we might very well have to eat whatever we could in there anyhow. I opened it.

There was a package of vanilla ice cream. We could make ice cream shakes. Not ideal, and it wouldn't do much to warm anybody up, but it would have to do.

I mixed up all the ice cream with the powdered milk and the hot chocolate mix, poured some of it into mugs, and gave it to the kids.

"Aren't you gonna have any?" Chris asked.

"No. I already had breakfast." I felt a little guilty about the great breakfast I'd had at Mandy's place when the kids were hungry. But that was irrational. If I'd been hungry and taken some of the milkshake concoction, there'd be less for the kids.

They drank it up and wanted more.

"Okay, but let's save some for later," I said, pouring them each another mugful. I put the rest of it in a pitcher and put the pitcher on the back porch, where it would stay cold indefinitely. Although, right now, anywhere in the house would do for that.

"We don't know how long it's gonna be before we can get some more food."

"Can't you just go shopping?" Brianna asked, a chocolate mustache above her lip.

I smiled. "I bet most of the stores are closed. But I can try."

The house was chilly, and it certainly wasn't about to get any warmer. The kids helped me collect blankets, coats, old sweaters—anything that would hold in the heat. We made nests on the sofa.

"Why don't you guys get some books and paper and crayons and things?" I said. "You can snuggle down in the nests and stay warm."

Brianna stood in the middle of the living room, her chin stuck out. "I wanna watch TV," she said. "I don't want to get in some stupid nest. I'm not a bird."

Goddess, the cat, crept out from under the sofa and leapt onto the pile of fabric. Her two kittens, who the kids had named Inky and Stinky, tumbled after her, swatting at each other.

"The cats like it," Chris said, grabbing a book and climbing after them. He snuggled back and pulled an afghan over his legs.

"I'm afraid I can't do much about the TV not working," I told Brianna. "And I do have to go out and see if I can find any place to get some food. Your mom's still asleep, and she'll be hungry when she wakes up."

Brianna stuck her fingers in her mouth and looked away from me.

"She'll be fine," Chris said, looking up from his book. "Brianna, get your crayons and coloring book. I bet Jesse'll read us some stories when he gets back."

"True, that," I said, hoping I wouldn't be gone for too long and that I could find some food that the kids would like that didn't need to be cooked.

Pulling on the warm down jacket and unfolding the rain poncho, I said, "I'll be back as soon as I can."

I wondered if McDonalds would be open. I could maybe get each of them a hamburger or something. But I should check into that on the way back, so if I could get any, they'd be warm.

Even if I could find a store that was open and had food, money would be a problem. In the few short months since I'd been released from prison, the cost of the basic foods I depended upon—peanut butter, tuna fish, ramen noodles—seemed to have gone up and up.

But the kids needed to be fed.

Snug in the down jacket covered by the rain poncho, I headed across town where I hoped to find a grocery store open.

No such luck. Every place was dark and quiet. Where had everyone gone? The only sounds I could hear were the drilling of the rain onto hard surfaces and the rush of water from downspouts and in the streets. A dank smell filled the air, like the odor of cut flowers that had been left too long in a vase.

The Best Deals for Your Dollar store had been almost out of food yesterday when I was there, and if I thought about it, I had to admit that I hadn't really expected to find anyplace open.

The emergency shelter at the high school might be my best bet. It was a good walk, but if I went the long way around, I could make it on high roads. They had to have food, if they were letting people stay there. Maybe they were letting people take some home.

In the waning daylight, the school gave off an eerie glow that I could see from a few blocks away. They were getting lights somehow.

As I got closer, I heard a steady hum that became a roar as I got close. Emergency generators mounted on the backs of military-style trucks.

Several soldiers in fatigues hurried across the parking lot. More sat in the truck cabs, and a few stood out of the rain, leaning against the wall just under the canopy by the school entrance. Were they National Guard?

Uneasy, I almost turned around then and there.

But why should they care if I came in? Emergency services were available to all citizens, even if they were convicts on parole. Besides, how would they even know that? I had every intention of behaving responsibly.

As I approached the door, one of the lounging soldiers stood erect and eyed me. He had a sidearm, so he was probably an officer. "What are you looking for?"

My throat closed. I told myself he was just asking a question, not challenging me. I licked my dry lips and said, "Food."

"Hot meal being served in the cafeteria," he said. "Past the registration table and straight down the hallway. If you're just here for that, you don't have to register."

I had to remind myself to breathe before I could say anything. "Thanks." After the big breakfast, I wasn't that hungry, but under the circumstances, I knew better than to turn down a meal. And maybe I'd be able to pocket something for the kids.

The scene inside the school was chaos, with children shouting, people rushing in all directions, and a man with a bullhorn trying to make announcements. The bullhorn wasn't working.

I went past a table at the entrance, where harried workers were trying to take down the names of the masses of people who were milling round. I glanced through an open door as I passed by. Row after row of cots lined the gym floor.

Babies cried and mothers tried to keep toddlers entertained enough to prevent them from running amok.

I continued to the cafeteria, where a line of hungry people snaked around the walls. This might be my only chance for a hot meal for who knows how long. And then, if I managed to scrounge up anything else, I could save it for the kids. I joined the line. It moved surprisingly quickly along.

The woman in front of me, with three school-age children hugging her sides, greeted the volunteer who was handing polystyrene plates and plastic forks. "Y'all working here instead of at the church?"

Another young man behind the serving line beamed at her. "Yep. We've moved the soup kitchen up here for now. The church kitchen isn't flooded, but it's got no power. And they need groups who know what they're doing if they're going to feed all these people." His gaze swept over the ever-lengthening line.

"Well, I must say, y'all know how to run a soup kitchen. I always say, best meal of the month is when y'all running it."

The young man's smile broadened. "We try."

The line moved forward, and he handed me a plate, fork, and napkin.

Some of the people were being picky about the food, refusing some of what they were offered. Years of prison chow had left me less than fussy, and I didn't turn down anything. I got a slab of meatloaf, a mound of mashed potatoes, a spoonful of creamed corn, some kind of greens—it looked like kale—and two slices of white bread. I picked up a very welcome cup of coffee from the assortment of drinks at the end of the line and made my way to a table.

I made a sandwich out of the bread and meatloaf, wrapped it in the napkin, and shoved it in my pocket. The kids could split that. Mashed potatoes, corn, and kale weren't going to travel as easily, so I ate them. The coffee probably wasn't all that great, but I'd been so long without any it tasted like a gourmet blend.

A volunteer carried a tray of desserts around, handing out pieces of apple pie and squares of cake.

I took a big square of cake and another napkin. The frosting might come off, but I could bring that to the kids, too.

The crowd kept coming, and they needed the space at the tables. I finished up, threw my trash away, and drifted out to the hallway to see if I could find out anything useful.

The line for showers in the gym locker rooms was impossibly long and not moving. The first aide station was packed. I skipped them. At the end of the hallway, another line was moving along pretty well. I wasn't entirely sure what it was for, but I stepped close to the woman manning the table to try to figure it out.

Food bank distribution. Just what I needed.

I got in the line. When I got to the head of the line, the woman didn't even look up. "Name?" she asked.

My chest tightened. What kind of trouble could I get into here, especially if Mr. Ramirez found out I'd been taking any kind of emergency assistance? He thought parolees should be paying their own way.

"Jason Dempsey," I murmured, hoping she wouldn't ask how to spell it or anything. I figured it sounded close enough to Jesse Damon that if I got caught in the ruse, I could use the excuse of the noise level for the misinterpretation of the name.

She didn't bat an eyelash. "How many in the family?" she asked.

"Four."

"How many children under the age of two?"

"None."

"Under the age of five?"

I thought for a minute. Brianna was six. "None."

"Under the age of ten?"

"Two."

"Race?"

I blinked. Why did she want to know that? Kelly's complexion was dusky, and she had that magnificent mane of thick, dark hair that I loved. Was she some kind of racial mixture? Or even Native American? And if she was, then of course the kids would be. It had never occurred to me to ask.

The woman glanced up. "We just need it for our statistics. Won't make any difference in what you get."

"White," I stammered.

"Anyone over the age of 65 in the family?"

"No, ma'am."

"You have any way to cook food?"

"Not right now."

She made a few check marks on her paper and selected a yellow card from an array of various colors in front of her. "Take this two doors down and hand it to the person at the door. They'll help you get what you need."

I took the card. Some people were going into the first room. It was piled high with food, but I went to the second door like I'd been told.

That room, too, was piled high with food. The guy at the door glanced at the card, handed me a few plastic bags, and said, "You can have four bags of food. Nothing in this room needs to be cooked, although some of it, you might rather have heated up if you get the chance."

A few other people were examining packages stacked on the counters and tables.

Since I had to carry everything a fair distance, I started with the boxed food. Cereal, raisins, crackers. I took three jars of peanut butter and found a canned ham, which would be a real treat. I tried to think about what the kids should be eating and what they might like. A five-pound block of sliced yellow cheese. Powdered milk. A cardboard canister of fruit-flavored drink mix, which probably had no nutritional values, but they'd like it. Canned items would be heavy, but I took a few cans of tuna and fruit cocktail. And a big can of canned government surplus cooked pork. I got a plastic bottle of barbeque sauce to put on that and then took a jar of mustard and one of mayonnaise.

There didn't seem to be any bread, which was too bad, but beggars can't be choosers. I was grateful for what I could get. The kids wouldn't go hungry for a while, anyhow.

My bags were pretty full. I tucked a few individual serving packages of beef jerky, string cheese, and cracker sandwiches wherever I could fit them.

The meals we could fix wouldn't be ideal, but they'd do. I thanked the guy at the door and went back out into the hallway. I knew the kids would be anxious, especially if Kelly was still in bed, so I wanted to get back as quickly as I could.

I tried to arrange the bags so they were balanced and I could carry them under the poncho to keep them dry. Then I flipped up the poncho's hood and stepped out the front door.

Behind me, someone yelled, "Stop! Thief!"

Who would steal anything in an emergency like this? And what would they steal?

The sleepy-looking soldiers snapped awake. They surrounded me, and a big blond one grabbed me by the arm.

CHAPTER 10

I stood still for a second, then backed up a couple of steps so my back was to the wall.

A petite female soldier stepped up in front of me, her eyes glinting gray underneath her fatigue cover. Her nametag read "Smyth," and she had sergeant's chevrons on her sleeves. Gesturing toward the bags I was carrying, she asked, "What you got there?"

"Stuff from the food bank," I said.

"You mind if we take a look?"

They were going to look even if I objected. I said, "No," and handed them to two other soldiers standing next to her.

"Keep your hands where we can see them," she said.

If I let my hands hang by my sides, they would be half-hidden by the rain poncho. I raised them and put them behind my head, fingers interlaced.

"You got any weapons?"

"No, ma'am."

"You mind if I have one of the men pat you down?"

I did, but again, I saw no point in objecting. "No, ma'am."

She nodded to a soldier standing off to the side. He avoided my eyes as he reached under the poncho and ran his hands over my pockets, sticking his hand in one and pulling out my wallet and keychain with its solitary key to my now-flooded apartment. He flipped open the wallet, examining the two ID cards and the pathetic few dollars. He glanced at the sergeant, then shoved them back in my pocket. "One of the ID cards is a prison ID, but he don't got nothing we got to worry about."

It was a thoroughly unprofessional search. I could have had a gun shoved down by my groin, or a hunting knife in my boot, and he wouldn't have found it. But then, soldiers weren't usually in the business of frisking suspects.

"Don't see nothing but food in these bags," said the guy who'd taken the bags. He pulled out a few boxes of cereal, handed them to another soldier, and rummaged through what was left in the bag.

"Me neither," the other agreed, peering into the bags.

I looked over at the doorway, where yet another soldier had escorted someone out of the school building. I recognized him as Diffy, the fork-lift driver from second shift at work. What kind of beef did he have with me?

A small crowd had gathered, staring.

The sergeant turned to face him. "You're the one who says this man is a thief?"

Diffy smirked. "Yeah. He's a criminal on parole. And he's a child molester."

She looked backed toward me.

How much should I tell her? They had seen the prison ID, so Diffy's claims couldn't be a total surprise to them. "I am on parole," I said, "but I sure as hell ain't no child molester."

"Yes, he is." Diffy nodded his head. "You can look him up on the sex offender registry online."

I glared at him. "You do that. You won't find me on it."

The woman leaned back on her boot heels and looked back at Diffy. "And I suppose you've looked him up?"

"Well, not me, personally," Diffy stammered. "I mean, I don't got a computer. But lots of the guys at work have. And he's there."

She shook her head. "Even if you're right about that—and I don't see how you can be sure if you haven't looked it up yourself—so what?"

Diffy set his chin. "Sex offenders aren't supposed to be near schools. And for sure we don't need the likes of him staying here. There's kids all over."

"Looks to me like he was leaving. Until we stopped him."

"Well, he shouldn't be here at all."

She raised her eyebrows. "Who put you in charge of who can be here and who can't?"

He shrugged. "Common sense say we don't need him here."

"And what has all that to do with him being a thief?"

"His type'll steal anything they can get their hands on. I know. I work with him."

I refrained from answering him. I'd never stolen anything, at work or anywhere else. From him or anybody else.

The sergeant sighed. "What do you think he stole?"

"Look in those bags."

"We have."

"Well, what's he got?"

"Food."

"Then he's stealing food."

"It's kind of hard to steal from a food bank. They give the food away."

"To people who need it."

"And what makes you think this guy doesn't need it?"

"That's an awful lot of food for one person."

She took a step back. "Maybe he's getting it for more than one person. And why is it any of your business, anyhow?"

"He's stealing from the people who really need it. Families with kids."

She just shook her head. "Why don't you just go back inside?" she said. "Let the people who are in charge make the decisions about who gets what."

The soldier who had searched me took him by the arm. "Come on, buddy." They went back inside the building.

She turned back to me. "You can put your hands down," she said.

I lowered my hands.

"Is all that for just you?"

"No. I'm taking it back to my girlfriend's place. She's got two kids. And no electric, so we can't cook anything for them."

"Well, take your bags and get this food home to them."

I picked up the bags.

The crowd started to drift away toward the entrance.

"What are you on parole for, anyhow?" one of the soldiers asked.

The crowd paused to listen.

Reluctantly, I answered, "Murder."

* * * *

When I got back to the house, I piled the bags on the kitchen table. The light that shone through the kitchen windows was dim, but it was enough to see by.

"Sort it out and decide what we should fix next," I told the kids.

Kelly was nowhere in sight. I went upstairs to check on her.

She was snoring gently, still covered by the bedding.

In the kitchen, Brianna lined the boxes of cereal up in a row. "You got some pretty good stuff," she said.

Chris looked up from sorting the food into stacks by type. "Is Mom okay?"

"Yeah. We might as well let her sleep."

I pulled the meatloaf sandwich and cake from my pockets. They weren't too badly squashed, and the meatloaf was still a bit warm. I stirred some of the drink mix into a pitcher of water and poured two cups full.

Fruit and vegetables were in short supply. I filled a bowl with raisins and put it on the table in front of the kids. That would have to do.

Chris wolfed his sandwich down. Brianna tore hers into little pieces, but she ate every bit. They each took a handful of raisins.

"Will you read us some stories?" Brianna asked.

Nodding, I said "We could do that. Or we could play a game, like Candy Land."

Chris grimaced. "That's for little kids."

"Maybe, but it's fun," I said.

Brianna stood up. "I have some books in my room. I'll go get a few," she said.

"Will you read some Harry Potter?" Chris asked. "I like that, but it's hard for me to read."

I got up. "Sure. We'll take turns. First, let's go see how the stuff we hung up to dry is doing."

Not dripping wet was the best I could have hoped for, but the sheet and pajamas hadn't even reached that point yet. I stared at the mattress pad in the bathtub. I didn't see any hope of getting that dry any time soon. Maybe I could put some towels under a clean sheet on Brianna's bed.

At least the kids had dry clothes. I had them each put on another pair of socks and a hoodie over the shirts and sweaters they already wore.

Trooping downstairs again with a stack of books, we settled onto the couch, snuggling together and pulling the blankets around us. Gradually, we went from chilly to comfortable to cozy. Maybe the situation wasn't ideal, but I couldn't think of much I would have traded for it.

We'd been reading for a while when we heard Kelly's footsteps in the hallway upstairs. She went into the bathroom, then back to her room. I was just thinking maybe I should go up and check on her again when she came downstairs.

She was wrapped in her bathrobe. I hoped for her sake that she had something warm on underneath that. Her feet were shoved in old slippers.

Brushing her hair back from her face, she glared toward us. "When did you get here?" she asked.

Since she knew the kids were here, I assumed she was talking to me. "A little while ago. The kids were hungry, and there didn't seem to be much that didn't have to be cooked in the house, so I went and got some food."

She looked out the window, where the rain was coming down steadily, although it was nowhere near as heavy as it had been earlier. "The stores are open?" she asked.

"No. Pretty much everything's shut down. They've got the high school set up as some kind of emergency headquarters, with cots and a soup kitchen and a food bank. They let me have some food that didn't need to be cooked."

Her nostrils flared. "You're eating out of a food bank?"

"Well, yeah. I mean, that's what a food bank's for. And there's not much else available."

"And you're feeding my kids food bank stuff?"

"It's food. And they have to eat, too. We got some pretty good stuff. You could fix yourself something."

"No thanks." She tossed her head and sat down in a chair. "And what are you doing?"

I'd have thought it was obvious. "We're reading books," I said, holding up the one I had been reading. "And keeping warm."

"You kids should have woken me up," she said. "I would have gotten up and fixed you something to eat."

Chris looked down at his hands.

"We tried," Brianna said in a small voice, "but you said we should go away."

Kelly wiped her eyes, then lifted her hand to her head. "I need a cup of coffee."

I shrugged. "There's no hot water, but there is some instant coffee. I suppose you could try to mix some of that with cold water and drink that. It'd be some caffeine. I did get some powdered milk, and there's sugar."

She wrinkled her nose. "I suppose it's better than nothing." But she made no move to get up.

"Do you want me to see if I can mix some up for you?" I asked. "And maybe you could have something to eat. Cereal with powdered milk."

Her face contorted, and she swallowed hard. She was probably pretty hung over.

"Or maybe a few dry crackers," I amended.

Getting unsteadily to her feet, she said, "What have you given the kids to eat?"

"Meatloaf sandwiches from the soup kitchen. Some raisins. And I made up some fruit drink."

"And cake," Brianna piped up. "Jesse had one big piece, so he gave us each part."

"First food bank, and now soup kitchen?" Kelly said.

It didn't seem so bad to me. "Yeah."

Pulling her bathrobe tighter around her, she said, "I don't need charity to feed my kids."

"I didn't see much to fix with the stove not working," I said. "And I sure as hell didn't see any place to buy food. If you think it's 'charity' and you don't want to take it, you could make a donation to the food bank to cover the cost. After this whole mess goes away."

Money was always tight, but it was going to be tighter as long as we couldn't work. If Quality Steel was closed for a whole week, Kelly could draw unemployment compensation, but that was nothing like a whole paycheck. I didn't have enough quarters of work credit to be eligible for it, so I wouldn't even get that.

She glared at me. "I can take care of my kids myself, thank you."

"You weren't exactly doing a great job when I got here earlier."

Her body stiffened. "And what's that supposed to mean?"

"The kids were up and hungry," I said, "and you were asleep."

"Where were you last night?" she demanded. "I thought you said you were coming over here."

"I got caught up in a few things and couldn't get over here. Besides, I didn't promise—how could anybody promise anything with what's going on now?—I said I'd try. And I did try."

"Not hard enough," she said, her face flushed. "While you were holed up somewhere, probably warm and dry and well-fed, I was up half the night waiting for you."

"And drinking," I couldn't help pointing out.

Kelly's voice rose. "What business is it of yours, if you couldn't even be bothered to get here?"

"You shouldn't be drinking around the kids."

Brianna leaned into my side and sobbed. I took a look at Chris. He was sitting still, staring at his hands. They didn't need to be hearing all this.

"Look," I said, getting up. "Let's drop this for now. You're up, and there's some food in the kitchen, no matter where it came from. Maybe I can go back out and see if I can find out what's going on."

"So now that you've finally shown up, you're walking out on me?" Her voice was shrill.

"I'm not thinking of it like that," I said. "You're getting mad. So am I. The kids don't need to hear this nonsense. Give us a few hours; we might be able to talk without yelling at each other. I'll go see how my apartment is doing. Maybe I can get some stuff out of there."

"You gonna come back?"

"If you want me to." I reached for the jacket and poncho. "But remember, I got no control over what's going on out there. So if I'm later than you expect, or if I can't make it at all, don't get mad."

She took a deep breath and shoved her hair back again. "You're right. Okay."

At the door, I turned to look back at the kids. Brianna had buried her face in the blankets. Her shoulders were heaving. Chris continued to stare at his hands.

How the hell could we be doing this to those poor kids?

I closed the door behind me.

CHAPTER 11

Water continued to rush through the streets, but it wasn't topping the curbs anymore. Bits of debris made landfall in the wheelchair cuts at the corners.

The new boots from Mandy's ex weren't soaked through. That was a unique and welcome sensation. They were leather, like my work boots, but even when I waded across the streets, they stayed fairly dry inside. They must have some kind of waterproofing finish.

I was pleasantly warm in the clothes she'd given me, and the rain poncho was very effective at keeping me dry. Who cared if I looked like a walking tent?

Staying long-term at Kelly's place didn't seem to be a viable option. We weren't getting along well enough.

I'd told her that I was heading out to check on my apartment, but I was pretty sure everything would be a soggy mess. Since it was a basement located downhill from here, it might still have a few feet of water in it. A discouraging thought.

How soon would Mandy and Nicole be leaving on their trip? Then I'd have a place to stay for a little while, at least. I didn't want to ask them if I could move into the carriage house until they gave me a date.

I could never come up with the deposit for a new apartment. And as long as Quality Steel was shut down, I wasn't earning any money. What money I had would be pretty much eaten up by parole expenses when I reported this week. Although, maybe the parole office would be closed. That was a basement, too.

Open for appointments or not, they'd want their money for this week anyhow, so I'd better make sure I had it.

As I approached the intersection where I'd been turned back last time, I could see that the saw horses were still there, but they were moved off to the side of the street. The tape attached to them was torn and flapped in the wind. It didn't extend across the road anymore. The tape was yellow with black lettering—"Caution: Do Not Enter." No one was manning the barrier anymore, so I slipped past.

As I rounded the corner to my street, emergency lights lit up the drab brick walls and glistened off the wet surfaces. Several patrol cars and a fire engine. What now?

They seemed to be gathered around my building.

I stopped and tried to focus through the dim light and rain.

They seemed to be gathered around my stairwell.

My throat started to close, and I had to fight down the urge to turn and run. That might attract attention, and somebody might decide to investigate. Instead, I hugged the dirty brick walls until I came to the recessed entry of an abandoned shoe repair shop. I slipped in and positioned myself so I could observe the situation without being readily seen.

Beyond the patrol cars and the fire engine, an ambulance was parked haphazardly, blocking the street. In the best of times, there wasn't much traffic to worry about. This certainly wasn't the best of times.

The vehicles sat in flowing water that came up a few inches on their tires. The firefighters, wearing their boots and yellow turn-out coats, were sloshing around with impunity, but the cops and the medics hunched in the rain.

The water flowed from the street down into the stairwell, which seemed to be pretty full.

Great. If the water was that high in the stairwell, I could just imagine how deep it was in my apartment. I was probably too late to save the mattress. Not that I was about to go wading through all those emergency responders to get anywhere near the place.

The medics took a gurney from the back of the ambulance and lowered the wheels. They pushed it through the water all the way over to the railing around the stairs. Two firefighters waded down a few steps, and another positioned himself at the top. Something was floating in the water. Something big. They maneuvered it near to the head of the stairs.

When it got straightened around, they lifted it out of the water and toward the gurney. It looked like a human body.

In spite of the cold, sweat dripped down my neck. Somebody floating in my stairwell. Could the person be alive? At a time like this, with the whole city in disarray, they wouldn't have wasted all those resources on somebody they already knew was dead, would they?

They lifted the person onto the gurney. One of the hands flopped off the side and hung there. Someone adjusted a spotlight so the medics could work.

The light caught bright orange. With purple stars. The vest was wet and flattened, but I recognized that expensive down vest.

Pounding in my chest made my lungs ache. Benji?

How could Benji be there again? Even with all the emergencies they were dealing with, surely no social service employee would have lost track of Benji enough to let him get back here.

But the body they were strapping onto the gurney was too tall to be Benji.

Hadn't Benji mentioned that Aaron had bought both of them orange vests with purple stars? Was it Aaron?

And if it was, what was he doing floating in my stairwell?

Maybe he was unconscious and would be able to explain when he came around.

One of the medics went to the back of the ambulance and came back with a blanket or something. He lifted the dangling arm and settled it next to the rest of the still form. Then he covered the entire thing. Including the face.

It was a dead body.

The dead body was probably Aaron.

Aaron had been found dead in my stairwell? What was he doing there?

I tried to convince myself that there was a good possibility that they would find out he'd drowned. But why would he have been in the water?

Or knowing his history, maybe he'd ODed.

Just so it didn't turn out that he'd been murdered and left in my stairwell.

Guess who would be the first suspect.

Even if there were any possibility that somebody would answer any questions, I wasn't waiting around to find out.

I slipped out of the store entryway and walked as sedately as I could manage toward the end of the block. After I turned the corner, I picked up the pace a bit and turned down an alley where I wouldn't easily be noticed by anyone in a passing vehicle. I didn't think I had to worry too much about people on foot—with the rain, anybody who was out walking would be in a hurry to get to their destination. Including me.

That sounded like a good idea, but I was having trouble coming up with a destination. I couldn't go home—even if I waited until the emergency crews left, my apartment was flooded.

I'd mooched off Mandy and Nicole enough. The body in the stairwell changed everything. Before I went to see them, I'd have to figure out a way to tell them I might not be able to house sit for them. If I got picked up for questioning about Aaron, there was an excellent possibility I'd be held for a parole violation. Or worse. Despite trying to keep the jail population down during the emergency, they could always make room. That would solve the immediate dilemma of where I would be staying, but I didn't really welcome that solution.

Maybe Aaron's death wasn't murder, I tried to tell myself. He could have died a natural death. Well, maybe not a natural death. But an OD or something that wouldn't implicate me.

Fat chance.

After the little run-in with Diffy, I really didn't want to head to the high school. I might not be welcome there.

Which brought me to Kelly. Would she have settled down by now? If she had, she might let me stay there for a little while.

She might even have rethought her opposition to the food bank and soup kitchen. We could take the kids for a hot meal there.

The fire engine trundled by the entrance to the alley, followed by the ambulance. No need for the siren or flashing lights to clear the way to the morgue.

It didn't look like Benji was going to be left with Aaron ever again. I wondered if Social Services had managed to track down his mother. Now they had bad news for her about her other son.

Benji was probably in an emergency foster home. Not great, but at least he'd be someplace warm and dry, with food available.

Staying in the limited shelter of the alley to give the emergency vehicles some time to get away from the area, I tried to think it through.

Whenever they caught up with me, the police would want to question me about Aaron's death, I was sure. Even if they could identify the cause of death and could tell I had nothing to do with it, they'd want to know what he'd been doing in my stairwell. They might not go looking too hard for me until things were back to normal, but it was something I'd have to deal with sooner or later.

I would have no answers to give them. What was he—or his body— doing in my stairwell?

Or suppose I was wrong and it wasn't him? The body was the right size and shape, the vest matched the one Benji wore, but it was possible it wasn't Aaron, wasn't it?

Okay, if it wasn't Aaron, who was it? And what was he doing in my stairwell? That might not be any better.

Despite the warm jacket, I shivered. Water was dripping off the edge of the poncho and soaking the lined blue jeans. Cautiously, I walked to the entry to the alley and peered down the street.

The flood of water that had been hugging the curbs was expanding again, meeting in the middle of the road. This wasn't a good place to stay.

I left the alley and went to the corner, just to see if the coast was clear at my apartment. It wasn't. The patrol cars were still there. As I watched, one of the cops unrolled some crime scene tape and strung it along the railing by the stairwell.

So much for natural death theories. They might be too busy with the current flood emergency to put a lot of time into investigation at this point, but they'd get to it soon enough.

Turning back toward the center of town, which stood on higher ground, I felt a wave of exhaustion. I wasn't thinking clearly. Maybe I should just go to the police station and turn myself in. It wasn't that far a walk. Save everybody a lot of grief.

That was probably not a good idea. First thing they'd wonder would be how I knew about Aaron. Then they'd almost have to lock me up, even if they were trying to keep the jail population down until the crisis passed. Any brownie points I earned by surrendering so they didn't have to look for me wouldn't be particularly useful if I picked up a conviction on Aaron's death. The minimum I could expect for a second homicide conviction was a life sentence. Probably life without parole.

Turning myself in would mean I lost any control I had in what happened to me. If I could think this through and come up with what might have happened to Aaron, at least some of the cops would listen.

And there was the little fact that I hated being locked up. I wasn't about to voluntarily give up the freedom I had, even with all the hassles that came with it.

I passed by the sunken entrance to the parole office and felt a grim satisfaction when I realized that it, too, was filled with water. The grungy waiting room would be even grungier.

Why couldn't Aaron's—or whoever's—body have been found in that stairwell? That would have saved me from a lot of the grief I was sure was coming my way as soon as a detective was assigned to the case.

I had a horrible feeling I knew who that would be. In a small city police force where everyone had to be flexible, Detective Belkins had seniority and was the most experienced homicide detective they had. And he hated my guts.

Walking past the library and the other county buildings, I peered at the windows and doors. Except for the police station and the jail, they were all dark.

The one church was still closed, and the other was well lit and showed a lot of activity, but I gave it wide berth.

I continued downtown. The stores and restaurants were all closed. The streets weren't entirely deserted, but the occasional vehicle was mostly a utility crew truck or some other type of emergency responder.

Was it too soon to head back to Kelly's? My gut twisted at the thought of the kids sitting there listening to our little spat. They deserved a hell of a lot better. Maybe I should just ease myself out of Kelly's life, before they got too attached to me. They'd had more than their share of losses already—their parents were divorced, none too amicably. Their father insisted on his visitation with them and was trying to get custody, but it was because he was trying to put the screws to Kelly, rather than because he cared about them. When he was supposed to have time with them, he mostly left them with his mother and aunt, neither one of them in particularly good health right now. And he'd recently been in a DUI accident with them in the car.

Not that Kelly didn't drink. Look at last night and this morning. She hadn't been able to take care of the kids. Chris tried hard, but an eight-year-old shouldn't be left taking care of himself, much less a six-year-old sister who wet the bed and hid in the closet.

Was I making things better or worse for them by sticking around?

It wasn't like I hadn't realized that adjustment to life on the street was going to be hard. But who knew how a woman and a couple of kids could grab my soul and tear it into pieces?

Or that I'd have to think all the time? In prison, I'd had few choices and little control over anything. This whole making decisions was more difficult than I had ever imagined.

All the problems that would be solved if I were locked up again. That distinctive clang of a cell door shutting behind me would mean I didn't have to worry about anything anymore. Maybe for the rest of my life.

* * * *

When I knocked on Kelly's front door, she opened it. Even without hot water, she'd cleaned herself up. Her hair was redone in a neat braid. She was dressed in regular clothes, but she was wearing a thick hoodie over them. And boots.

The house was cold.

She stepped aside so I could come in.

I looked around. The blankets and quilts we'd snuggled into on the couch were still in place, but the kids weren't there. "Where are the kids?"

"In their rooms."

"Are they warm enough there?"

Shrugging, she shut the door behind me. "I guess. They didn't want to stay down here with me." Tears formed in her eyes. "What kind of monster am I? My own kids would rather be up in their cold bedrooms than stay in the room with me."

I put my arm around her shoulders and drew her to me. If I was feeling bad about this, how was she feeling? "You're not a monster. But you do have to think about how the things you do affect them."

She didn't pull away. In fact, she buried her face in the wet poncho and shuddered. Her warm female scent, now a bit on the funky side and still mingled with the factory smell of oil, filled my nostrils. It wasn't unpleasant in the least. I buried my nose in her hair and inhaled, holding her for a moment.

"Let me get the poncho off," I said, moving her back a step and pulling it over my head. I stripped the puffy down jacket off, too, and laid them on the stair railing. Then I gathered her to me and steered her to the couch.

She leaned into me and laid her head on my shoulder. "I don't know what to do," she moaned.

I grabbed one of the blankets and wrapped it around her. "Stop drinking, for one thing."

She ignored that. "I can barely make the mortgage payment. My credit card is maxed out. I'm afraid I might have to apply for emergency heating assistance. Now we're probably gonna miss a few days of work. I can't afford a short paycheck. And I'm behind on paying my lawyer. If I don't keep up those payments, he won't go to court for me, and Fred will get custody of the kids."

Fred was her ex. If Fred had been a decent parent, the kids would be better off with him. But if anything, he drank more than Kelly did. "The kids need a responsible parent," I said. "And when you're drinking, you can't be a responsible parent."

She pushed away from me and glared at me, her eyes narrowing. "And I suppose you're someone to talk about being responsible?"

I wasn't at all sure I was the right person to do it, but somebody had to challenge Kelly's tactic of trying to turn the issue away from her drinking. "Maybe not," I said, "but whatever I am or aren't, it don't change the fact that you're the kids' mother, and when you're drunk, you're doing a lousy job of it. The kids are the most important thing in your life, and you're messing up."

"So." She tossed her head. "What do you think I should do?"

"Get help."

"I can handle this myself."

"Yeah, sure. That's what all junkies say."

"What did you call me?"

I steeled myself to repeat it. "Junkie."

"I don't use drugs."

"Just because you can buy it in a store and can't get thrown in jail for possession don't mean it won't destroy your life and your family."

She sat up straighter and glared at me.

"Nobody asked you."

"Yeah, you did."

"Well, butt out. This isn't that much of a problem. Nothing I can't deal with."

I was this far in. I might as well finish it. "That's called denial."

"What?"

"Denial."

She gave a bitter laugh. "And what do you think I should do?"

"Join Alcoholics Anonymous."

"AA? Those 'My name is Kelly, and I'm an addict' meetings?"

"That's NA—Narcotics Anonymous. It's the same idea, only for alcoholics."

"You think I'm an alcoholic?"

I bit my lip, then said, "Yes."

She stood up and strode through the kitchen and into the bathroom off the laundry room. The door slammed so hard, it shook the whole house.

Well, *that* was a successful intervention technique. If she was using drugs, I'd have thought she'd gone to take a hit. Since she'd always been pretty open about the drinking, I didn't think she'd be hiding booze in there.

My better judgment said I'd better get out of there before she came back out of the bathroom.

The thought of the kids made my stomach twist. I wondered if I could go upstairs and say goodbye to them. Instead, I just sat there stupidly. Probably hadn't done any good at all, and probably ruined any relationship I had with Kelly, or might have had in the future. She was right. Who the hell did I think I was?

Kelly came back so quietly that I didn't hear her, and I was still sitting there like a lump.

Her eyes were swollen, and her nose was red.

I scrambled to my feet and reached for my jacket and poncho.

She reached out and put a hand on my arm. "Jesse."

"Yeah?" I paused with one arm in the jacket.

"Suppose you're right? Suppose I am an alcoholic?"

Staring at her, I said, "Well, like I said, then you got to get help."

"You don't think I could stop drinking on my own?"

"Nope. Most people can't. They need something. The twelve-step programs are pretty successful."

She tossed her head. "I'm not religious."

"You don't have to be religious, at least not in the Sunday-go-to-meeting sense. Just recognize that there's a higher power you can lean on when you need to, when you can't make it on your own."

"I think I can make it on my own."

"What d'ya mean?"

"I can stop drinking on my own."

"Well, if you can, great. But if you can't, you need to have backup."

"Watch me."

I scratched my four-day beard. "You gonna give it an honest try?"

"Yep."

"Starting when?"

"Starting now."

"You gonna pour out all the booze you got in the house?"

"I already have."

"All of it?"

"Yep."

No point in disagreeing, even if that was at best an iffy scenario.

I slipped my arm back out of the jacket sleeve and put it and the poncho back on the stair railing. Reaching out, I put my arms around her and drew her to me. "I hope you can do it. If there's anything I can do to help, let me know."

"You're right about what I'm doing to the kids."

Everybody's "higher powers" were different. Most people thought of it as God.

In a way, maybe hers were the kids. I knew a lot of people would do things for their kids that they wouldn't do for themselves. Kelly was one of them.

She snuggled up against my chest, her hair tickling my face, and cried. I buried my nose in her hair, breathing in her distinctive smell. It might not be perfume, but it was Kelly, and it smelled good to me. I stroked her back. I longed to lead her up to her warm bed and hold her until she stopped crying. And see where it led us.

Too bad the kids were awake.

I pulled her over to the couch, and we sat down with her still nestled in against me. Her shoulders heaved, and she made soft mewing sounds. I wasn't sure what I should be doing, but just sitting next to her, cradling her in my arms, seemed to be working okay. She shivered, and I pulled a blanket over us.

Eventually, her breath became slow and regular. She'd dozed off. My arm was falling asleep, but I wasn't about to move it.

Goddess jumped up on and settled down next to us, purring. Inky and Stinky followed.

I closed my eyes and wished we never had to move. I dozed.

"Jesse? Is that you?" a small voice said from the stairs.

"Yeah, Chris," I answered. "Want to come sit with us?"

"Has Mom stopped being mad?"

"I think so. She's asleep."

"I'll see if Brianna will come out of her closet."

"She's hiding in the closet again?"

"Yeah. Mom was yelling, so we went upstairs. And Brianna went back into her closet. She's been doing that a lot lately."

"Go see if you can get her out. And we can figure out what we're going to do about getting something to eat."

CHAPTER 12

"Kelly." I shook her gently.

She shifted slightly. "Hmmmm?"

"Kelly, do you have gas in the car?"

"Yeah. I filled it up before I went to work last."

"That was smart. Maybe you could take the kids and drive over to the high school? You could get a hot meal."

She sat up. "A hot meal at the high school?"

"Yeah. They're running a soup kitchen there. It's too far for the kids to walk. Especially in this rain."

"I'm not going to any soup kitchen. Neither are my kids."

I sighed. "Kelly. Be reasonable. The soup kitchen is set up so people who don't have any power can get a hot meal. It's not like some kind of regular charity or something."

"No? You don't pay for it, do you?"

"You certainly can. They'd appreciate any donation you wanted to make. But I'd think your best bet would be to wait until things settle down and make a donation then. We don't know how long we're gonna be out of work."

"So it is charity. At least for now."

"The kids are hungry. And they need a good, hot meal."

After the little scene with Diffy, I had planned to avoid going back to the high school. And now it was likely that the cops would want to talk to me about Aaron. They might not be looking hard right now, with all the other emergencies that they needed to attend to, but if I was seen and recognized, they'd probably haul me in.

I debated saying something to Kelly about Aaron. After all, she worked with him, too. When he showed up. But she felt bad enough already, and knowing he was probably dead would just make her feel worse.

Kelly's face was set in a stubborn frown. She looked so much like Brianna that I had to smother a grin.

I sighed and said to Kelly, "If you don't want to come in and get anything to eat, maybe you could just drive us over. I'll take the kids in."

She frowned at me. "And where would I be?"

I shrugged. "You could stay in the car if you wanted. Or go see if you could find anything out."

"About what?"

"About when they expect the rain to stop and the flooding to go down. When they're gonna open the bridge again. If any of the stores are gonna open anytime soon. Stuff like that."

Kelly shook her head. "I got food here for the kids. We don't need no soup kitchen."

"They won't starve," I agreed, "but it's more like snacks. Do 'em some good to get a real meal. Do us some good, too."

"I can fix them grilled ham and cheese sandwiches and tomato soup…" Her voice trailed off. "But I guess I can't use the stove."

"That's right. And we probably shouldn't open the refrigerator. The stuff'll keep for a few days without power if we don't open it and let any warm air in."

She shivered. "And where would we find this warm air to let in?"

I laughed. "You're right, it wouldn't be warm air. But it still won't be as cold as the air in the refrigerator."

Kelly smiled back. "I sure hope not."

Chris came down the stairs, Brianna trailing behind him, and pulled his jacket closer around him. "We could have more peanut butter and crackers," he said. "And Jesse made a whole big pitcher of the fruit drink."

Kelly looked at his pinched little face. Did she realize how hard he was trying to please her? "Okay." She pushed back the blanket covering her. "Let's go to the high school. You can get something to eat, and I'll see what I can find out."

She got her keys and a raincoat. We all headed out to the car. The kids piled in the back seat. The starter in her old station wagon was reluctant to catch in the dampness, but eventually, it kicked over. She let the engine idle for a few minutes to warm up so it wouldn't stall. Welcome heat began to flow from the vents on the dashboard.

The gathering darkness created shadows beneath all the trees. The deserted streets were wet, with rivulets running down either side, but we didn't hit any standing water. That was a decided improvement.

"I'll drop you and the kids off at the entrance." Kelly pulled up in front of the school. "I'll find a place to park. Where is the soup kitchen set up?"

"In the cafeteria," I said.

"I guess that makes sense. After you get something to eat, come out and look for me. I'm going to see if anyone has any news."

They were serving chicken pot pie. I looked at the already-filled trays of people heading to the tables. It was heavy on the veggies and gravy, a little light on the chicken. But it was hot. And it smelled wonderful. The kids and I got in line and each took a tray.

"This is like school lunch," Chris said. "You get a tray, and they put food on it for you. And you never really know what you're going to get. It's fun."

It reminded me more of the prison chow hall, which ran about the same way, only with correctional officers all around. And I never would have called that "fun." I hoped the school meals the kids got were of better quality than the prison food.

Brianna took her tray. "I wish we could get school lunch all the time." I was surprised. "You don't get school lunches much?"

Chris shook his head. "Usually we carry. Mom says school lunches are way too expensive."

We got up to the serving line. The server put big scoops of the pot pie in our bowls. The kids were going to skip the little packets of baby carrots and celery sticks, but I made them take some, along with a square of cornbread. They each got a carton of chocolate milk and one of orange juice. I took a cup of coffee. I thought about saving it for Kelly, but decided that if she wanted one, she could swallow her false pride, or whatever it was that made her think she didn't have to ever take any help, unlike the rest of the world, and come get it herself.

I led the way to the back corner and took a seat with my back facing the wall. Always the safest place when there was a crowd, especially when most of the people were strangers. The kids sat on either side of me and dove enthusiastically into their bowls of pot pie.

A voice said, "Hey, Jesse, that you?"

I looked up to see a tall, dark man, dressed in a jacket that was much too thin for the weather and balancing a tray. His skeletal face was framed in a bushy beard.

"Banjo?" I asked.

"Yeah, man. Mind if I sit here?" He gestured toward the table.

"Go for it, man."

Compact in his movements, he placed the tray on the table and slid into the seat. "Long time, Jesse. How ya doing? And where the hell did you get the kids?"

I grinned. When I was in prison, Banjo and I had been assigned to the same cell for a few years. We came from very different places and were going in very different directions, but we had developed a deep respect and friendship for each other. "My girlfriend's kids. When'd you get released?"

"You got a girlfriend? Will miracles never cease?" He unfolded the paper napkin and wiped his hands. "I got a mandatory release last week. Just in time for this damn storm. No job, no car, no money. Just the clothes on my back. Great timing, huh?"

"True, that." He wasn't asking for help, and I didn't have much to give him, but if he was truly desperate, I could give him a few bucks. It might go for drugs, but then, it might not, either.

I drained my coffee cup and thought about getting a refill. The crowd was growing by the minute, and I'd have to push my way over to the table with the coffee. Well as I knew Banjo, with his sense of responsibility—or rather lack thereof—I was a bit leery about leaving him with the kids. "Where are you staying?" I asked.

He grimaced. "For right now, with some bikers who took over an abandoned warehouse, down on 67th Street. But it's a warehouse on high ground. So it's okay for now."

I knew where he was talking about. "Predators?" I asked.

"Yeah. Old Buckles—you remember him? Commissary clerk who's doing life on the installment plan?"

"Yeah." Old Buckles was Kelly's dad.

Banjo took a forkful of pot pie. "Well, Old Buckles got in touch with a few of the guys." He grinned. "Smuggled cellphone. You know how much that's happening?"

Since I'd never had anyone to call when I'd been locked up, I hadn't paid much attention to the cellphones that got smuggled into the prison. But given the exorbitant rates charged for a call by the company that ran the official phone system, I knew that even generally compliant inmates were tempted to use them.

"Anyhow, he told them to let me stay there while I ran a few errands for him out on the street."

I knew how Old Buckles's mind worked. "Running a few errands, or settling a few scores?"

Banjo paused with another forkful halfway to his mouth and grinned. "Both. He says this snitch, this meth junkie kid, set him up for this last bit. Either that, or this reporter bitch. He wants me to find out what goes. And take care of anything that needs taken care of."

"This meth junkie kid" sounded suspiciously like Aaron.

And "this reporter bitch" sounded like Carissa.

I didn't like the direction this was going in.

Banjo would use techniques I wouldn't to find things out. If he did figure out, though, what had happened to Aaron and who might have wanted him dead so badly, I'd like to know that. It might be very useful information to pass on to the investigating police if they tried to pin

Aaron's death on me. Which, if it turned out to be homicide, they would, when the emergency situation settled down and they really had time to start really looking for me.

I nodded at the kids. "These are Old Buckles's grandkids."

Banjo stopped chewing and looked at them. "His daughter is your girlfriend?"

"Yep."

He raised his eyebrows. "Well, with Old Buckles for a daddy, I can see where that explains why she don't think you're too much of a badass. Next to Old Buckles, you're practically a boy scout."

I wouldn't have put it like that, but I knew what he meant. I was at least trying to live as a law-abiding citizen. Old Buckles was an outlaw biker through and through. The only respect he had for the law was because they could lock him up. And they did. Repeatedly. As Banjo said, doing life on the installment plan.

Banjo threw his head back and laughed. "A boy scout on parole for murder."

Grinning sheepishly, I shrugged. "What can I say?"

"Not a whole hell of a lot. Where'd you meet this girlfriend, anyhow?"

"At work. Quality Steel Fabrications. Midnight shift."

He sighed. "Straight job, huh? You always liked your work routine. How're you doing with it?"

"Pretty good. The pay's okay, and it's got benefits."

"I bet. Like the women who work there, huh? A lot more besides this one? Maybe I ought to try to get a job there. They all put out?"

Banjo could be crude. I glanced meaningfully at the kids. "No. Kelly's the only woman on the shift. She gets a college girl to come stay overnight with the kids when she's working."

His gaze followed mine to the kids, and he took my hint. "You stay at her place?"

"Not all the time. I got a little basement apartment. Or I had one. I think it's pretty well flooded out now. So I don't know where I'm gonna be staying." I wasn't about to tell Banjo about the possible arrangement with Mandy and let him know that a nice house with nice furnishings was about to be empty for a few weeks.

Especially since there was now the distinct possibility that I would be locked up for Aaron's murder and not be able to keep an eye on it. I'd better tell her fairly soon so she could have a chance to find someone else to stay in the carriage house.

We stopped talking as one of the soup kitchen volunteers came around with a tray of desserts. Chris chose a brownie from the selection.

Brianna got all shy and wouldn't take anything, so I took a few cookies for her. Banjo and I each went for apple pie.

As the kids finished, I stood up. "I got to go find their mother," I said.

"When you give them back, you want to come up to the warehouse with me?"

I shook my head. "Not right now. Mind if I put that off for a little while? Like maybe tomorrow? I was figuring I'd go home with Kelly and the kids for tonight. I hope."

He leered. "Hoping to get lucky, huh? Sure. Tomorrow's fine. You know where the warehouse is?"

"I think so. Back in an alley, with a chain link fence with a gate? And a guard house?"

"Yep. You been there?"

"Yeah."

I helped the kids gather the trash onto their trays and carry them over to the trash cans and table where the dirty dishes and trays were stacked. We went out into the teeming hallway. With this press of damp humanity, how was I ever going to find Kelly?

Keeping as close to the wall as possible, a habit I'd picked up in prison, I guided the kids in front of me, making slow progress down the hallway. In the half hour or so we'd been in the cafeteria, dozens, maybe hundreds, more people had shown up. Where had they all come from?

The sound of a TV news broadcast came from a small lobby by one of the stairwells. They'd have to give some kind of a report on conditions and when things might begin to return to normal. And Kelly might be listening to it, trying to get some information.

We inched our way down the hall and into the room.

Several of the soldiers stood around, monitoring a huge TV that was apparently hooked up to one of the generators. We made our way against a wall. I scanned the people in front of us. Kelly was about five foot four and had long, dark hair. She would be hard to pick out from the back.

A cheerful weatherman assured us that it would continue to rain overnight, with some possibility of tapering off in the morning. Meanwhile, the river was over flood stage, but had just about crested. Most of the snow in the mountains was already washed away, so unless the rain became much heavier than expected, we could hope to see gradually improving conditions. And power companies all over the east coast had sent utility crews to help restore power in our area, although it might be over a week before all repairs were made and power completely restored.

The view on the screen switched to dramatic still photos of the flooding, with a running narration in the background.

A car teetering on the edge of a bridge, its wheels mere inches above the level of the water. The interior of a flooded furniture store, mattresses floating on the dirty water. A fire hydrant gushing even more water into the street.

Me standing waist deep in a flooded street, looking more than moderately demented, clinging to a rope and handing an obviously frightened woman up to someone standing on the curb.

"Isn't that you, Jesse?" Kelly stood by me, her hand on my arm.

"Yeah."

"Is that where you were when you didn't make it over to my place?"

"For part of the time."

"You look kind of rough there. And you have to have been soaked. It must have been cold."

"True, that. It was cold."

"Obviously you managed to get out of the water. Why didn't you come over then?"

"I wasn't really thinking straight. Kind of disoriented."

"You mean, like hypothermia?"

"Probably."

"So did you end up at the hospital?"

"Nah."

She frowned. "Where did you go?"

"You remember Mandy Radman? Sterling Radman's wife?"

"Sterling Radman who worked at Quality Steel? Until he got busted for that fake ID scheme?"

"Yeah. I don't think there can be too many Sterling Radmans around here."

"What about her?"

"She was there. She gave me a ride. She did want to take me to the hospital. But I talked her out of that. So she took me to her house."

Kelly drew back. "You stayed at her house?"

"Yeah. And she gave me some of the clothes that he left behind."

"I wondered where you got that nice jacket and new boots."

"They used to belong to Sterling Radman. I don't guess he'll need them in the federal pen he's headed to."

Kelly was staring at me with her eyes narrowed. "You stayed at Mandy's house overnight. Where did you sleep?"

We didn't have an exclusive arrangement, Kelly and me. I would have been happy to, but Kelly didn't want to commit. And between my uncertain future and her having to worry about the kids, I could understand. Who knew how long it might be before I was locked up again?

So why was she getting bent out of shape?

"On a couch," I said reassuringly.

"I know you and she had some kind of dealings before Radman was arrested. Does Mandy…" Kelly sought for words to ask what she wanted to know.

"Some kind of dealings" had been Mandy wanting me to either kill her husband or recruit someone else to do it. But I knew what Kelly was getting at. "Does Mandy want to start something with me?" I asked.

"I guess that's what I meant."

"Nah. I think, since this whole thing with Radman and all, she's done a lot of thinking. Probably with a therapist. Even if I was in her class—which I'm definitely not—I'm not the type she's interested in."

"What do you mean?"

"She's got a girlfriend. And they're planning to get married."

"Shhhh," someone hissed at us.

We turned our attention to the TV, where the announcer was reading a list of things closed for the entire week. The schools, of course. Most businesses—including Quality Steel, our employer.

That wasn't a surprise, but the short paychecks would hurt both of us.

Videos began playing on the screen, with the announcer describing the scenes.

The screen showed ice floes crowded around the supports of the bridge, threatening to knock some off the pilings. National Guard troops waving off traffic. The bloated bodies of several expensive Holstein dairy cows trapped with other debris in floodwaters. An electrical substation under water. Several emergency response vehicles, their flashing lights throwing a lurid glow over the scene, surrounding a stairwell outside a rundown building.

I froze.

The only known fatality so far in this disaster, the announcer intoned. And authorities were unsure whether it was a drowning or a body dumped in the flooded stairwell. The identity of the victim was being withheld until next of kin were notified.

If I was right that it was Aaron, it might be a while before they found his mother. But at least they were already looking.

I wondered how Benji was making out. As well as could be, I hoped, aware that he was probably in emergency foster care, a fate I had a fair amount of experience with in my younger days, and one I would not wish on anyone. A lot had gone wrong in his young life now, and with Aaron dead and his mother still away and unable to get back, things might get a lot worse for him before they got better.

The camera caught the ambulance driving away and the cop unwinding crime scene tape and attaching it to the lamppost.

The announcer said that the police wanted to question a "person of interest" in the case.

I had a feeling I knew who that person was. I hoped they didn't have a picture to put up.

"Let's go," I whispered to Kelly.

* * * *

The house was cold. We played board games around the dining room table, a candle supplementing the feeble light from the window, until our fingers got so stiff that Kelly sent the kids to get their gloves.

"I hope the pipes don't freeze," she said, pulling aside one of the front drapes to stare out the window at darkening sky. A few pinpricks of light showed in the distance. Nothing like the lights on an ordinary night in this comfortable residential section of town.

"Not likely." I stepped up next to her and put my arm over her shoulder. She snuggled in close. "It'd have to be freezing out there, under thirty-two degrees. And we'd be getting snow, not rain."

"I guess. Maybe I should get a kerosene heater."

"You could. How often does this happen?"

"Power go out? Every once in a while."

"All over town?"

She thought. "No. Usually, it's just pretty localized, and they get it back up in a few hours. I can't remember Quality Steel ever being shut down like this before. And I've worked there for over ten years."

"Generators are expensive. You'd have to think about whether the expense was worth it, for just once in a while like this."

Brianna came in, several books clutched in her mittened hands. "Can you read to us now, Jesse?" she asked.

I glanced at Kelly, who put a hand on the child's head and smiled. Despite the cold, I felt a warmth in my chest. I loved it when she smiled like that.

"Sure," she said. "Jesse can read to you. I'll go upstairs and see if I can't find some extra blankets and things. Once it gets all the way dark, we may as well go to bed. We won't be able to see to do much else."

The kids and I settled back into the nest we'd built on the couch, and I read to them until the light from the windows failed.

"Come on up and get in bed," Kelly called. "It's going to get colder as the night goes on."

My breath quickened at the thought of snuggling down into Kelly's soft bed. We'd keep plenty warm.

Kelly had found clean sheets for Brianna's bed. The ones we'd hung up weren't dripping anymore, but they certainly weren't dry.

"Should I leave on my jacket and gloves?" Chris asked.

"If you want," Kelly said, smoothing the bedding. "Definitely wear a hat to keep your head warm."

After they both were tucked in with teddy bears and a tiny flashlight next to the beds, we went into Kelly's room. It was too dark to see much. I stripped down to my long underwear. I was hoping they wouldn't stay on too long.

Kelly went into the bathroom and came back wearing her long, fuzzy bathrobe. And socks. I was betting she didn't have much on under the robe. She lay down.

I slipped into bed next to Kelly, pulling the heavy blankets over us. The bed was cold. That was okay—we had plenty of time to warm it up. She lay on her side, facing away from me. I snuggled into her back, burying my face in her long dark hair. Of course, there'd been no opportunity for showers, but she'd put some kind of scented lotion or powder on her neck. She still smelled of sweat and oil from the factory. And woman. I reached my arms around her, feeling her soft warmth, and pulled her closer. She turned her head, and her mouth reached for mine.

Her kiss had an alcoholic, but minty taste to it. Mouthwash. I wished I'd thought to use the mouthwash I knew she kept in the bathroom. I hadn't even brushed my teeth.

I forgot about that as her tongue sought mine. My hands eased under the soft warmth of the robe. She wasn't wearing anything underneath it.

The door opened. "Mom?"

Kelly sighed and pulled away from me.

"What is it?"

Brianna said, "I can't get warm."

Chris was right behind her. "Neither can I."

"Can we get in bed with you?"

"Well…"

I leaned back against the pillow. "It is cold. We'll get other nights."

"Okay. I guess," Kelly said, shifting and gathering the robe around her.

Brianna climbed in next to Kelly, and Chris next to me. We pulled the blankets up around us. I'd heard something about people who slept this way all the time. They called it a "family bed" or something. I couldn't say I wasn't disappointed at the turn of events, but it was cozy. And I could see the satisfaction in it, lying so close to people I cared about.

I just wondered how they handled the whole sex aspect.

And I hoped Brianna wouldn't wet the bed.

CHAPTER 13

When I woke up, dim light shone through the window. Dawn. I lay there for a few minutes, enjoying the warmth of the soft bed. Kelly was snuggled up on one side of me, her breath coming in deep, regular sighs. Chris was on the other side, curled in a ball, his butt and feet pressed against my thigh.

Trying not to disturb anybody else, I lifted my head and looked over beyond Kelly. Brianna lay there, her tiny face relaxed more than I'd ever seen it when she was awake.

I glanced over at the nightstand. The digital alarm clock's face was blank. The power hadn't come on.

Silence except for the sound of the sleepers' breathing. It took me a minute to realize what that meant. No drumming on the roof. It wasn't raining!

Careful not to let too much of the decidedly cold air under the covers, I slipped out and climbed over Chris, then tucked the bedding around everyone again. I stood for a few seconds, just looking at the peaceful trio.

The chill cut that short, so I grabbed my clothes and went to the bathroom.

After I'd washed up as best I could in the icy water from the faucet, I reached for a towel to dry myself.

The ones that hung on the towel racks were all damp and cold. Not surprising. I opened the linen closet and took a clean one from the diminishing stack there. If nobody could get laundry done soon, we'd all have to rethink our definition of usably clean clothes and linens.

As I pulled it out, something tucked behind the stack fell over with a clunk. I looked closer.

A half-empty bottle of Southern Comfort.

Had Kelly lied to me about pouring out all the alcohol in the house? Or had she stashed bottles in so many places throughout the house that she'd forgotten about this one? And how many others were still hidden in various places?

Remembering the alcohol and mint on her breath as I'd kissed her last night, I looked in the medicine cabinet. Sure enough, a big bottle of mint mouthwash stood there. I took it down and sniffed it. It was mostly minty smelling, but there was a faint undertone of alcohol.

Didn't alcoholics frequently use mouthwash to mask the smell of alcohol on their breath?

My gut twisted. I didn't want to think that Kelly had lied to me. On the other hand, it would do no good to any of us if I became the classic enabler who wanted so much to believe what she said that I overlooked the obvious.

I left a note saying I was going out to check on my apartment. I addressed it to all three of them, since I was pretty sure only Chris could read well enough to make it out.

Outside, the rain had stopped, but the streets were full of debris and downed tree limbs. A utility truck with its lights flashing wound its way down the street and stopped next to a pole at the corner. Maybe Kelly would have her power back on soon.

How long before the city was operational again?

The time I had to try to figure out anything useful about Aaron's death might be very limited.

If I could find out who else might have had a beef with Aaron, I would have something to tell the detectives, who would start looking for me in earnest as soon as the chief of police was satisfied that most of the city was safe and secure.

Banjo might have found out something, and I'd told Banjo I'd stop by the abandoned warehouse where he was staying with some of the Predators. I turned in that direction. My apartment could wait.

Despite my best efforts to keep my distance, I'd been inextricably mixed up with the Predators when one of them had attacked Kelly. At first, the cops were sure it had been me. Old Buckles, who'd been out on parole and staying at Kelly's place, hadn't been quite so sure I'd been the attacker, but he'd been open to the possibility. Turned out it was a biker named Razorback, but he was dead now.

I'd had a couple of run-ins with Funky Joe, but they'd been minor and not worth the trouble it would cause the gang to track me down to settle it. But what would they do if I showed up in their midst? Offer me a beer, which I'd better take, and answer a few questions about Aaron? Tell me to get lost and lock the door? Beat me senseless and stomp me to death, then toss my body somewhere it was not likely to be found?

Assuming they didn't decide to implement the third option, I didn't see I had much to lose.

I heard the whine of chainsaws, but didn't see many people. A patrol car passed going in one direction, a cherry picker with an out-of-state logo on the door going the other way. The streets were a mess. In the lower areas, and wherever there was a depression in the ground, dirty water stood. If the storm drains were working at all, it was sluggishly, and water pooled around their grates.

The alley that led to the warehouse climbed up from a flooded street. Water dripped from the roof and ran down a gutter on the side of the alley. The rusted gate stood partially open. I eased through it.

A guard shack stood next to the entrance to the truck yard. A pole barrier blocked the entry effectively for any vehicles, but I was on foot. I stepped around it.

Someone was in the shack. I went up to talk to him, but he was asleep, his gray bandana slipping over one of his eyes. His head leaned back against the wall. Empty beer cans were scattered on the floor. A few unopened ones sat on the desk. Yet another, this one open and tipped on its side, lay next to the man's hand.

The door hung half-closed. I stuck my head in. The small space smelled of stale beer and urine. The guy's dark blue jeans had a darker stain in the front. I wrinkled my nose.

I really didn't want to touch him, so I said, "Hey, dude."

He didn't stir.

I stepped inside. The rank odor was worse. I put a light finger on his cheek. He was warm, so he was probably still alive. "Hey, dude," I said again.

He lifted his hand to swat mine away from him. "Go 'way."

So he definitely was still alive.

I backed out of the shack and headed up to the main warehouse.

It couldn't have been used for its intended purpose for a good long time. The concrete truck yard was cracked and uneven, and some of the weeds growing through the cracks were the size of small trees. The edges of the loading bays were crumbling. Trash, now very wet trash, lay everywhere. A set of stairs with a crooked railing ran up to an empty doorframe on one end of the dock. I went up the stairs and into the warehouse.

If it had ever had lights, they weren't on now. It was a good bet that the electric bill hadn't been paid for months, if not years, and somebody had probably jerry-rigged a connection from a neighbor's hookup to supply minimal electricity.

Right now, though, nobody around here had access to electricity to steal. And this desolate neighborhood would likely be one of the last to see it restored.

I stood for a few minutes, waiting for my eyes to adjust to the dimness. It didn't smell quite as bad as the guard shack had, but the odor of stale beer and marijuana mingled with a whiff of an organic decaying odor. I wondered if something had died in there and was rotting in a corner.

A few men were stretched out on packing crates and decrepit tables, sleeping. It was cold and dank in there, and I shivered. A fire in a thirty-gallon drum smoldered in the center of the room. It had provided a bit of heat, but now, no one was awake to feed it. They were all passed out drunk or high and beyond caring much about the temperature. Looked like they'd had a party the last night, flood or no flood.

Water dripped down a wall and ran across the stained floor and out under the overhead doors of the truck bay.

In stark contrast to the squalor all around, a gaggle of well-kept choppers rested on their kickstands against the back wall. They were all bright colors and polished chrome, their extended handlebars and custom-painted gas tanks catching what light was available in a burst of jeweled reflections.

I went across the open space to an office in the back. For the first time, I heard voices.

There was no door. I knocked on the doorframe.

A beefy biker looked up sharply, his eyes hidden behind dark shades. I wondered how he could see anything at all.

"Who the hell are you?" he growled, yanking a smoldering blunt from his mouth. "And how the hell did you get in here?"

Banjo unwound himself from an old office chair and stood up. "Jesse Damon," he told the others. "Tigerman, I know him. From the big house. Old Buckles knows him, too."

Tigerman leaned back in his decrepit office chair. "Yeah?"

"Yeah. Met him when I did my first bit at the big house. Got to know him pretty well."

"Yer cell buddy or something?"

"Eventually. But he saved my bacon when I was a stupid hopper, right off the bus from diagnostics."

Tigerman snorted. "How the hell did he do that?"

"I got myself into a tight spot in the yard first day. Somebody asked me what set I was with, since I was a loner back then, before I hooked up with any of you guys. Like to beat the crap out of me there and then."

A cloud of pungent smoke drifted out of Tigerman's mouth and nostrils. He eyed the blunt again and said, "And?"

"I was just a dumb kid. Jesse, here, he stepped up and said, 'He's with my set. You wanna make something of it?' The other guys just eyed me and drifted off."

"What set are you with?" The first guy waved his blunt toward me. "Deadmen Inc.?"

I shook my head. "I keep to myself. No gangs."

"Then why the hell did they back off?"

Banjo shrugged. "I was never quite sure. It was either everybody knew he was totally crazy, or he had the street cred, I guess."

I had to laugh. "Must have been crazy. It sure weren't no street cred. I'd been off the street for years by then."

Tigerman grinned. "Had a rep inside, though, huh? Old head?"

"I sure was an old head by that time."

Banjo grinned. "We got assigned to the same cell a little while later. I paid off the tier clerk, so he arranged it. Jesse didn't care much one way or the other. But all the time we spent in the same cell, I never did ask you, Jesse? Why'd you stick your neck out and step in like that? You didn't owe me, and you didn't know me."

It was my turn to shrug. "You was a scared new kid. I remember what it was like. Guys sizing you up when you walk by, making clucking noises. Fresh chicken. Didn't want to see them think you had to stand all by your lonesome. No point letting them take advantage of you if I could head it off."

"Before I got locked up, I thought I was tough stuff."

"Yeah." A strand of wiry hair had escaped from my ponytail. I brushed it off my face. "We all think that. But we learn. And some of us remember."

Tigerman lumbered to his feet and held out his hand.

His grimy paw completely engulfed my hand.

One of the other guys stood unsteadily and put out his hand. "Animal here," he said.

Tigerman offered me the blunt.

I said, "No, thanks. You know how long that stuff stays in your system?"

"So? The longer the better."

"I got to see my PO this week. He can piss me if he wants. I can't afford to test positive."

"What, you afraid of getting locked up again?"

"You'd best believe that."

"It ain't so bad. I been locked up lots of times."

"And I only been locked up once. For twenty years. I'm looking at almost another twenty backup time."

He raised his eyebrows. "Must have been a serious charge."

He was fishing. I wasn't about to satisfy his curiosity. I narrowed my eyes and stared into his dark glasses. I said, "It was. I try to keep my nose clean. At least until I'm off supervision."

He scratched himself. "Then what the hell are you doing here? Most of us are convicted felons. You still under supervision, you could get violated for being here."

He wasn't telling me anything I didn't know. "You know a dude named Aaron? Aaron Stenski?"

"And if I did?"

I took a deep breath. "I'm trying to figure out what he's been up to."

"What d'ya mean?"

Might as well level with them all, at least to a certain extent. "I know he was boosting cars and running errands for the chop shop some of you guys was running."

"Whoa." Tigerman backed up a step. "I sure wasn't part of nothing like that."

Banjo reached for the blunt. "Old Buckles told me all about Aaron. They started calling him Gopher. Buckles says he's a snitch." He inhaled deeply.

Tigerman laughed. "Gopher. I like that. 'Cause he was always running errands?"

The pungent smoke streamed from Banjo's nostrils. Then he said, "Yeah. Buckles said he'd 'go fer' anything you sent him to do."

Laughing again, Tigerman took the blunt back for another drag, then offered it to me again. I shook my head, and he handed it to Banjo.

Banjo rolled it between his fingers. "Buckles says he thinks maybe Aaron set him up, with this newspaper lady. It was pictures she took of him out partying that got his paroled revoked. I'm supposed to look into it and maybe settle the score."

I looked at Tigerman. "So you guys don't know much about what he's been up to?"

"Didn't say that. Some of the guys we used were careless, but that guy Aaron is pretty useful. And Buckles is right. He is a snitch."

"You sure?" I noticed they were using the present tense. Either they didn't know Aaron was dead, or they were pretty good at this.

"Yeah. He's pretty dumb." Tigerman took the blunt. "He'll believe anything he hears if he thinks you aren't talking to him. So he's a great way to send stuff to the cops that you want them to hear, but can't tell them outright."

"You mean like stuff that's going on that you want stopped?" I shook my head when he offered it to me again.

"Some of that," he said, looking critically at the burning end. "But mostly just, what do they call 'em, red berries? Like when you send 'em off in the wrong direction?"

"Red herrings?" I asked.

"Maybe. Like, you want a clear road for a midnight run, so you talk about planning a big heist at a truck stop in the opposite direction. So this guy Aaron, he sneaks back and snitches, only the info he's got is wrong. Then they're keeping an eye on the truck stop, not where you want to go."

"Good technique if you can make it work," Banjo said. "But how many times can you pull that?"

Tigerman grinned, showing broken and blackened teeth. "Quite a bit, when you come right down to it. Next time the snitch is around, you talk about how you had to call off the gig cause there were so many cops out on the road in the area. That gets them thinking that maybe they weren't careful enough, or at least they headed it off, so they're waiting for the next time Aaron brings them a plan."

"What kind of heists do you make Aaron think you're trying to pull?" I asked.

"Mostly hijackings. You know, semis with loads of computers or TVs. Then you not only got the truck to sell, you got the cargo, too. Used to be big business." He shook his head. "But we stopped doing much of that a while ago."

"Why?"

"Too dangerous. They've infiltrated the buyers. Sting operations and such."

"How about the chop shop?" I asked.

"That was just dumb." Tigerman leaned back. "A couple of the younger guys, they set that up. I mean, we was doing okay taking cars and driving them straight down to the port. They'd be loaded quick on a ship and be off to Africa or South America, a lot of the time before the owner even reported them missing. Especially if you took them from long-term parking at the airport."

"Old Buckles said Aaron was looking at luxury cars around here," Banjo said.

"Yeah." Tigerman tried to take another toke, but the blunt had gone out. He peered at the end. "And that was stupid. You never piss in your own backyard. Even if it's easier."

"Then why were they doing that?" I asked.

"Just not patient enough." Tigerman patted his pockets, looking for a match. "When you're boosting cars for export, you can't do a damn thing until the right ship is port, with the right set of dispatchers and night watchmen who'll look the other way. You got to get the merchandise and get rid of it quick. And the ship should be just about ready to sail. So you can go a few weeks sometimes between jobs."

Banjo pulled out a lighter and handed it to Tigerman. He asked, "So they decided to do something to fill in?"

"Yeah. Some of us tried to tell 'em they was playing with fire, but Razorback—he used to run the excavation business with his old lady. But I think she ran it more than he did—he told them they could use the garage if he got a cut."

I nodded.

"You hear about Razorback?" Tigerman asked.

"He's history," I said.

"Yeah. He's dead. His old lady Black Rose is gonna go down for it." Tigerman leaned back and looked at me. "What did you say your name was?"

"Jesse Damon."

"The same Jesse who Black Rose tried to frame for Razorback?"

"The same."

Tigerman reached down and picked up a jug from behind the desk. "Here. Have a drink. No piss test is likely to pick this up."

"True, that." I didn't really want a slug of whatever they had in the jug—probably dago red wine, maybe mountain dew from a backwoods still—but if I wanted any more information from them, I'd have to play along. Alcohol didn't stay in the system the way drugs did. It would work itself through in less than a day. I hefted the jug up to my shoulder, balanced it on its side, and put my mouth on the opening. When I raised my elbow, it tipped up and flowed right down my throat.

Mountain dew, hell. White lightening was more like it. Or rotgut. I took a few gulps, trying to keep from coughing it up. My nostrils tingled, and my eyes watered.

Banjo grinned and reached for the jug. "Good stuff, huh?"

I passed him the jug and wiped my mouth. "I haven't had anything like that in a long time." Ever, if I was honest, but I wasn't going to tell them that.

Another biker lurched into the office from the warehouse. He stood unsteadily, his eyes not focused, and reached for the jug. I handed it over.

He was Funky Joe, the guy I'd had a few problems with. But if he wasn't challenging me, I was more than willing to let bygones be bygones.

Balancing the jug precariously on his shoulder, he took a huge swig and passed it to the next guy. When it came back to me, I tried to just take a small sip, but when I hefted it on my shoulder again and tilted it up, I got a lot more than I'd bargained for. I gulped it down, trying not to choke.

Funky Joe peered at me. "Where do I know you from?"

I held out the jug, but he didn't take it. I put it on the battered desk.

"Ain't you the guy Old Buckles had me bring here once?" He raised his fist and took a step toward me. "And then you beat the crap out of me? What the hell are you doing here?"

Tigerman stroked his unkempt beard and looked at me thoughtfully. He reached out a boot and prodded two other guys who had slept through the conversation to this point. They got to their feet. Someone's hand went into a pocket and came out with something that looked like a closed switchblade.

I straightened up and looked Funky Joe in the eye. I clenched my fist, but I didn't raise my hand.

"Hey, maybe we better be going," Banjo said to me.

Sounded like a good idea, but I had to figure out a way to do it that wouldn't put either one of us in danger.

"Wait a minute," Tigerman said. "Ain't you the guy was doing Old Buckles's little girl?" That would be Kelly, who didn't fit too many people's definition of "little girl."

Banjo took a nervous step toward the door. "Didn't you say you had to get back?" he said to me. "Come on, I'll walk you to the street. You in touch with any of the guys from the old cell block?"

I ignored Banjo. To Tigerman, I said, "Sometimes I hang with her, if that's what you're saying."

He sneered. "So Buckles, he told everybody to kind of leave you alone, did he?"

"If he did, that's on him. I never asked for no protection."

Funky Joe moved forward, his fist still raised. "Well, Buckles ain't here right now. You and me got a score to settle." He swung his fist at my head.

Not a smart move for a person who's as wasted as he was. I stepped back. Funky Joe missed and stumbled, falling to his knees.

One of the men snickered.

Scrambling to his feet, he ran at me, his fists flailing. I would have expected him to fight smarter than that.

This time, I feinted a step to the left, then quickly moved to the right.

He staggered past me and lost his footing, falling again.

The snickers grew louder.

He muttered something that sounded like, "You bastard," and got to his feet. Glowering, he lowered his head and charged at me.

I stepped aside, and he ran headlong into the wall.

The snickers became guffaws.

Funky Joe lay on the floor, dazed. Or worse.

Tigerman stepped up to him and nudged him with one heavy boot. Funky Joe jerked his arm and moaned.

"Well, he ain't dead," someone said.

All eyes turned toward me.

"What ya gonna do?" Tigerman asked.

I looked at the men standing around, then down at Funky Joe. "Leave," I said. "Can't kick a man when he's down."

Tigerman nodded. "Good plan."

Banjo took my elbow and steered me out. "Come on."

When we got through the warehouse and out on the truck yard, he said, "I don't think Funky Joe likes you much."

"You got that right."

"Maybe you best not come around again," Banjo said. "What do you want to know about this dude Aaron for, anyhow?"

I thought about how much I should tell him. Not much, for his own sake. Thinking before he blurted something out was not Banjo's strong point. What he didn't know even the best interrogator in the world couldn't manage to pull out of him. Otherwise, all bets were off on what he'd say to whom.

"I got my reasons," I said. "And I'd say you ought to lay off looking too hard for him, too, at least for a bit."

He looked thoughtful. "You mean not ask any questions, either?"

"The questions part is probably okay. That'd be up to you. How much you find out so far?"

"Not a whole hell of a lot. You know his mama inherited money or something from his daddy? And they hadn't even been an item for a long time. She'd even gotten married and had a kid by somebody else."

I nodded. That kid would be Benji.

"I was figuring maybe Aaron got some money, too, and disappeared with it. From what I hear, though, the disappearing'll only last as long as the money lasts. Which will be until he stuffs it all up his nose. Or mainlines it into his arm."

I nodded again.

"He's got two older half brothers, y'know. His daddy's kids. Different mama. They might want some of that money, too."

I tugged the jacket collar closer around my neck. "Yeah? They think they're not gonna get their fair share?"

"Aaron's mama already got her fair share and then some. I'd be pretty pissed, myself, if my daddy's ex got a hunk of his hard-earned money and I didn't get none."

"Have you talked to the two older brothers?"

"Not yet. One is this guy, Jumbo George. He's supposed to be real fat. Obese, like, as in can't get around too good. He's got a head shop over on Middle Street. And Nick, who I guess is normal-sized, drives a truck."

"Local or long distance?"

"Long distance. He's an owner-operator. One of those Peterbilt Cabovers with a sleeper."

That was an expensive truck. He'd have to be doing pretty well for himself if he was the owner.

We reached the guardhouse, where the occupant now lay on the floor, snoring loudly.

Banjo looked at him. "That's how you got in without anybody knowing. Great lookout."

I chuckled. Was I being fair to Banjo, not telling him Aaron was dead? I didn't want him to get in any trouble if it came out he was poking around, and even if he thought he was being careful, he'd probably say things that could be interpreted as threats. "Hey, dude. I mean it when I say don't go looking too hard for Aaron."

He raised his eyebrows. "I take it you got a reason for telling me that?"

"Yeah."

"But you're not gonna tell me what it is?"

"'Fraid that's right. At least for now."

"But you still want me to tell you anything I find out about him?"

I shrugged. Put that way, it seemed pretty unfair. "Yeah."

"Look. I'll see what I can find out without being too obvious."

"Okay. Meet you back here tomorrow?"

Banjo shook his head. "I think you'd be better off not coming by here again so soon. How about we meet in a bar or something?"

"No bars open until the electric power's back on."

"They'll restore it to commercial places quicker'n to residential areas. And downtown quicker'n other places. You know Mickey's Bar, down by the courthouse?"

"Yeah." By the conditions of my parole, I wasn't allowed to drink. And I wasn't supposed to be in bars. But what were the chances I'd get caught, especially with all the cops working round the clock on disaster relief?

"About eight or nine tomorrow. If it's open." Banjo said.

"Okay."

"Or no later than eleven," he said.

That wasn't a particularly helpful time frame, but I knew Banjo well enough to know there was no point in trying to pin him down further.

"Otherwise, I'll meet you in the alley that runs next to it."

I could see myself waiting in the alley for a few hours tomorrow night and Banjo never showing. But I knew I'd take the chance. "You got it," I said.

"I'll tell you what I can find out. If I do, though, you got to give me something back, too."

"Don't know what I can tell you." Since I knew Aaron was dead and Banjo didn't, that wasn't entirely true. I said, "Maybe I'll see you tomorrow night." But I didn't make any promises.

* * * *

I didn't have much experience with alcohol at all. As I left the warehouse and the sidewalk rippled in waves in front of me, I realized this must be what drunk felt like.

The weak winter sun peeked through the clouds, shimmering oil slicks on the pools of water lying everywhere. I concentrated on putting one foot in front of the other. Maybe I'd better go back to Kelly's and get a nap before I checked out my apartment.

Jeez. My head was spinning. What did people see in getting drunk like this? If this was how people felt when they were partying, I sure didn't want to have anything to do with it. Right now, I would be happy if I could keep on my feet.

A few blocks farther on, and my head was spinning. I leaned against a lamp post, trying to get my bearings. An odd glow surrounded me on the sidewalk. Trying to puzzle that out, I looked up at the light. The light was lit.

The electric power must have come back on, at least in this section of town.

Moving my head like that was not a good move. I grabbed onto the pole to keep from falling.

My head spun worse. I was puking into the street before I realized I was going to be sick.

A car came by, giving me wide berth. I leaned over, my sides heaving. At least I was getting rid of whatever alcohol was still in my stomach.

A sour taste filled my mouth. I wiped my lips with the side of my hand, bringing away a rope of slimy saliva and puke.

Hunching inside my jacket, I stepped back up on the sidewalk and made my way to Kelly's house.

The steps up to the porch seemed steeper than the last time I was here. And they'd somehow gotten uneven. By gripping the handrail, I managed to climb up the steps.

The curtains were drawn, but I could see light around them. So Kelly's power was on, too. We could cook and do some laundry.

But first, I needed to get some sleep.

It took me a few tries, but I stabbed the doorbell.

The door opened, surprising me. I don't know what I expected, but I took a step back to keep from tumbling over. Chris stood there looking at me.

"Mom!" he shouted. "It's Jesse. He's drunk."

CHAPTER 14

Chris opened the door for me. I stumbled toward the sofa and collapsed, closing my eyes.

When I looked up, Kelly was standing over me, her arms folded. Chris was staring at me, and Brianna was hiding behind her mother's legs.

"Kelly." I was having trouble forming words. "I..."

She shook her head. "Just lie down and get some sleep," she said, pushing my shoulder back and reaching for a blanket.

How was I going to get my boots off? Was it worth the effort?

I felt someone—Kelly—lift my feet up onto the sofa and begin unlacing the boots.

Everything was spinning, and I couldn't keep my eyes open.

When I woke up, the room was dark. My head ached, but dully, not like the brain-splitting headaches I'd heard some people describe as hangovers. I licked my dry lips. My tongue was dry, too.

Quiet voices and the scent of frying bacon came from the kitchen. I wasn't hungry, but the smells didn't make me want to throw up.

The room was pleasantly warm. I sat up and took off my jacket, tossing it onto an overstuffed chair. I was a little dizzy when I leaned down to put on my boots.

I stood in the doorway to the kitchen, leaning against the doorframe and taking in the homey scene. A pot of soup simmered on the stovetop. BLTs seemed to be on the menu. Kelly sliced tomatoes. Chris manned the toaster. Brianna, kneeling on a chair, carefully spread mayonnaise on slices of toast and lay strips of bacon on them. I could have stood there forever, just watching them.

Chris looked up. "Jesse!" he said. "You want a sandwich?"

Kelly turned and glared at me, her eyes smoldering.

My voice was dry and cracked. "No, thanks. I'm not that hungry."

"You're hungover," Kelly said in a steely voice. "You can fix yourself a cup of coffee."

That sounded really good. "Thanks," I croaked, and then moved to take a mug and the jar of instant coffee from the shelf.

"You were drunk." Kelly turned back to the cutting board. Her knife chopped down on the tomato, cutting uneven, ragged slices.

"True, that." I filled the mug with water and put it in the microwave.

"After you got me feeling bad about my drinking."

I sighed. "You're right."

"And made me get rid of my booze."

"Yeah." Not a good time to point out that I'd found the bottle in the linen closet.

"So what's with that?"

"I know what it looks like—"

"Looks like hell. I know what it is."

Did I have any possible answer to that?

Chris took two finished slices of toast, handed them to Brianna, and put two more in. He looked at me, a worried frown on his face. "There's some vegetable soup, too, Jesse. From the stuff you got us. Maybe you want some of that?" There was a hitch in his voice.

"Thanks, no." The water wasn't finished heating up, but I grabbed it out of the microwave and dumped a spoonful of instant coffee in it anyhow. The water was lukewarm, and the coffee crystals clumped.

Kelly's voice rose. "So you got nothing to say for yourself?"

I took a gulp of the coffee. It was terrible and lumpy. But I knew it contained caffeine, and I was pretty sure I'd feel better if I managed to choke it down. "You want me to explain—"

"No need to explain. First you get all holier-than-thou about my drinking and what it's doing to the kids. Then you go out and get drunk. And come back here. Let the kids see you drunk. A bit hypocritical, don't you think?"

"Yeah. I wasn't thinking straight."

"Of course you weren't thinking straight. You were drunk."

I couldn't deny that. "I guess I shouldn't have come back here like that. I'm sorry."

"You're sorry?" Kelly's face was turning red. "You shouldn't have come back here like that. You shouldn't have gotten drunk in the first place."

If I looked hard enough, I thought maybe I would see steam coming out of Kelly's ears. The kids hadn't moved, but they appeared somehow smaller, like they'd shrunk. I chugged the rest of the contents of the mug and managed to keep from coughing it back up.

"Hey," I said. "You're getting upset. I'm gonna get upset. Let's discuss this when we're calmer."

She took a step toward me, the knife in her hand. "Calmer? Calmer? You want me to be calmer?"

I didn't know if she and her ex had ever gotten into it physically, but I wasn't going to take a chance. Especially not in front of the kids.

"I'm going to leave now. Before we say something we regret and can't take back. Or do something we're gonna regret." I didn't look at the knife in her hand.

"Yeah?" She sneered. "What are you gonna do? Murder me?"

Wordlessly, I turned and went through the living room and toward the front door, snatching my jacket from the chair where I'd dumped it.

A glint of glass poking out from behind the cushion of the chair caught my eye. I paused to take a closer look. A partly empty bottle of Southern Comfort, on its side.

Now was not the time or place to say anything about that bottle, either.

I went out the front door, closing it as gently as I could.

* * * *

Jumbo George's head shop was near the bottom of a hill. That part of town that was in flux from solid working class. It was hard to tell whether it was being gentrified by the young professionals who had come to work in the shiny high-tech buildings that were springing up on the edge of town, or sinking into abandonment and poverty, like the section of town where my apartment was.

The perfect neighborhood for a head shop, which was located in a row of older, but picturesque two-story brick buildings.

The streets and sidewalks were damp, but a few areas had standing water. Soggy debris lay everywhere. Where people had started to clean up, upholstered furniture and misshapen boxes sat along the curb. The sound of whirring emergency generators hummed from a few buildings, and a few lights showed in the daytime dimness, but most of the interiors were dark.

If Jumbo George lived over his storefront, would he be there, trying to get his business going again? I thought it was a good bet—certainly what I would be working on if I had a business. A small stack of boxes and garbage bags were piled in front of the building by the street.

As I approached it, the front door opened, and an enormous man backed out, dragging a garbage bag. I caught a damp whiff of patchouli from inside.

The man was not only tall, he was also immensely obese. He wore a tie-dye shirt that was so big, I wondered if its origins had been as a tablecloth. And the seat of his blue jeans were so expansive that the back pockets were actually on the sides.

That had to be Jumbo George.

Halfway across the sidewalk, he paused, panting, his breath coming in big gasps.

I walked up to him. "This going on that pile?" I asked, grabbing the bag and nodding toward the trash by the curb.

He raised his flushed bearded face and nodded. His hair was pulled back in a ponytail that hung halfway down his back. His clothes had a heavy scent of patchouli, too, but I also picked up an underlying unwashed body odor.

Well, I hadn't had a shower in a few days, either.

I swung the bag to the top of the pile.

The man straightened up and wiped his face. "Thanks, bro," he said.

I held out my hand. "Jesse Damon."

He took my hand in his. It was pudgy and damp and totally swallowed my hand. "George Stenski," he said. "Most folks call me Jumbo George."

I nodded. "I worked with your brother Aaron."

He scowled. "Half-brother," he said. "Different mothers. He was a cute little monster, when he was a kid."

I raised my eyebrows. "Have you heard anything about him lately?"

"I heard he was dead," Jumbo George said, raising the hem of his tablecloth shirt and wiping his face with it. "But I don't know if it's true or not. Can't say as it'd be much of a loss if he was. Except maybe to his mama."

He pressed his hand to his chest, still breathing heavily. "I got to go and sit down," he said, taking an unsteady step toward the door.

I grabbed his elbow—it felt like I imagined the Pillsbury Doughboy would feel—and reached to hold the door open.

Bracing against me and the doorframe, Jumbo George struggled inside. Once we got through the door, the scent of the patchouli mixed with a damp mildew smell was so strong as to be nauseating.

The interior was dim, and it took my eyes a few seconds to adjust. He continued to work his way deeper into the shop, shifting to support his weight on the counter that ran the length of the store.

A massive recliner sat in a back corner. Jumbo George struggled toward it. When he reached the end of the counter, he paused. He'd have to let go to make it the few steps to the recliner.

I took his arm again. I could feel the flesh quivering under my hand. Leaning heavily on me, he turned and backed his broad rear end toward the chair. When he was poised above it, he bent his knees and collapsed into it.

His breath continued to come in gasps.

"Hey, man," I said. "You don't sound real good. You want I should call an ambulance or something?"

He coughed, his chest heaving, and held up his hand. "No!"

I was afraid he was going to die of a heart attack or something right here in front of me. Something else I'd probably get blamed for. I wondered if 9-1-1 was working now. And if he had a working phone.

He shifted his weight in the chair and closed his eyes.

My throat tightened. "Jumbo George?"

"I'm all right," he said, his breath coming now in gasping wheezes. "Asthma. Looks a lot worse than it is. I just have to catch my breath."

"Do you have an inhaler anywhere around here?"

He coughed again. "I dropped it when there was half a foot of water in here. I don't even know where it is now. And it's probably ruined. Damn thing's expensive."

I looked around. Sure enough, a damp line showed about six inches above the floor on the walls and the counter. I had no doubt the recliner was damp for at least the bottom six inches. Maybe more, if the water had wicked its way up.

"All this dampness can't be good for your asthma. And there's probably all kinds of horrible molds and mildew starting to grow."

He took another shuddering breath. "You're probably right. But I don't know what the hell I can do about that right now."

"Maybe you could go stay upstairs or something until it dries out a little more."

"Fat chance." He laughed, but it turned into a deep cough. Rolls of flesh on his chest, neck, and arms trembled and heaved. "I haven't been able to make it up the stairs in a few years. And if I did get up there, I might never get down again."

"So where do you stay at?" I asked.

"Right here. The back room's got a bathroom with a shower. And I got a little refrigerator and a microwave. All the modern conveniences."

"Can I get you anything?"

"Nah. I don't want to open the fridge—maybe the food'll still be good when the power goes on. And I'm not sure I'd trust the water supply. Sewage might have backed up into it."

That unpleasant thought had occurred to me, too. But the people who ran the shelter at the high school seemed confident that the water was okay. Or maybe the National Guard had set up a water purifying system.

"Look," I said. "I can't just leave you like this. What can I do to help?"

He opened his eyes and studied me. "You really mean that?"

I considered. "Well, yeah. I mean, I don't got much else to do."

"You could get some of the crap on the floor moved out to the trash pile. I could pay you. A little."

"Well, okay. But how's that gonna help you?"

"Any cleanup you get done is something I don't got to do. I'm not so sure I can get much done anyhow. I sure can't open up shop until this mess is cleared out. And if I don't open shop, I got no income."

I looked around again. I must have been getting used to the patchouli scent. It was still there, but it wasn't choking me anymore.

It was obvious that Jumbo George needed the help. On the plus side, if I helped him, it would give me a chance to talk to him about Aaron. Maybe find out about his father's tangled finances, what the possibility was of him having anything to do with Aaron's death.

Although it was equally obvious that, unless he was a terrific actor and had some help with the physical part of dumping the body, Jumbo George could not have been directly responsible for Aaron's body ending up in my stairwell.

On the minus side, if Mr. Ramirez, my parole officer, ever found out I was working in a head shop, I'd have lots of explaining to do. As well as potential paraphernalia charges. There was also a good chance Jumbo George was himself a convicted felon and someone I wasn't supposed to associate with. But if I didn't ask, I could honestly plead ignorance of that.

Of course, after being at the Predator's lair and arranging to meet Banjo tomorrow, I didn't know why I was even worrying about this.

Jumbo George's chest had stopped heaving quite so badly.

"How'd you hear Aaron might be dead?" I asked.

"This skinny newspaper bitch, she came by. Stuck her camera in my face and took a bunch of pictures. Said she wanted to ask some questions. I thought it was gonna be about getting the business going again after the flood, and any publicity is good publicity. So I said okay."

It was a long speech for him, and he had to stop to catch his breath. "But then she said some shit like 'Do you know your brother's dead? He might have drowned,' and started snapping more pictures. I guess she wanted me to cry or something."

Sounded like Carissa. That was something she'd do without it even occurring to her that maybe it was more than a trifle insensitive.

"I thought she meant my other brother, Nick. He's a trucker. He had a pickup scheduled. When he heard the new bridge was closed, he said he was gonna try to find another way over the river. I thought maybe he was on a bridge that wasn't rated for his rig, and it collapsed or something."

"So how'd you find out it was Aaron, not Nick?"

"She said he'd been found in a flooded stairwell across town. That didn't sound like anywhere Nick would be. I said that, and she said no, it was my brother Aaron."

"What did you say then?"

"Not a word. I grabbed the damn camera and threw it in the water. What right does she have, coming around, telling me crap like that, whether it's true or not, just so she can get a picture for her paper? Damn bitch."

"How'd she react?"

"Started fussing about her camera getting all wet. Said it might not work right."

I was fascinated. I'd been tempted myself to do something to that camera, but I'd never quite dared. "Did the water ruin it?" I asked.

He snorted. "That I don't know. But it didn't work real good after I stomped it."

Despite the seriousness of the situation, I laughed. "Too bad you couldn't get a picture of her face when you did that."

He grinned. "Yeah. That'd be a picture worth having."

I looked around. "What needs to be done first?"

"I was trying to get the wet stuff on the floor sorted out and the stuff that's no good in garbage bags and out to the curb. Sooner or later, they're gonna come around with trucks and take it all. For free. But if you don't got it out in time, you're gonna have to pay a trash hauler later on."

The "wet stuff" was mostly mud, papers, and cardboard boxes.

"Suppose you get the stuff out of the boxes you want to keep, and I start shoveling the mud into garbage bags."

He looked at me. "So you are gonna help?"

"Yeah. I got a little time."

"I can't pay you much."

"Tell you what," I said. "You got rooms upstairs?"

"Yeah. It's, like, a little apartment. Nick stays there when he's in town."

"Well, my apartment's in a basement. It's flooded out." I didn't tell him it was where Aaron's body was found. "You let me stay here a few days, until I get some stuff straightened out about where I'm gonna stay, I'll help you clean up."

Jumbo George looked at me and scratched under his beard. "Deal." He held out his hand.

I shook it. "Deal."

I lifted boxes that threatened to fall apart onto the counter. Jumbo George sat on a stool and unpacked them. His huge butt covered the entire top of the stool and overlapped it all around.

Most of the boxes had hard goods like hookahs and key chains with little coke spoons on them. That kind of stuff could be washed off and sold. A few had items like rolling papers and postcards that would never dry off and be salable. I showed them to Jumbo George, and he agreed that I should just toss them into the garbage bag.

We worked most of the afternoon. Finally, Jumbo George sat back and looked out the display window into the gathering gloom. "Ya hungry?" he asked.

"Yeah."

He fished in his pocket for his wallet and took out two twenties. "Wanna go see if they got Mickey D's up and running?" he asked. "You know they're gonna have their electric on soon's anybody. Wouldn't be surprised if corporate didn't send them a big generator."

"True, that," I agreed, taking the twenties. "I can go see. What'd ya want?"

"I got a case of root beer in the back, so nothing to drink," he said. "And by the time you get back here, the fries'd be greasy. I like those quarter pounder things, but the stuff off the dollar menu is a better deal. So get some of those dollar burgers."

"How many do you want?"

He cocked his head and looked at me like I didn't have good sense. "Forty, of course," he said. "Or thirty-eight, or however many you can get with the sales tax."

I hiked the couple of blocks over to McDonalds. Sure enough, it had power. So did the buildings lining the street toward the courthouse for as far as I could see. I got two big bags of burgers and headed back to Jumbo George's.

He was dozing in his recliner. As far as I could determine, that had to be where he slept. If he didn't go upstairs, I saw nowhere else.

He opened his eyes. "You're back," he said.

"Of course I'm back. Where'd you expect me to go?"

He shrugged his mighty shoulders. "I dunno. Just take the forty bucks and take off, I guess."

"I wouldn't do that. Then you wouldn't have anything decent to eat." I wasn't sure forty dollars of fast food burgers was *decent*, but that's what he wanted.

"Yeah. Well." He heaved himself to his feet and lumbered to the back room.

"Can you get that fridge pack of root beer back there and put it on the table?" he asked me.

I set the bags of burgers down and lifted the cardboard case onto the table. It was covered with mud. The wet packaging fell away.

"Guess maybe we ought to wash these off before we drink them," Jumbo George said, eyeing a can streaked with the mud. He carried an armful to the sink.

I put the cardboard in a new garbage bag and put the rest of the cans in the sink. Then I helped him carry the rinsed-off cans back to the table.

He pulled out a very sturdy chair and dropped his bulk into it with a sigh. I sat down in an equally sturdy chair on the other side of the table. Jumbo George dumped the burgers out on the table and raked a pile of them over to him. Then he opened three cans of root beer and lined them up next to the burgers.

Glancing up at me, he said, "Ain't you gonna eat?"

I opened a can of root beer and unwrapped a sandwich. For a buck, it wasn't bad at all.

When I finished that one, I took another.

Jumbo George unwrapped two sandwiches and stuffed them into his mouth, washing them down with half a can of the root beer.

"What can you tell me about Aaron?" I asked him.

"What's to tell?" Jumbo George stuffed another burger in his mouth and talked around it. "When my mom died, my dad started running around like a teenager. Then he showed up with a floozy and told us she was our new mama. Didn't go over well. She was pretty, yeah, but she was only looking at his money."

"Did your dad have a lot of money?"

"Oh, yeah. He started a printing business. It was doing okay, but then he figured out, you donate campaign crap to the politicians, they pay you back when the government's bidding printing jobs."

"If it's bid, doesn't everybody have an equal chance?"

"That's what he thought at first. But then he realized the people who were the insiders got tips ahead of time, so they could bid smarter. Once he did that, his government work took off."

"Which party did he donate to?"

Jumbo George took another burger. "Both of them. And any other little splinter group that showed up at election time."

I blinked. "That meant no matter who got in, they kind of owed him?"

"That's the idea. So he had a good business."

"What's that got to do with Aaron?"

"I'm getting to that. Gina, Aaron's mom, got pregnant. Nick and I think it was before they got married, but maybe not. Aaron was a skinny little baby. Maybe he was just early. Don't matter much, though."

"Did you and Nick live with them?"

"Yeah. We was teenagers. As soon as we finished high school, we was out of there."

"College?"

He threw back his enormous head and laughed. "Not college. Why'd you think that?"

"If your dad had enough money, I'd think he'd pay for college for you."

"I suppose he might have. If he thought we was smart enough. He always said we was dumber than dirt."

"So you just left?"

"Well, he did offer to help us start out. He paid for Nick to get his CDL. Then after he drove for a while and said he wanted to buy a truck, Dad bought him a brand spanking new Peterbilt Cabover with a thirty-six-inch sleeper. Bright red. He's been contracting out as an owner-operator ever since."

"And you?"

"I wasn't as big as I am now, but I was pretty hefty. Dad said I disgusted him. But when I said I wanted to be a shopkeeper, he bought me this building and gave me enough to get inventory." Jumbo George chuckled. "He didn't know it was going to be the best-stocked head shop for four states around that he was financing."

"Was he upset when he found out?"

He shrugged. "Not really. I mean, Nick and I'd both been in trouble, and he knew we smoked weed. I think he just wouldn't have been quite as generous if he'd know what I was buying with his money."

"And the cops leave you alone with the head shop?"

"Pretty much. I'm careful. I sell lots of neutral goods, like the plastic skulls and incense and shit. All kinds of trail mix. Some tobacco so I can justify the rolling papers and hookahs. Don't sell much of that, though. And I keep an eye on what's getting media attention. When something hits big, like bath salts or K-2 spice, I stop carrying it. Let the damn independent convenience stores take the heat."

"Was he doing anything for Aaron?"

"Aside from paying for rehab a few times, I'm not sure. He thought he was disappointed in Nick and me, he just had to wait for Aaron. I mean, Aaron was in trouble from the get-go. First picked up for distributing CDS when he was fourteen. In school, no less."

"Was he living with your dad by that time?"

"Hell, no. Gina started running around on Dad right after Aaron was born. He didn't want to believe it, but he caught her red-handed, so to speak, in bed with the guy who cut the grass. So he got a divorce. And they both got married again. Dad was smart enough, though, not to have any more children."

"But he still felt responsible for Aaron?"

"Yeah. He wrote up his will and got insurance and all so there'd be enough money for Aaron until he got to be eighteen. And then some to set him up, like Nick with the truck cab and me with the shop."

"What happened when Aaron turned eighteen?"

Jumbo George drained another can of root beer and shrugged. "By then, Dad was pretty much losing it. He sold the business when he started to go downhill. Suzanne, his new wife, took pretty good care of him. But he was bonkers. And he'd get all paranoid whenever anybody tried to talk money with him. He was sure we were all trying to steal it. So I have no idea if he changed his will or anything."

I finished a third hamburger. They were small, but three was all I wanted.

He eyed me. "That all you gonna eat?"

"Yeah. I had enough, thanks."

"Suit yourself." He finished the rest of the burgers and three more cans of root beer.

I gathered up the wrappings. Then I collected the cans. Under ordinary circumstances, I'd separate them and rinse them out for recycling, but I had a feeling the city sanitation department wasn't going to be too concerned about recycling for a little while. I dumped them all on top of the wrappings in a garbage bag.

Jumbo George pushed himself back from the table and belched. "When you go to the top of the stairs, you're in the main room. It's got a sink and a stove and a refrigerator. The bathroom is right next to them. The room off to the right is Nick's. The one on the other side of the room used to be mine, when I could still get up the stairs. That's the one you can use if you want."

"Thanks. Where do you sleep now?"

He gestured at the recliner. Just like I'd thought.

"That can't be any too comfortable," I said.

"Beats lying down flat. I can't breathe then. And I can get up out of it. If I lie all the way down, I have a lot of trouble getting up."

Without lights, the narrow long storefront was filling with shadows. Soon, it would be hard to make anything out.

"Might as well get some sleep," Jumbo George said. "Flashlight batteries died last night."

I pulled one of the tiny flashlights from my pocket. "Here. You can't see a whole lot, but it's better than nothing."

He pushed the button on the front, and a tiny, but strong beam of light shot out. "Neat!" he said. "Can I use this?"

"You can keep it. I got a few more. They're, like, five for two dollars. When the store has them."

"Thanks. I'll have to think about stocking them." he said. "One more thing."

"Yeah?"

"Do you think you could go upstairs and get me a blanket or two off of Nick's bed? He's probably not going to be back tonight, and I've been freezing at night."

I could sympathize. I'd spent many a night in a cold cell with just one thin blanket, wearing all the clothes I owned and trying to get warm. Although "owned" was the wrong word. As a prison inmate, they might be mine to use, but I couldn't really say I "owned" them. I had been a ward of the state, and the state owned everything.

"Sure," I looked around and didn't see any stairs. "How do I get upstairs?"

"Door in the backroom wall, next to the refrigerator. You might be glad you got the flashlight. Them stairs can be pretty dark."

The door next to the refrigerator looked too narrow to be anything but a storage closet, but when I opened it, a rickety flight of equally narrow stairs led up into the gloom. I wondered how long ago it was that Jumbo George had been able to navigate those stairs.

The little apartment had two windows, both overlooking the alley behind the building. There must be another apartment up front, too. Probably bigger. Those stairs probably led up from a door in the front of the building.

The rooms here didn't smell of patchouli, but they didn't smell much better. At least the stuff up here should be dry.

I heard a dripping sound.

Unless the roof leaked.

It was coming from the center of the main room. As I watched, a big drop of water fell from the overhead light fixture and splashed into a puddle on the floor.

I went into Nick's room. The smell here was stronger and worse. Cigarettes, marijuana, dirty clothes heaped on the floor.

Sweeping a grimy, but cozy-feeling quilt off the bed, I bundled it up and looked around. I also grabbed a knit afghan that Jumbo George could tuck around his shoulders. As I left the room, the edge of the quilt brushed a pile of papers off the nightstand. I kept going, figuring I could pick them up when I got back upstairs.

As I opened the narrow door to the kitchen, Jumbo George was coming out of the bathroom. He took a few pathetic blankets and a pillow from a shelf under the store counter and waddled over to the recliner. He spread one blanket on the recliner, then maneuvered himself into the chair, lying on top of the blanket. Struggling, he tried to spread the other blankets over his bulk.

I took the remaining blankets from him and flipped them over him. Then I laid the quilt on top, smoothing it evenly over him and making sure his feet were well covered. His body took up so much of the chair that there wasn't room to tuck the edges in. Then I wrapped the afghan up around his upper body and neck. "You got a hat?" I asked him. "You ought to be wearing something on your head."

He grinned. "Nope. No hat." He flexed his shoulders. "This feels good. You sure you don't want to move in here? I could use someone to put me to bed like this every night."

I laughed. "I'm sure your brother Nick would love having somebody else move in."

Pulling out the tiny flashlight, I went back up the stairs to go to bed myself. Not much to do in the dark like this. One thing, I'd been getting enough sleep lately.

CHAPTER 15

Back upstairs, I went to check out the accommodations. Not luxury, I was sure.

The bathroom was grungy, but not filthy. A good scrubbing might improve it somewhat, but the old fixtures were worn and stained. The other bedroom—Jumbo George's, when he could make it up the stairs—was so small I wondered if he'd ever really been comfortable in it. Everything was dust-covered, as if no one had entered it in a long time. A spider colony appeared to have taken up residence in the far corner.

I opened the window a crack to let some fresh air in. Then I went into Nick's room to pick up the stuff I'd knocked down.

It was mostly paperwork—letters, bills, ripped envelopes. I tried not to mess them up any more than they already were, but the stack kept sliding. Finally, I sorted them into several piles.

Gripping the flashlight, I looked under the bed to see if I'd missed anything. Sure enough, a few pieces of something white showed in the narrow beam of the flashlight. I couldn't quite reach them, so I lay on the floor and pulled them out.

Another stack of envelopes, these ones new, with names on them. Phil. Reggie. Jason. Denver. James. Diffy.

Diffy.

Diffy wasn't a common name. The only Diffy I knew was a forklift driver on the four to midnight shift at Quality Steel. Who didn't like me.

And Denver. Wasn't that the name of the driver who'd been looking for Aaron the last night we'd worked?

I picked up the envelope with Diffy's name on it. The flap was tucked in. Pulling it out, I looked inside. A piece of paper with a list of numbers and letters. Some of the numbers might have been dates. But I couldn't make any sense out of the rest of them. A tiny plastic baggie with a resealable zipper was in the bottom. I took it out. It contained a little white powder.

Cocaine? Powder meth? I was tempted to lick a finger and get a bit to taste, to see if it had the bitter taste I'd expect.

Not a smart idea. I had no notion how much—or how little—it would take to show up in a drug test. While Mr. Ramirez didn't regularly test me when I showed up for parole appointments, he had the right to, anytime he felt like it. And the last thing I'd need was to test positive.

I put those envelopes onto the nightstand and looked a bit more closely at the other things.

One was a big manila envelope. "Aaron" was written on the outside. I only hesitated a moment before I looked at the contents.

A few pictures. Aaron by himself. Aaron and Benji. Aaron standing next to his battered blue pickup. Aaron and an older lady, possibly his mother.

The envelope also contained some legal-looking documents. The only legal documents I was familiar with had to do with criminal cases, but these looked a lot like them, only the state wasn't one of the parties listed.

I sat down on the edge of the bed and shone the narrow beam of light on the pages. They outlined some kind of financial settlement, repeatedly referring to "Aaron Stenski, minor" and "Gina Michaels, guardian."

Of course, Aaron was no longer a minor. Or wouldn't have been if he were still alive. Because of the heavy machinery, overhead conveyors, etc., the child labor laws would not have permitted him to be hired at Quality Steel until he was at least eighteen.

Perusing a bit further, the papers seemed to be outlining child support arrangements and how they would be affected by various events, including the youngest child, Aaron, reaching eighteen or graduating from high school, or the death of one Gustav Stenski.

Also mentioned were George and Nicholas Stenski, children of Gustav, and Suzanne Stenski, his wife.

The papers stated that Nicholas had received $125,000 to purchase a truck cab and establish himself in business. George had received a similar amount to purchase and stock a retail store. Therefore, fifty percent of the estate would go into a trust fund for Aaron after his eighteenth birthday to provide him with the means to set himself up in business.

The remaining forty percent of the estate would be divided among the other two sons and Suzanne, also in trust funds. If an heir died, his trust fund would go to his issue. If he had no issue, it would be distributed to the other trust funds according to the same formula.

I didn't know much about estate law. Could he really set it up so if someone died, the money would go back into trust funds for the other heirs? The paperwork seemed to indicate that.

A list of assets added up to a staggering $2,765, 250.

That meant that Aaron's fifty percent would be $1,382,625.

Ten times what either Jumbo George or Nick had gotten.

Assuming, of course, that Aaron was alive to collect anything from the trust fund.

* * * *

Jumbo George was up and piling mud-encrusted merchandise in the sink when I got downstairs.

"Only got cold water, but I can get a start on it," he said, holding a leering gargoyle up to the light.

I looked around the shop. It was in a lot better shape than when I first got there, but it was still dirty and cluttered. And it still stank of mildew. Jumbo George had lit a whole sheaf of incense sticks on the counter, but I wasn't sure that the smoky patchouli scent was much of an improvement.

"You think you can walk down to that McDonald's again?" Jumbo George asked.

"Sure."

He pulled a twenty out of his pocket, stared at it, and added a five. "Get some coffee. The biggest size. And as many breakfast burritos as you can."

The McDonald's was packed. It's an ongoing mystery to me how stores can be out of stock, roads can be blocked, supply lines can be almost nonexistent, but the fast food restaurants are up and running as soon as the power comes on and the employees can get there.

For the money, I got two huge cups of coffee and a bag stuffed with the breakfast burritos.

"Haven't had any coffee in days," Jumbo George said as he took the top off his massive cup and inhaled the aroma. He took a huge gulp. "That's good."

I put the bag of burritos on the table and took a sip of my own coffee. It hadn't been as long for me, since I'd had some at the high school and then the cold instant at Kelly's, but I'd missed it all the same.

We sat at the table again. Jumbo George wolfed down a few burritos and half of his coffee.

"What ya got planned today?" I asked him, taking a second burrito.

He shrugged. "Same old, I guess. Keep cleaning up and see if I can't get this place in shape to open whenever the power comes back on. How about you?"

"I got to check out some stuff," I said.

"Like your apartment?"

"Yeah. I bet that's a mess. And I got to find out when Quality Steel is working again. That's a good job, and I wouldn't want to lose it."

Jumbo George unwrapped another burrito. "Seems like it's kind of hard to get fired from there, isn't it? I didn't see him much, but I know Nick said Aaron was always goofing off, missing work, stuff like that. And he never got fired."

"Yeah." I wondered how much I should tell him. He'd as much as said he didn't care much about Aaron. But it was his brother. "Some people thought Aaron was untouchable because he was keeping an eye on the drug deals and stuff in the shop."

Jumbo George snorted. "Running the drug deals in the shop would be more like it. Aaron's a druggie, no doubt about it. If he needed a fix and thought selling his mother's eyeballs would get it for him, he'd do it. No problem."

I let that statement hang in the air between us.

"When you say 'keeping an eye on' the dealing, you mean, like, snitching?" He took another gulp of his coffee.

"That's what some people said."

"To the cops?"

"Yeah. And the cops asked the company to keep him on while they investigated a few things. So he didn't get fired."

"You know," Jumbo George said, "Nick said Aaron was beginning to hang out with a bike club. Predators. That's where he was getting a lot of his shit from. If they thought he was rolling over on them, he'd be toast in no time."

I took another drink of my coffee. This container was huge. "Unless they were using him."

"You mean, like to find out what was going on?"

"Yeah. And to send fake information."

He raised his shaggy dark eyebrows. "Interesting. But a dangerous game. As soon as they were done with him, or he proved a liability, they'd off him."

"I imagine they would." I drained my coffee. "But if they did that, I don't imagine the body would ever be found. They're pretty good at hiding bodies."

We finished our breakfast, and I began sweeping the wrappings into the bag. "Your brother Nick ever haul for Quality Steel?" I asked.

"Sometimes." Jumbo George finished his coffee and looked sadly at the empty cup. "That's where he found out a lot of this stuff about what Aaron was up to."

"Was that a good-paying gig?"

"I think so. He's just getting into it. Talking about buying a flatbed trailer so he can haul anybody's stuff, instead of just the big companies that can provide a trailer. Says steel makes a good load—it's so heavy, you hit your weight limit fast. Not like some things, where they try to stuff just a little more into the trailer no matter how full it is. That kind of shit takes forever to load and unload."

I got to my feet.

Jumbo George looked up at me. "You gonna come back and help out any more?"

"I might. If you want. Especially if you'll let me sleep here again."

"Hell, you can move in, for all I care."

That was the second time he'd mentioned something like that. I wondered if he was really lonely. He sure couldn't get out too much.

As I walked down the street, I thought about going to see how Kelly was doing, but decided to wait until we got back to work, which I hoped wouldn't be too far in the future. We both needed the money. At work, we could talk things out a bit without the kids overhearing. If she wanted to talk to me.

I should go by Mandy's and see how her plans were coming along. Maybe warn her I might be locked up again soon.

And my apartment—what kind of shape was that in? I almost hated to find out.

Not to mention that I needed to look into if Quality Steel was planning to reopen any time soon. And if the parole office would be open for my weekly appointment. I wasn't looking forward to that.

Going to see Mandy won out.

Mandy's neighborhood was in much better shape than the area around Jumbo George's. It was higher ground, so it hadn't been flooded. No debris stood in the streets. I heard the whine of a chainsaw and saw tree limbs piled neatly, awaiting pickup by the town's trucks. The traffic lights were blinking instead of operating on their synchronized cycles, but they did have power.

I went past the hedge that surrounded Mandy's property and up on the gingerbreaded porch. Wiping my feet on the doormat, I lifted the bronze knocker and let it fall.

Nicole opened the door. "Jesse! Good to see you!"

"Good to see you, too. How are you two getting along?"

"Fine. The power came on yesterday. Mandy decided to go out and get some food and things. She figured the towns away from the river ought to have a reasonable supply of most essentials."

"So Mandy's not here?"

"No."

If Nicole didn't want to let me in, I wouldn't blame her. "I just came to check on whether you still wanted me to come house-sit at some point." I didn't say anything about the clothes I'd left behind, since I didn't really have any place to take them right now.

Nicole opened the door wider. "Come on in. I was thinking about fixing some lunch. Are you hungry?"

After the breakfast burritos, I wasn't really, but I wasn't about to turn down any reasonable offer of food. "Sure," I said, stepping into the entry hall/laundry room.

"I made some potato soup," she said, "and a loaf of bread. Bread is one of those things that sells out fast in the stores."

That sounded good to me. As I entered the kitchen, it smelled good, too. Fresh baked bread.

Nicole's nose, though, wrinkled and she turned her head. "You haven't had a chance to take a shower?" she said.

I should have thought of that. By this time, I must have been pretty ripe. "No, ma'am." I took a step backwards, toward the door. "I can come back later. When I've found someplace to clean up. And maybe Mandy's back."

"Nonsense. You can take a shower here. I've washed the clothes you left here. Except for the jacket. So there's something for you to change into."

I followed her back into the laundry room with its little bathroom tucked in a corner. It was bigger than the one in my apartment. She got two fluffy yellow towels off a shelf and handed them to me. "I think there's soap and shampoo in the shower," she said. "I'll put your other things on top of the washing machine."

The shower felt good. The soap and the shampoo smelled better. And when I got out, the yellow towels were pure luxury.

I looked in the medicine cabinet to see if there was a bottle of mouthwash. There was. I hadn't brushed my teeth in a while, so I took a big swig and swished it around in my mouth. That would have to do.

As promised, my own clothes were folded neatly on top of the washing machine. I put them on and pulled on the now-dry boots. Someone, probably Nicole, had cleaned them up nicely. I took what I had been wearing and tried to fold them as well as I could. I took a good sniff. They were pretty rank.

Back in the kitchen, Nicole had set the table for two. "Sit down."

Awkwardly, I sat. She put a big bowl of the soup in front of me and a plate with slices of the fragrant bread in the middle of the table, along with butter and some fancy jars of different preserves and honeys.

"What are you up to?" she asked.

"I got to go check out my apartment," I said. "I want to see how much of my stuff is salvageable."

"You can bring it over here," she said, "and put it in the carriage house, since you're going to be staying there for a few weeks anyhow."

I tipped my bowl up to catch the last of the soup in the spoon. "I'm not so sure about the house sitting while you and Mandy go on your honeymoon trip…"

A cloud settled over Nicole's face. "You decided you can't do it?" she asked.

"It's not that…"

Her eyes tightened. "You don't want to do it because we're a lesbian couple and you don't approve?"

"No! Ain't none of my business. Except I'm glad Mandy found somebody she can be happy with. That damn Radman was just out to take advantage of her. I think the reason he could manipulate her was because she was lonely. So if she's got a good relationship with you, she'll be a lot better off. And I'm happy for her."

"Then what's the problem?"

I shifted in my seat and looked away from her. "I'm just afraid I'm gonna be locked up again."

"What'd you do?" she asked.

"Nothing! Well, nothing bad enough to get locked up for."

"What do you mean?"

"Well, I been associating with convicted felons. Which I'm not supposed to do. But as long as there weren't no crimes committed, they're not gonna think it's that serious. I hope." I stared at the assortment of jars, trying to decide what I wanted to try.

She stirred the soup in her bowl. "Is that all?"

"It's all I've done," I said. "But I think they want to question me about some other shi…stuff." This wasn't the place to say "shit."

"Like what?"

"You been watching the news?"

"Yes. They keep showing that picture of you rescuing that lady from the car in the water."

I grimaced. "You see about some guy, got pulled out of a stairwell. Dead?"

"I remember something about that. The only casualty of the flood. So far. They thought he might have drowned, but they were treating it as if it were a homicide. That one?" She lifted the spoon and sipped the soup.

"Yeah. Well, it was a guy I worked with and who tried to set me up a few times. They know I don't like him."

She leaned back in her chair. "So you're afraid they might think you were responsible?"

"Yeah."

"Did he have any other enemies?"

"Lots."

"So why would they be looking especially for you?"

"Well, for one thing, because it was the stairwell outside my apartment where he was found. And I was the last person who they knew was driving his truck. Stuff like that."

She eyed me. "I can see where they might want to talk to you."

* * * *

A work crew was assembled on the sidewalk and stairs outside the parole office. All the crew members wore blue jeans and orange hoodies with "Inmate Trustee" stenciled on the back. From the county detention center. I looked around, but didn't see a corrections officer supervising them. Maybe they all had work release status.

I sidled up to a guy who was sweeping up a pile of trash. "The parole office open?" I asked.

"Nah. Gonna be closed all week." He cocked his head and looked at me. "Can you read okay?"

"Yeah."

He pointed to a white placard attached to the wall. "Then better you should read it yourself than have me tell you and maybe mess it up."

I went over to it, excusing myself to the person who was trying to scrape some ugly muck off the concrete in front of it.

The posted notice confirmed what he'd said. Basically, they were skipping a week. Fees wouldn't be excused, though, so bring double the money next week. If there was a problem—low battery on an ankle monitor, situation where a parolee needed permission for something—they gave a number to call, since the offices were closed and not all PO's cell phones were active. Show up for treatment at outside providers as scheduled. Otherwise, therapy and treatment groups held at the parole office would be resumed next week. And all appointments set for this week would be honored next week.

"Honored" wasn't the word I would have used, but its meaning was clear enough.

My next appointment would be over a week away. They'd probably detain me at that meeting, if they hadn't caught up with me before.

Next stop was my apartment. No power in that part of town. No signs of a cleanup, either. A downed tree blocked the road. It had hauled electric lines along with it.

The crime scene tape was still there, but it was torn and flapping in the wind. I hesitated only a minute before I slipped down the stairs, my key in my hand.

Inside was very dark. And it smelled as bad as Jumbo George's place, minus the patchouli. A few inches of water and who knows what covered the floor.

I pulled out the tiny flashlight and shined it on the walls. A watermark five feet high showed on the wall. The cheap paneling that came up to a chair rail was sagging away from the wall.

The sinks were still full of water. In the bathroom, the toilet was full to the brim. Grime covered the shower stall to the same five feet above the floor.

My throat closed. It may not have been much, but this little one-room apartment was the only real "home" I'd had in years. And it had been mine.

I could stay at Jumbo George's for a few days. I still wasn't sure when Mandy and Nicole would want me to house-sit, but maybe I could move in there early. At this point, I didn't want to count on Kelly's place as a possibility.

Was I in total denial? Let's face it. As soon as things settled down and the law enforcement personnel were free to return to their regular duties, I'd be picked up and brought in for questioning concerning Aaron's death. Then I wouldn't have to worry about a place to stay. I'd have a temporary bunk in the county detention center. And likely a permanent one back in a state prison.

My chest felt heavy. Angrily, I wiped tears away from my eyes with my sleeve. Sniveling wouldn't change anything. I might as well just keep acting like I wasn't going to spend the rest of my life in prison. Even if it was an illusion, it was one I valued.

And who knows? Maybe I would find out something that would throw suspicion somewhere else. Maybe Banjo would have picked up rumors that would give me a lead.

Yeah, right.

I got down the laundry basket I'd lashed to the overhead pipes. Surprisingly, the clothes in there weren't very damp. They did have a musty odor, but if I could hang them up for a while somewhere, they might be okay.

The mattress was a total loss. The bedding didn't look much better, but a run through a big washer at the laundromat with plenty of bleach might make a difference. For now, though, I'd leave it here.

To really take a look around and see what else I could manage to save, I'd need a better flashlight. Lifting the laundry basket and its contents, I went out of the apartment. I stood in the landing to lock the door. No point leaving it unlocked—even if there wasn't much of value in there, I might be able to find some more stuff later.

Several inches of water stood on the cracked concrete, not moving at all toward the drain. The storm drain system must still be flooded, at least in this part of town.

I carried the laundry basket back across town to Mandy's house. As I lifted the knocker on the front door, I looked down at my boots.

They had been clean when I'd put them on earlier. Now, they were caked with mud. And probably sewage from the backed-up drains.

When Nicole answered the door, I declined her invitation to come inside and stand on the nice rug. "Look at these boots. They're filthy."

She frowned. "We've had mud in here before."

"Yeah. But I'm afraid I was walking where the sewers might have backed up."

"The sanitary sewers? Or just the drain sewers?"

"Both, I imagine. When the storm sewers get clogged, they spill over into the sanitary sewers. And then both overflow. It's a mess."

She wrinkled her nose at the thought. "We haven't had any problems with that," she said.

"That's good, ma'am. But other sections of town have." I didn't explain to her that, when the lines below were blocked and she flushed her toilet, the contents would come spilling out of drains farther downhill. Like those in my apartment.

"Okay. Do you want to put your things in the carriage house, or in the garage for now?"

"The garage is fine."

She came out with the keys to the garage. "You work at Quality Steel Fabrications, don't you?"

"Yes, ma'am."

"On the news, they said any shop employees who could make it in should report at eight tomorrow morning to get the plant ready for production Monday."

Quality Steel was getting ready to reopen? First good news I'd heard in a while. "That's not my shift," I said.

"The announcement said any employees. They especially want wheelwrights, setup men, and lift drivers."

"Lift drivers. That's me." I'd show up. I needed the money.

I wondered if Kelly would be there.

* * * *

On my way back to Jumbo George's, I stopped at Tex Mex's takeout for a big bucket of chili and a slab of cornbread. I was well aware that he would eat the vast majority of it, but he'd fed me for two meals, and I owed him.

There were still no lights in any of the windows, but the street showed a bit more activity, with the staff of a ladies' specialty shop down the row busy washing the exterior and show windows. It was a bit uphill from Jumbo George's, so it might not have sustained any water damage.

The door to the head shop stood open. Loud, argumentative voices reached me. I could pick out Jumbo George's, but I didn't recognize the other one. I stopped on the sidewalk outside. Maybe I should come back later? But then the chili would be cold. The temperature was above freezing, but it was still damp and cold. Warm food was a comfort, perhaps more so to someone with an appetite like Jumbo George than to most people.

I stepped inside and let my eyes adjust to the dimness.

Jumbo George was leaning his bulk on the counter, his chest heaving. Another man, much skinnier, stood on the other side of the counter. His fists were balled, and his face was fierce.

Coughing, Jumbo George waved a hand at me. "This here's the guy I was telling you about. He's been helping me clean up. I told him he could stay upstairs. In my room."

The other guy swung to face me, his chin and lower lip stuck out. "You were messing with my stuff," he said.

This must be Nick.

I put the chili and cornbread on the counter. No sense it getting spilled if there was a fight. And no sense me being handicapped by holding it.

Firmly planting my feet and squaring my shoulders, I braced myself. I let my hands hang by my sides, hands curled slightly, but unclenched, and narrowed my eyes into a version of the prison yard stare that had served me well for years. I glared back at him.

"I got George here a few extra blankets. And I knocked some stuff off the nightstand. So I picked it up. You got a problem with that?"

"You had no right to touch my stuff."

"You missing something?" I asked.

He glanced at Jumbo George, looking a bit confused. "Well, no, but…"

Jumbo George straightened up, propping himself up with his arms. "If you ain't missing nothing, what's your beef?" he demanded.

Nick's face was set in a stubborn pout. "It's my stuff."

"Nobody's disputing that," I said.

"Do you want your blankets back?" Jumbo George asked. "I'm sure Jesse would bring them back upstairs for you."

"The hell with the blankets." Nick turned on his heel and stalked out. We watched him go.

"What was that all about?" I asked.

Jumbo George shrugged. "He came in and went upstairs to get something and got all bent out of shape. At first I thought it was because I had his nice quilt, but it because he was afraid you'd gotten into his stuff."

"I did pick up what I knocked down," I said, "but I left it all there for him." I didn't add that it had the little envelopes of white powder, probably some kind of CDS, all neatly packed in envelopes with names written on them. Or that I'd looked at all the legal paperwork.

"Well." Jumbo George heaved himself off the counter and nodded toward the bucket. "What that you got there?"

"Chili. And some cornbread. I thought we could both use some warm food."

"Bring it on," he said, making his way to the back of the store.

I rummaged in the kitchenette for two bowls and a pair of spoons. Dishing it into the bowls, I said, "I hope you like chili."

"Chili's food, ain't it?" he said. "Of course I like it. There's another few cases of root beer back there somewhere. Get one, will you?"

I found an unopened fridge pack. "I take it that was your brother Nick?"

He grinned. "Yeah. Piece of work, ain't he?"

I shrugged. "He fly off the handle like that a lot?"

"He can be touchy. Been worse than usual lately."

Breaking the cornbread in pieces, I took one and waved my hand at the rest. "Take some."

Crumbling a piece into his chili and stirring it, Jumbo George peered across the table at me. "You know," he said, "you look like somebody who can take care of yourself. But I have to say you looked downright scary just then. I wouldn't have wanted to challenge you to a fight. You done hard time?"

I nodded.

"How much?"

"Twenty years."

He raised an eyebrow. "And you're how old?"

"Thirty-seven."

"That's more time down than on the street. From when you was a kid."

"Don't remind me." I took a spoonful of chili.

"You manditoried out?"

I shook my head. "Parole. Another twenty backup time."

"So you got to watch your step?"

"Yeah. I don't need no more trouble in this lifetime."

He scratched under his beard. "Nick told me about Aaron. Might have been murdered. You know about that?"

"Hadn't heard the murder part. But it doesn't surprise me. Aaron was mixed up with all kinds of shit. And he wasn't real smart about it."

"You can say that again. Nick's afraid that when they investigate the whole thing, they'll find out some shit he's been involved in with Aaron. Drugs, I think."

"Could be. Aaron was into drugs."

"And Nick's afraid Aaron was a snitch."

I looked up. "Not much doubt about it. Aaron was a snitch. Police informant."

Jumbo George winced. "So do you think somebody offed him?"

"I dunno. And don't care. Just so they don't think it was me." But that's exactly what they would think.

By the time the light was getting too dim to work, we'd gotten a lot done. The ruined merchandise had been discarded, the muddy things rinsed off, the floor scraped down to basic tile, and the shelves restocked.

"I'll go over everything again with hot water and detergent when I have hot water," Jumbo George said, eyeing the display cases under the counter with satisfaction. "And I'll get everything out of the front window, scrub the area down, and put in a new display."

I had my doubts he could do all that by himself, but he'd done a lot already, so he might surprise me.

Thinking of the agreed-upon meeting with Banjo, I said, "I got to go meet a friend. You okay for supper?"

"Yeah. One advantage to selling a lot of trail mix is I always got plenty of food."

CHAPTER 16

As Banjo had predicted, Mickey's Bar had electricity. It might be the only place dispensing alcohol for miles around, and it was hopping. They'd drawn their usual crowd and a whole bunch of others.

It was on the corner of a row of storefronts with apartments above. I checked to see if the laundromat was open. I really needed to be doing my laundry soon. It was.

Cars lined the street. A pair of fancy choppers stood in one space, their chrome and extended forks gleaming in the streetlight.

I hesitated before going in. That was silly. I was a lot more likely to be seen loitering on the sidewalk in front of the place than if I went in and sat in a corner, minding my own business.

Banjo was already inside, sitting at a table with a couple of bikers. All of them were sitting facing the room, so I couldn't see the backs of their vests. I would have taken bets that they wore Predator colors.

Springing to his feet, Banjo shouted, "Jesse! Come sit with us."

I edged over to the table and pulled out a chair, then placed it so my back was to the wall. Banjo was already half-sloshed. He waved toward me expansively. "This here is my old cell buddy—the best guy you could ever share a cell with! He had my back when I was a snot-nosed kid, just locked up for the first time."

The bikers stared at me intently, but didn't say anything.

Banjo gestured at them. "Spider and Nuke," he said by way of introduction.

"The next round's on me," Banjo said, heading toward the bar without asking anybody what they wanted. He returned with both hands full of beer steins, plunking them down in front of us.

I knew I shouldn't drink, but I didn't see how I could decline without dissing Banjo, and if I nursed it and kept it to just the one, I should be okay.

"We was just talking about Aaron," Banjo said, taking a big swig of his beer. "Ain't that who you wanted to know about?"

"Yeah." How much did he know? And how reliable would any of it be if he was drunk?

"You know he's dead?"

"I'd heard that."

Banjo shook his head. "First they thought he might have just OD'd and drowned. But then they said he'd been hit on the head. Probably unconscious when he fell in the water."

"Or was put there," Nuke said ominously.

"But he did drown?" I asked.

"Yeah. Funny, that. They found his body in a flooded stairwell, pretty far away from where he lived. Not near where he worked, either. What do you suppose he was doing over there?"

I shrugged. I wished I knew.

"Plenty of people had beefs with him," Banjo went on "He had a finger in everything he could find. Boosting cars; dealing drugs, especially to truck drivers; lifting anything he could get his hands on."

"Snitching," Spider said.

"Yeah. Ain't no surprise he ended up dead. Serves him right." Banjo looked mournfully at his empty stein, then glanced around. Mine was still almost full, but everyone else's was empty. "I'll get another round," he said, rising from the table and gathering the empty steins.

I wondered where he was getting the money from. Better not to ask.

He plunked the beer steins down again, including a full one in front of me. I was going to have to drink more than I wanted to. Remembering how I'd felt the last time I tried drinking, I wasn't looking forward to that. But this was commercial beer, not somebody's home-distilled corn liquor. Maybe it wouldn't make me as sick. I took a small sip.

When Banjo was settled in his seat, I asked, "Anybody hear anything about how Aaron got along with his brothers?"

Spider said, "He had a kid brother. Turn up with the kid in all kinds of dumb places. In a stolen car. At a buy. Stupid."

"Didn't he have older brothers or something?"

The biker shrugged. "Not that I ever knew."

"Older brothers?" Banjo said. "I heard something about one, runs a head shop in town. And another one, who's a trucker. That's how come he could sell to them. Had an in, somebody they knew."

"Where'd he get the shit?"

"Predators got a good business going."

Nuke reached over the table and smacked Banjo across the face. "Don't be putting nobody's business out in public," he said.

Banjo rubbed his cheek. "Sorry. Didn't mean no harm. I mean, Jesse, he's cool."

"But we're in public. Anybody could be listening."

I changed the subject. "How you doing since you got sprung, Banjo?"

He brightened up. "Okay. I been thinking about moving south, though. Too cold here."

"You off supervision?"

"Will be in two months. Done most of my backup time in lockup." He laughed. "It's too easy to violate."

I was uncomfortably aware of that fact.

A loud commotion broke out across the room. We ignored it. I lifted my beer to take another sip.

A body crashed across our table, slamming against me and Spider. My beer spilled down my jacket. Well, that would be less I had to drink.

The guy's arm came up and knocked Nuke across the face. Nuke stood up and grabbed the guy by the throat. He crashed his head into the guy's forehead and kneed him in the groin. The guy collapsed on the floor, moaning.

If he were moaning, he couldn't be dead.

A crowd began to gather.

The bikers stood up and downed the rest of their beer. They started to elbow their way past the onlookers toward the door. Their Predators colors were visible on the backs of their vests. The crowd parted to let them through.

A woman dressed in a skimpy shimmering outfit, a cocktail glass in her hand, pushed her way up to the front. "Uh, Fred?" she asked, looking at the guy who lay there. "You feel okay?"

I could have told her he didn't feel okay, but he probably wasn't really hurt. I peered down at him.

He looked familiar, but I couldn't place him.

"You gonna get up, honey?" the woman said, nudging him with the pointed toe of her shoe. "Uh, Fred?"

Fred? I looked closer. Fred. Kelly's ex. I'd only seen him a few times, and then his face wasn't all twisted up in agony, but that was definitely him.

Was that a siren I heard in the distance? If somebody had called the cops, they might be here any second.

"Banjo." I grabbed his sleeve. "Let's go."

"Go?" he said, cradling his empty mug. "The party's just getting started."

"You can stay. I'm out of here."

"Suit yourself."

Flashing lights showed through the front window. I looked around and saw a fire exit in the back wall. Probably led to the alley. I slipped through the crowd and out the door.

I breathed the cool night air. It cleared my head a little. I hadn't drunk more than half the first beer, so I should be all right.

The security light placed high on the wall threw grotesque shadows. Overfilled dumpsters lined the alley. A few cars were parked haphazardly.

The police probably wouldn't be poking around back here. If they'd wanted to catch anybody, they wouldn't have used the siren. The whole point of that was so that the troublesome elements would disperse before they arrived. Now they'd have to do something with the injured Fred.

Dodging trash blown by the wind, I strode down the alley toward the far end. I needed to get off the street. Jumbo George's place sounded like a good bet.

As I passed the last car parked in the alley, a small voice called out. "Jesse?"

I stopped and looked at the open window of the car. "Chris? Is that you?"

"Me and Brianna," he said.

"What are you doing here?"

"Waiting for Dad. He told us to wait while he went into the bar and got something for us to eat. We're hungry. And he's been gone for a long time. I don't know if he's still in the bar."

What was this with adults leaving kids in vehicles? First Benji, now Chris and Brianna.

"He's still in the bar, all right," I said. And not likely to be able to take care of his kids any time soon. "Your mom know where you are?"

"I don't think so," Chris said. "Just that Dad was supposed to take us out for dinner. Then bring us back home."

"Is your mom home?"

"I think so."

I debated what to do. I couldn't leave the kids here in the car. I could go find one of the cops, and when the report went in that Fred had left them in the car while he was in the bar, fighting no less, it would help Kelly with her efforts to get full custody.

But if Kelly had been drinking when they contacted her to come get the kids, they might put the kids in emergency foster care. And I wasn't particularly anxious to get involved with the authorities myself.

Driving the car, with the kids in it, to Kelly's might be an option. The last time I tried driving without a license, though, it hadn't ended well. Fred probably would claim the car was stolen.

"Do you think we can call your mom to come get you or something?" I asked. I didn't have a cell phone, but maybe Banjo did. I'd have to go back in the bar to find out, though.

"Dad left his cell phone on the charger here," Chris said. "He said not to call anybody, though. He said he'd get in trouble, and it'd be my fault."

"Give it to me. If anybody gets in trouble, it'll be my fault."

Chris handed me the phone. I stared at it blankly. People used them all the time. But how the hell did it turn on?

"Do you know how to use it?" I asked Chris.

He took it back and did something to it. It lit up, and images started blinking on the screen. I stared at it. How did it work?

Eventually, the scrolling images stopped.

"You just punch the phone number in on the keypad," Chris said, "and hit 'send.'"

Awkwardly, I pushed the buttons for Kelly's home phone and then the send button.

The phone made a few weird noises and then buzzed. The word "ERROR" showed up on the screen and kept blinking.

"Did you put in the whole area code?" Chris asked.

"No."

"Then you have to reset it and start over."

"How do I do that?"

Chris took the phone back again and did something to it again. Then he handed it back.

I punched in Kelly's entire phone number, area code included. The phone rang.

"Hello?" she said.

"Kelly?"

"Yes," she said impatiently. "Who is this? Is it you, Jesse?"

"Yeah."

"What did you want?"

"Well, I'm with the kids."

"The kids? Chris and Brianna?"

What other kids could I possibly mean? But I said, "Yeah."

"What are you doing with the kids?"

"Fred left them in the car while he went into a bar. They're cold and hungry. Maybe you should come pick them up."

"Where the hell are you?"

"You know Mickey's Bar on Middle Street?"

"Yes."

"The car's parked in the alley behind it. Down at the other end."

"I'll be there in ten minutes."

A patrol car eased around the corner at the other end of the alley and crept toward us, its searchlight moving over the walls and parked cars.

I slid into the car and sat in the front seat. I was less conspicuous. And warmer.

The kids huddled in the back seat, a thin blanket wrapped around them. I wished I had something to feed them.

The patrol car passed by without stopping. I hadn't realized I was holding my breath until I had to gulp in air.

An ambulance screamed by the end of the alley. We just sat. It rounded the corner, and we could hear it screech to a stop. I wondered if they were picking up Fred.

Kelly's old station wagon finally pulled up. Chris climbed out. Brianna was sleepy and limp. I picked her up and carried her.

Climbing out of her car, Kelly rushed up and took Brianna from my arms. She opened the back door to her car and laid the child on the seat. Then she looked at Chris, who was clinging to my waist. "What happened?" she asked.

Chris hung on to me tighter. "Dad told us to wait for him and to not use the phone or we'd get in trouble. But Jesse called you to come."

"It's all right," Kelly assured him. "You won't get in trouble for Jesse using the cell phone." She stepped up to take his hand.

Her face inches away from my jacket, she stopped and sniffed. "You smell like a brewery," she said. "You've been drinking again."

CHAPTER 17

"Was me, I'd be looking for another job." Hank scratched his cheek.

I'd read him off the list of tasks for this shift, circling the important stock numbers and quantities on the paperwork, and handed him back the clipboard. He took it and scanned the circled numbers. He couldn't meet my gaze.

A motley crew had assembled at eight a.m. at Quality Steel Fabrications to prepare the plant to reopen. I'd expected the dayshift foreman to be working. But it was Bucky, from second shift. Who didn't like me in the least.

If he'd noticed me before I'd punched in, he might have told me to leave. Then I'd have to file a grievance with the union to get paid at all. Once I showed up, I was supposed to get a minimum of two hours pay. And after I was punched in, it would be a minimum of four hours. Bucky wasn't going to let four paid hours go, so I knew he'd have me working that at least.

"Jobs are hard to come by these days," I said to Hank as I adjusted my hard hat. "Especially if you're on parole."

He nodded, tucking the clipboard under his beefy tattooed arm. "Them forklifts cost a pretty penny. If'n they're looking for somebody to blame, it's probably gonna be you."

"I get that. The lift was assigned to me."

"Don't seem fair. But the fact remains, it was signed out to you. And it ended up crashed. Right over the edge of a loading dock. They'll say, where the hell were you?"

"Taking a leak. We always park the lift there if we're gonna run into the head."

He peered at the clipboard, the floor—anywhere but my face. "You left it running."

I sighed. "Yeah. We always do that, too, if it's just gonna be a few minutes. Never had a problem with it."

"Until now."

"True, that. Now, it's a problem."

He shifted his considerable weight from one foot to the other. "Who else was around that could have done it?"

I had an idea, but I said, "You got me. Wouldn't you think a security camera would have caught the whole thing?"

"You'd think. But there are lotsa blind spots."

"Do you think they'd let me look at the tapes or whatever?"

He shook his massive head. "Nope."

"John might."

"Maybe. Probably not. And he's not working now. I hear he's got flood damage at his place. Fences down. When you got livestock, like he does, you got to see to that. Bucky's in charge now."

"And he don't like me," I said.

"He don't got to like you. Or nobody else. Just got to get the work done."

I wiped a trickle of sweat from my face with my sleeve. This was a good job. I couldn't afford to lose it. "Might be. But he was coming on duty when it happened."

"Yeah. It was a Saturday overtime. One of his lift drivers was working, too. Diffy."

Hank was thinking along the same lines as I was. I thought back to that morning. The foreman had been hurting for a plating room lead man, and he'd been trying to talk Hank into at least part of another shift. At double time. "You worked daytime, too, that day, didn't you?"

"Yeah. Part of it. I didn't want to, but they needed somebody to oversee tearing down the platers. That takes a good six hours. I worked that long." He looked over at the platers, now idle. "Good money. But the time comes when it ain't worth it."

I found it hard to envision that, but then, I'd never been offered two overtime shifts, back to back, after I'd worked a whole regular week. "So did anything…funny happen?"

He scratched his head under his hard hat. "Kind of. Diffy, he was all over the place. Had to track him down, a few times, when we needed stuff moved. You wouldn't think you'd have to—we weren't running full production, so he should have been able to keep ahead of it. I thought he'd be out in shipping mostly, but every blasted time I needed to find him, he was in the warehouse."

"The warehouse?" That was funny. All he should have been doing there was picking up parts and dropping off finished products. That didn't take much time.

"Yeah. And you know, there were a couple of other guys going back there. Guys who didn't have no business back there that I know of."

That was even funnier. Usually, the foremen ran a tight ship. Production workers were clocked in on a job, with a quota to meet. Everybody got two ten-minute breaks, one in each half of the shift, and an eighteen-minute lunch. Other than that, it would be unusual for anyone to be away from their work station.

Unless they weren't punched in and working. Then the foreman might not even realize they were in the shop.

"You think you know what you got to do?" I asked Hank.

He frowned. "Yeah. I hope so."

"I'll be by every now and then. Flag me down if you need to."

"You think Bucky's gonna work us the whole shift?" Hank asked.

"I'm sure you'll get the full eight hours. He might send me home early if he can. But I'm the only lift driver on—there's not a lot he can do if he doesn't have a lift driver. Whether he likes me or not."

Hank grinned. "Don't think there's any question about that. He don't like you. And if he can get you fired over that damaged lift, he'll do it."

I thought for a minute. "You think it'd do any good to talk to the union rep?"

"Can't hurt. At least give him a heads up. He'll do what he can." He turned to unlock the cabinet that contained test kits for the contents of the plating tanks.

I pulled on my work gloves and reached for my own clipboard.

Hank finally met my gaze and shrugged, his tiny eyes clouded. "Good luck with everything."

I swung up on the forklift. Not my usual one—that was lying somewhere a mangled mess. Probably back in the locked repair cage.

Who the hell had snagged it while I was in the john? And why would anyone send it off the edge of a loading dock like that? I could see some of the clowns I worked with deciding it would be a good joke to drive it around the corner or something so I'd panic when I came out and it was gone. Absolutely hilarious.

I'd panicked, all right.

It couldn't have been strictly an accident, somebody who didn't know how to drive it and lost control. The overhead door to the bay had to be opened. Not a big deal—the button that operated it was set in the wall right next to the door. It had certainly been closed when I parked and went into the john. On a cold, rainy night like the other night, for sure I would have noticed an open truck bay door. But someone would have had to open it deliberately.

And no one was hurt. My best guess was that whoever had stopped it at the very edge of the drop off, climbed off, and gunned the engine so it crept forward and toppled off.

But it shouldn't move without some weight on the seat.

I remembered Diffy's pants, wet to the knees. If he'd driven it off the edge, I'd expect him to have been hurt.

What was he up to, spending so much time in the warehouse on a Saturday overtime shift?

Could I ask Victor, the union steward, to see if he could review the security tapes? There were cameras all over, but the shipping department, where outside truckers and their helpers were often wandering around more or less unsupervised, was particularly well covered.

Bucky came by about two thirty and told me to punch out. It wasn't a whole shift, but the money would be welcome.

* * * *

I spent the rest of the afternoon sorting through stuff in my apartment to take to Mandy's garage or throw out. There wasn't much of mine left there.

The soaked furniture and the mattress had come with the apartment and were the landlord's financial loss, not mine.

Last time I was there, I'd left the window open in the hopes of getting some fresh air through the place, but it hadn't made any difference, I noticed. The wet mattress still smelled funky, and the furniture seemed to be growing a layer of slippery algae. Or maybe it was mold. Whatever it was, it was pretty nasty.

I hoped the landlord had flood insurance.

The floor was slippery with mud. And sewage. The day was much brighter than it had been the last time I was there, and I could see better. I wasn't sure that was a good thing.

In the bathroom, a circle of even fouler muck than everywhere else surrounded the drain. That half-used bar of soap would have to go. And there on the floor, in the muck, was the toothbrush I'd been missing. It followed the bar of soap into the trash bag. Looked like nothing else of mine was left in the bathroom.

Next, I tackled the kitchenette. I never kept much food, but I didn't think what there was would be salvageable. Definitely not the opened package of powdered milk and oatmeal. Why hadn't I put them in the basket I'd tied to the pipes? Or the bread. I hesitated over the jar of peanut butter—it was tightly closed, and that stuff was getting expensive—but in the end, I tossed it. I did keep a couple of unopened cans.

I didn't have too much kitchenware, but it should clean up all right. I piled the kettle, the frying pan, my two plates, and my two bowls on the dresser. The dish drainer should be okay. The almost-new, but soggy roll of paper towels were an obvious discard. The cutlery would have to be wrapped in something so it wouldn't poke holes in the bag. I tossed two forks, three spoons, and a paring knife toward the dresser. One of the forks slid right over the slippery surface and disappeared over the edge.

Served me right for being too lazy to walk over there and put them down carefully.

I went over to retrieve the fork, but it was nowhere in sight. With the toe of my boot, I scraped through the muck on the floor, but it wasn't there.

It had to be somewhere. I pulled the dresser away from the wall.

Without the dresser pushed up against it, a half-sheet of the wall paneling sagged away from the chair rail. It was in such bad shape now that I didn't see how pulling it out a little more so I could look behind it would do any more damage. The paneling would have to be replaced when, or if, the landlord decided to renovate the place so he could rent it out again.

I gave it a yank and moved aside so what light came through the window would reach back there. Peering into the space behind it, I caught a reflection of something metallic catching a glimmer of light. I pulled the paneling out farther, finally ripping it away from the wall.

The fork was there. So were a few grimy coins. And something else. I picked it up. It was round, heavy, about the size of a bracelet, and completely covered with the muck.

I took it over to the sink and turned the faucet. No water. I couldn't wash it off. Carrying it, I went outside and up the stairs, looking for a fairly clean puddle. Or at least one that didn't smell entirely foul.

As I swished it around in the water, bright colors began to wink up at me.

It was a heavy band of some kind of jewelry, set with stones. Not really right for a bracelet, but something like that. It looked familiar.

A cat collar.

A few months ago, a cat had showed up on my doorstep in the middle of a nasty snow storm. Of course I'd taken her in. She'd seemed to hate her collar, scratching at it, and I'd taken it off and tossed it on the dresser.

The weirdos in the storefront church upstairs had reclaimed the cat, saying she was their "goddess." They worshipped her. She slept in a "gold" box that was really just painted wood and wore the jeweled collar.

When one of the members had mentioned it missing, I'd given the area a half-hearted search, but never found it. I hadn't worried too much about it. The cat didn't like wearing it.

The cult leader had claimed that the collar was expensive. I had no doubt he was right; a plain cat collar at the Best Deals for Your Dollar was a couple of bucks, so a fancy one like this might run ten dollars or more.

The entire church kind of fell apart when the leader was locked up. I took the cat in again and took her and her kittens to Kelly's, where the kids loved them and the cats had a good home.

Claims were made that some of the jewels set in the collar might be real and the collar worth a fair amount, but it didn't seem likely to me. They also said the box the cat slept in was real gold, but it was gold-colored paint on wood.

Now I had the collar back. And I wasn't sure what to do with it. It didn't belong to me, for sure, but the members of the tabernacle hadn't been around much lately, and I knew some of them had decided to leave the area.

I dried it off with the tail of my T-shirt and stuck it in my pocket.

Not much else left here for me to do. It wouldn't make much difference if I tried to clean up more, and without any running water, I didn't think I could do it anyhow.

I put the kitchenware in the bag with the cans of food. I picked up the bags and headed out. As I closed the door behind me, I turned and gave the room one last look. It hadn't been much, but it sure had beaten a prison cell.

A convenience store on the corner had a pile of discarded furnishings and merchandise at the curb. I dumped the bag with the trash on top of it.

The neighborhood where I'd be staying when I was house-sitting was much nicer than this one. And its electric power had been restored. Mandy's house was one of the oldest in town, and it was still one of the nicest. But not one of the most expensive—the McMansions just outside the city limits had that distinction.

When I dropped these things off at her place, I could ask when I could move into the carriage house. Until then, I could just go to Jumbo George's.

I skirted the county complex, where the lights were on, and turned down Mandy's street.

A few people with chainsaws were working on some of the downed trees in the street. Between their pickups and the trees, the street was almost impassable.

I went down an alley behind well-kept and picturesque old houses. Water pooled in low-lying spots. Some of the fencing around the yards was down, and trash cans littered the pavement. A few garages, their doors firmly shut and locked, faced the alley.

Some of the houses had lights shining through the windows, but most of the interiors were dark. A number of them had outdoor security lights, mostly motion activated. I saw no cars or people. None of the backyards contained dogs. Most residents seemed to have found someplace else to weather the emergency.

I set off a light with a motion detector as I passed a closed garage. I heard a car behind me and stepped to the side of the alley, hugging the garage door. Maybe the car would pass without splashing me too badly.

It was a patrol car, and it stopped in front of me, angling in so I couldn't pass.

My throat swelled shut.

I could try to turn and go the other way, but they'd just chase me down. And charge me with fleeing and alluding.

Both front doors of the car opened, and two officers stepped out. It was Cunningham and Richards, the same team who'd stopped me in Aaron's truck. They had wanted to haul me in, but the sergeant had nixed that idea. They hadn't liked being overruled then, and I doubted they were any happier about it now. That kind of humiliation stuck.

In this emergency, they'd undoubtedly been working long overtime shifts. Add that to grudge they probably carried against me, and I could count on them being in a particularly unfriendly mood.

Maybe they wouldn't recognize me.

Richards's hand went to the flap on her holster, unsnapping it.

They recognized me.

"What are you doing here?" Cunningham asked.

I couldn't think of anything that would sound anything like believable. "Just walking."

"Just walking, huh? In the alley here behind all these nice houses?"

I shrugged.

"All these nice houses whose owners voluntarily evacuated when the mayor suggested it?"

I hadn't heard of a call for a voluntary evacuation, but then, I had limited access to any media. Since I couldn't think of a reasonable response to that, I didn't say anything.

Cunningham poked me in the shoulder. "All these nice houses whose burglar alarms aren't working because they need to be reset after the power came back on?"

I hadn't thought of that, but of course that was true.

"And what's in that bag you're carrying?"

I glanced down it. "Just a few things I salvaged from my apartment."

"Yeah? Where's your apartment?"

"Over on Second Street. It got flooded out pretty bad."

"So you decided to come over here and see what you could 'salvage?'"

"No, sir."

"How about you drop the bag and face that wall." He indicated the garage wall next to the big overhead door.

Not too many options. I dropped the bag and turned to face the wall.

Richards stepped up, grabbed the bag, and backed up a few feet.

"Assume the position," Cunningham said.

I leaned my hands against the wall and spread my feet. I glanced under my arm and saw Cunningham pulling on rubber gloves.

"You got anything I should know about? Anything dangerous or illegal?"

I closed my eyes. "No, sir." Just a cat collar with possibly valuable jewels. But that wasn't dangerous or illegal.

As soon she saw I was cooperating, Richards dropped the bag and went back to the car to pick up the radio. I wanted to tell her they didn't need backup, but I didn't think they'd believe me anyhow, so I didn't.

Cunningham pulled my wallet, keychain, little flashlight, and the cat collar out of my pockets. I couldn't see what he did with them.

Then he ran his hands over my clothes, under my jacket, and between my legs. He took off my watch cap and shook it, then perched it back on my head.

Grasping one of my hands, he pulled it behind me and turned the palm out, then snapped a cuff on it. He did the same with the other hand.

"Turn around."

I did so.

Richards was holding the trash bag in one hand and the cat collar in the other.

"What'd you find?" Cunningham asked.

"Just a couple of pots and dishes, a few cans of food, and some silverware," she answered.

"Real silverware? Like sterling silver?"

"I don't think so. Just garden variety forks and spoons."

"No drugs?"

"Nope."

"And what do you think of the piece of jewelry?"

"I'm not sure." She turned it over in her hands. "But it's pretty heavy. And those gems might be real."

"You think it comes from one of these houses?"

"Could be. Where else would he have gotten if from?"

No one asked me directly, and even if I told them the truth, they'd think I was lying. And I couldn't blame them. The idea of a cat who was a goddess and lived in the church upstairs from my apartment was a pretty far-fetched notion to begin with. And then trying to explain that the cat had this collar, which got lost in my apartment…

It would even sound to me like I was lying.

"Why do you think he hasn't got more loot?"

"Maybe he's just getting started. But my guess would be that he's got a lot of stuff piled up near the back door of these houses to come back for with a car. But he could fit the bracelet in his pocket."

Cunningham reached over to take the cat collar. "Backup coming?" he asked.

"Nah. Dispatch still isn't working well. Didn't think there was much point unless we're gonna bring him in. And with the jail not having any power, we'd need something more than finding him walking down the alley with some jewelry in his pocket. Unless the jewelry was on a stolen property list."

Which, I thought miserably, it might well be.

"You'd better call the stop in anyhow. Make sure there's no warrants for him or anything."

Richards had my wallet in her hand. She pulled my ID out and headed to the patrol car.

I stood still, my stomach clenched in a knot. For sure somebody'd want to talk to me about the body in my stairwell.

I knew how uncomfortable and dangerous a lockup with only emergency electricity would be. My only hope was that they wouldn't want to be adding to the population.

She climbed out of the car again a few minutes later. "A BOLO. Be on the lookout. Wanted for questioning on a homicide," she said. "And they said they always have room for looters. Especially during an emergency like this. They're sending backup."

I wanted to say I hadn't been looting and they had no reason to think I had been, aside from the cat collar, but keeping my mouth shut seemed like the smartest move.

Another car pulled up, this one a black Lincoln I was pretty sure I recognized. And it meant more trouble. I closed my eyes and fought down the urge to try to dash off between the garages and through the yard.

For one thing, I wouldn't get far. My hands were firmly cuffed behind my back. I had no place to go where I could expect anybody to help me. And I'd certainly be facing new fleeing and eluding charges that would violate my parole.

Detectives Belkins and Montgomery got out of the car and came over. As usual, Montgomery looked like he'd stepped out of the pages of a men's fashion magazine. Belkins looked like he'd slept in his clothes and just rolled out of bed.

"Well, well," Belkins said, a nasty grin on his pasty white face. "What have we here?"

Cunningham hefted the cat collar. "Caught us a looter."

Montgomery raised the chiseled eyebrows on his handsome dark face. "Looting. That doesn't sound like you, Jesse."

I took a deep breath. Good thing Montgomery was itching for a promotion. He was careful to handle situations so they wouldn't blow up in his face. He would be reasonable. It was my best bet for getting out of this dilemma.

"No, sir," I said.

Montgomery turned to Cunningham. "Did you actually see him in one of the houses?"

"No. But look at what he had in his pocket." He presented the collar.

Montgomery took it. "Interesting. Jesse, where did this come from?"

He would listen. And he knew my history. He just might accept the story. "It belongs to that group that had the church upstairs from my place."

He nodded. "The tabernacle cult or whatever it is?"

"Yes, sir."

"I thought they more or less disbanded when their leader got in so much trouble."

"I haven't seen them around lately."

"So you couldn't give them their bracelet—or whatever it is—back to them." He was feeding me the correct answer to give, and I appreciated it.

I shifted my weight from one foot to the other. "It's a cat collar. For that cat they thought was a goddess. Truth be told, I'd forgotten about it. I just found it in my apartment."

"And how is your apartment?" he asked.

"A total mess. Uninhabitable."

He nodded. "I've been by."

"I just went by to see if I could salvage anything. And I found the collar."

Belkins took an unlit cigar out of his mouth and spit on the ground. "Could be that one on the stolen property list they circulated just before the flooding," he said.

Montgomery looked at him with respect. "You read that?"

"Not really, but Carissa did." Belkins eyes glowed. He had a thing for Carissa. "She said keep an eye out for it. There's a big reward."

"A reward for a cat collar?"

"Yeah. Before the storm, Carissa was gonna do a story on it. It disappeared from a jewelry shop where it had been taken for a repair. Belongs to some rich hotshot's cutesy young wife. She's got some kind of exotic cat."

Montgomery shrugged and turned to Richards, who still held the black plastic trash bag as well as my wallet and keychain. "What else was in the bag?"

"A couple of cans of food and a frying pan and stuff," she said.

He turned to me. "So where are you staying?"

If I stayed any length of time in Mandy's carriage house, I'd have to register the change of address with the parole office. But I didn't want to bring her into this right now if I could help it. I said, "A night here, a night there."

"Not at your girlfriend's place?"

I shifted from one foot to the other. "She's mad at me right now."

He laughed. "Seems she's usually mad at you. What's the point?"

What, indeed. My throat closed up, and my eyes stung. I didn't dare try to say anything.

"She get over that whole thing about that guy who raped her?" he asked.

"That's not something a woman ever 'gets over,'" I managed to say. "Scars like that don't go away."

"I suppose that's true," Montgomery said. "She still think you had something to do with it?"

I shook my head. "I didn't, and she knows that. But I got to let her take her time with this. She wants me over there, I'll be as supportive as I know how. She needs space, I'll give it to her."

"And if she don't want you at all?"

I almost choked on the words, but I said, "Then I leave her alone."

Richards was looking at me. A slight smile played on her lips, and she nodded approvingly. Maybe, since she was a woman, she'd understand a little better than the men did.

"So what's she mad at you for now?" Montgomery asked.

Admitting I'd been drunk would be an invitation back to prison. I shrugged again.

Belkins had taken the collar and looked up from his examination of it. "Damon will never convince me that he didn't have something to do with that rape. Just like his type to do something like that."

"What 'type' is that?" Richards asked.

Uniformed patrol officers don't usually question detectives. Belkins looked up at her and smirked. "Criminal types. Murderers. They should abolish parole. They let these guys out after they kill the first time, and next thing you know, some other woman's been raped. And probably left for dead."

"That doesn't even make sense," Montgomery said. "Jesse's victim wasn't even a woman. It was a male drug dealer."

Belkins shrugged. "Violent criminals are violent criminals. They got no respect for anybody else. They take what they want, and given half a chance, they kill if they don't get it. Leave 'em locked up, if you ask me. Unless you execute them. Probably a better solution."

He was fingering the collar. "These real jewels?"

He answered himself. "I guess if there's a big reward out for it, they are."

Another car pulled up. This one was a puke-green electric hybrid.

I recognized that one, too. I closed my eyes and sighed. Carissa, the reporter for the *Rothsburg Register*. No doubt with a new camera. Once again, not good.

The thin blonde in a skimpy dress and high heels climbed out of the car. She was carrying a camera.

Belkins grinned. "Carissa! Good to see you. Where have you been?"

The woman tossed her head so her layered, highlighted hair flipped back from her face. Her lips pursed as she tilted her head at Belkins and simpered. "Working, Honeypot. You haven't called me."

Belkins and Carissa were an unlikely couple, but they'd connected somehow. Montgomery looked like he was going to say something about hotshots with cutesy young girlfriends, but he didn't.

"Haven't had a chance," Belkins said. "Take a look at this." He held out the collar. "Think it might be the one there's a reward out for?"

Carissa lifted the camera and began snapping pictures.

"Hey!" Montgomery reached over and grabbed the collar. "That might be evidence. If anybody takes pictures of it, it ought to be over at the evidence room at the station. Not a reporter from the newspaper."

Carissa sniffed and turned her camera on me. "Jesse Damon. What are you under arrest for this time?"

I wasn't going to say anything. I tried to turn so she couldn't get a good picture, but I didn't dare make any sudden moves.

Belkins stepped between us, which I hoped would have the unintended effect of blocking her pictures. "Damon can't talk to you now, Snookums. Besides, you know anything he says is likely to be a lie. How about after I get off, you let me take you out to dinner. Got to be someplace open. We can talk about it then."

Richards, standing next to me, made a disgusted snorting noise. I glanced over at her. Her nose was wrinkled, like she'd smelled something rotten.

"Be careful," Montgomery said. "Carissa's a newspaper reporter, Belkins. She has to wait for a press release. Or call and ask the information officer. We can't make a statement."

Belkins reached out and took Carissa's hand. "Oh, we know the rules. You wouldn't take anything I said as an official statement, would you, Snookums?" He raised her hand to his mouth and kissed it.

Carissa wiggled her shoulders, turned her head, and giggled. "Oooh, of course not! I wouldn't want you get in trouble over little old me!"

Richards shook her head and walked back toward the patrol car.

Montgomery opened his hand to look at the collar. "This the only thing he had?" he asked Cunningham.

He gestured at the black plastic trash bag on the ground. "That and what's in that bag."

"Really?" Montgomery looked at me and raised his eyebrows. "What else do you have, Jesse?"

Cunningham answered for me. "Some kitchenware and a few cans of food."

Montgomery smiled. "Some looting, Jesse. You couldn't find anything better than that?"

I shook my head. "It's stuff from my apartment. I was trying to see what I could still use."

"And that's when you found the cat collar."

"Yes, sir. The tabernacle people, they were using it for their cat. Supposedly she was their goddess or something."

"And what happened to the cat?"

"I took her over to Kelly's place. And her kittens."

"Does Kelly still have them?"

"Yeah. The kids really like them."

He opened the bag and dropped the collar into it. "So what are you doing now?" he asked.

I tried to come up with a reasonable answer. "I worked a partial shift at Quality Steel. They're hoping to open up Monday."

"Have you been doing anything else for money?"

I didn't answer directly. "They said I can collect unemployment for while they're closed. Not as good as working, but maybe enough to tide me over. But I don't think I have enough quarters in the last year to get it. "

"And will you able to move back into your apartment?"

"I doubt it. I'll have to see what I can find."

Montgomery tied the bag in a loose knot. "Red Cross'll help find someplace. If you need a place to stay."

I hoped it wouldn't come to that. "Yes, sir. I'll look into that."

"When were you over at your girlfriend's last?"

I tried to think. "Maybe two days ago."

Belkins stepped up. He was still clutching Carissa's hand. "What are you jawing about? There's a BOLO out for him. We got some serious questions to ask him. Ain't you gonna have him taken in?"

Montgomery nodded. "I think that would be best."

My heart sank.

"Well, ask if the uniforms can take him in. Or call for transport. We don't have a cage in our car."

"Officer Cunningham, can you transport the prisoner to headquarters?" Montgomery asked.

"Yes, sir, if you'd like."

"Thank you."

Carissa had pulled her hand free from Belkins and was busy with her camera again. I wondered if the *Rothsburg Register* printing facility was functional. And if I'd show up on the front page of the newspaper again.

"Shall I tell them looting charges?" Cunningham asked.

Montgomery shook his head. "We'll be right behind you. I'll take care of it when we get there."

Belkins chomped on his unlit cigar.

"He'll be charged with the murder of Aaron Stenski."

CHAPTER 18

Nobody said anything about Miranda rights, even though Carissa was right there and she was a newspaper reporter. On the other hand, nobody was going to ask me any important questions in front of her.

It didn't come as a huge surprise that they'd issued a BOLO for me for questioning about Aaron's death. Even though I'd been acting as if it would never happen, I'd been trying to dodge cops whenever I could, aware that it was only a matter of time before I was picked up. At my next parole hearing, if they hadn't found me before that. After all, he'd been found floating in my stairwell. I'd never made a secret of the fact that I knew he was a snitch and thought he was trying to set me up.

Cunningham took me by the elbow and escorted me to the car. He opened the door and moved aside so I could slide into the back seat. He held his hand up to shield my head from striking the door frame. Then he leaned in to secure the seat belt. He might be annoyed with me, but he was a professional.

It was a fairly new car, with molded plastic seats that had a cutout in the back of the seat so my cuffed hands weren't caught between me and the seat. A lot more comfortable than the old kind, especially if I ended up spending much time waiting.

But it was only a little while before Richards slipped into the driver's seat. Cunningham climbed in a few minutes later and put on his seat belt.

"You okay back there?" she asked.

They didn't usually care. "Yeah," I said.

The car crept out of the alley.

"What the hell's going on between that newspaper broad and that detective?" Richards asked.

I didn't know if she was talking to me, so I said, "You talking to me?"

"If you got any answers and you want to tell us."

"Well, she's a reporter with the *Rothsburg Register*. She thinks she's got a great career ahead of her, so she's trying to get some feature stories. She's done one on the Predators bike club, and she'd like to do one on me."

"And she thinks that detective's gonna feed her info?"

"She don't think it, she knows it."

"What does she do? Sleep with him?"

"I imagine she does. Hell, she wanted me to take her to the Predators' clubhouse, and when I told her no, she offered to put out for me."

Cunningham laughed. "And did you take her up on it?"

I grinned. "No. I may not look like much, but I got my standards."

Richards chortled.

It was only a short distance to the police station. They pulled the car into the enclosed area marked "Prisoner Reception" and stopped the car.

Of course, I had to wait for Richards to open the door and lean in to undo the seat belt. She stepped aside to let me slide out, grabbing my arm as I stood up.

Montgomery was already waiting by the intake counter as we entered. Belkins was nowhere in sight. Nor, thankfully, was Carissa.

"Take him up to an interrogation room when you're done with him," Montgomery said. "I have a few things I have to check on. This communication slowdown is a real hassle."

I was frisked again and surrendered my jacket, steel-toed boots, and belt. I hoped someone had brought in my wallet and keychain and they'd all end up in the same property bag.

Then the handcuffs were snapped back on, this time in front with a waist chain, and I was escorted up a flight of steel stairs to an interrogation room. I was glad no one had decided I presented enough of a risk to require leg irons; climbing stairs with my ankles shackled was a skill I hadn't managed to acquire in twenty years of assorted tries.

I was deposited in a battered chair in front of an equally battered table. The room had battleship-gray walls with a large "window" on one side, which I knew very well was a one-way mirror. I would be under constant surveillance. There was undoubtedly a camera I didn't see recording every minute.

I didn't have long to wait before the door opened and Montgomery came in. He rested his butt on the edge of the table. My stomach knotted up. Montgomery was a good interrogator, and I knew I was well out of my league trying to keep up with him. He'd be careful, since he didn't want to bring a case that fell apart in a courtroom, especially if it was one that had attracted a lot of publicity.

And a second set of murder charges for a paroled murderer was likely to be big news, even though there was no longer a death penalty in Maryland.

I could only hope it wouldn't go that far, but I didn't have a lot of control over that.

The door opened again, and I could smell the stale whiskey and cigar before I caught sight of Belkins.

My throat closed up, and I had to force myself to breathe. Belkins wasn't too fussy about his interrogation methods. He thought once a murderer, always a murderer. He had no sympathy. There was no point in me trying to tell them I hadn't really killed anyone. My record said different.

He stationed himself behind me. The back of my head itched, waiting for an impatient smack if he didn't like my answers.

And no way would he like my answers.

"So." Montgomery looked at his manicured nails. "What can you tell us about Aaron Stenski?"

"That he's dead?" I said.

He nodded. "How did you know that?"

"Well, Belkins—Detective Belkins, he said you were bringing me in to charge me with murder. Of Aaron Stenski. So he must be dead."

Montgomery arched his well-groomed eyebrows. "Yes, he did say that, didn't he?" He glared over my head at Belkins. "Had you known before you heard him say that?"

How much should I let on I knew? It was always a problem. Tell him too much, and it led to other problems. But try to hide some of the truth, and he'd get me all twisted up in what I said and then turn it against me. I was sure this was being recorded.

If I refused to answer, he would tell Mr. Ramirez, my parole officer, that I wasn't being cooperative. That might end up in a parole violation hearing, and I could be returned to prison for my backup time. Almost another twenty years. That thought made my brain freeze.

"Not really," I mumbled.

Montgomery spread his hand in front of him and looked at his heavy ring with its green stone. "What do you mean, not really?"

I shrugged. "I hadn't seen him for a while. But I knew he was missing."

"How'd you know that?"

How indeed? Did Montgomery know about the little scene with Benji? Probably, if he'd been investigating Aaron's death. And if he didn't, he'd find out about it soon enough.

I took a deep breath. "He was supposed to be minding his kid brother, Benji. But he left the kid in his truck, down by the park. For hours. Even for Aaron, that was pretty irresponsible. If he could get back to the kid, he would have. So something must have happened to him."

I was babbling. I clenched my teeth to keep my mouth shut.

"And you know this how?"

I took a deep breath. "Benji got scared and came by my place. I found him sitting on the stairs when I came home from work."

The same stairs where they found Aaron's body floating. But I didn't volunteer that.

Montgomery picked an invisible bit of lint from his dark gray trousers. "Why would Benji go to your place?"

"I dunno."

He stood up. Montgomery towered over me. "Guess."

I shrugged. "It's all the way across town from where he lives, but he knows where I live. Or at least, where I used to live."

"Why do you say 'used to live?'"

"Have you seen the building?" I said.

Of course he had. He'd said as much.

"It got flooded out pretty bad. I can't live there now. Not unless they get it fixed up. And that'll take a while."

Montgomery took a step back. "And do you think Benji knew where you lived because he'd been there before?"

"Maybe. Not inside, but maybe outside."

"And why would he have been to your place?"

"I dunno. Aaron came by a few times. He might have had Benji in the truck." I was grasping at straws.

"And why did Aaron come by? To see you?"

There was no good answer to that. I just shook my head.

Belkins spoke from behind me. "To buy drugs?"

I tensed more, if that was possible. "No."

"You use, don't you?"

"No."

"But you deal."

"No."

Belkins coughed. "Judges always come down harder on dealers who don't use. They're in it to make money, not to support their own habit." He leaned in close. "Again. What do you use?"

I tried to move away from his whiskey and cigar breath, but I couldn't. "I don't deal. And I don't use. You can test me."

"You probably aren't just smoking an occasional joint. Stuff you use, it's probably out of your system by now. And the storm's interrupted distribution. So you might test clean."

"I ain't had a haircut since I hit the street. You can do that hair test thing." If they really decided to do that, they'd probably have my parole officer order it, and I'd have to pay for it. Still, it would be worth it if it convinced them I wasn't using.

Belkins straightened up. He kept his eyes on a piece of paper in his hand. "Bath salts, maybe? K2? Something like that, not illegal, but for sure not innocent. That doesn't show on standard tests."

This was going nowhere. I gave up trying to respond to his comments.

Montgomery just sat back and watched.

The silence grew. I was familiar with that technique. Most people can't stand too long a silence and feel compelled to say something. I had all the time in the world, and they had lives. I knew I could outwait them.

Belkins was the one who got restless. "So tell me about this kid, Aaron's brother."

"Benji?"

"If that's his name."

I could play the game on this level. "It is."

"So tell me about him."

"What about him?"

Belkins grimaced impatiently. "Why did he come over to your place?"

"I told you. Aaron told him to wait in the truck. But he never came back."

"Over by your place?"

"Close enough." I moved my hands a bit, trying to keep the blood circulation going in them.

"Close enough for what?"

"Close enough for Benji to walk over to my place."

Belkins leaned in close again. "This was when?"

"Friday morning."

"Why did he come to your place?"

"I dunno. He needed help. He said Aaron had pointed out where I lived to him."

"Doesn't that strike you as a strange thing for Aaron to have done?"

"Yeah. But Aaron does lots of strange things." I was careful to use the present tense. Even if I knew he was dead, I wanted it to seem like I hadn't fully absorbed that fact.

Belkins's hot breath was on my face. "Especially if he's buying drugs from you, and this is his kid brother."

I decided not to go into the meth Aaron had given Benji, so I just didn't respond.

"Damn it. Tell me something." Belkins slammed his hand down on the table in front of me. It was unexpected, and I jumped. Next time, was the blow going to land on my head?

Montgomery probably was concerned about the same thing. He got up and stepped between us. "Where did you see Benji?" he asked.

I'd already told them that. They wanted to see if I would be consistent. I said, "On the steps down to my apartment."

"He was hanging out in that stairwell?"

"Yeah. He was sitting on the steps when I got home from work."

"The same stairwell where Aaron was found floating?"

"Yeah." Damn, he'd gotten me. I hadn't planned to let on that I'd known that Aaron was dead, much less where his body was found.

Montgomery leaned in. His breath smelled of minty mouthwash. "And how did you know where Aaron's body was found?"

I shrugged. "I came by to see if I could get some of my stuff out of there before it all got soaked. There was an ambulance and a couple of squad cars there."

"So what did you do?"

"I watched."

"They didn't notice you?"

"I kind of hid in a store entrance."

"What store?"

"I dunno. Most of them are closed. I could probably pick it out if it's important."

"So what did you do then?" he asked again.

I closed my eyes. "I just left."

"Did you know it was Aaron?"

"Not for sure, but I thought it might be."

"Why was that?"

"Well, he'd kind of disappeared. And the body was wearing a bright orange vest. Just like the one Benji had. He told me they hadn't been home in a few days, and when he said he was getting cold, Aaron bought them these matching vests."

"You had reason to resent Aaron Stenski, didn't you?"

"Well, he sure wasn't my best friend. But I didn't kill him."

"Why was he not your 'best friend?'"

Angrily, Belkins shoved the table a few inches.

"Why are you bothering with this nonsense? We all know Damon's a murderer. We all know Aaron was a druggie who had his fingers in any dirty deal he could manage. Including Damon's CDS distribution schemes. Why wouldn't Damon kill him?"

Montgomery raised his eyebrows. "We don't know Jesse was involved in any CDS distribution schemes. There's no evidence."

"Who the hell needs evidence? He's a paroled convict. He'll do anything he thinks he can get away with."

"Even if we were sure that was true, we can't take that to the district attorney."

"Maybe not. But all we got to do is dig a little deeper, and we'll find the evidence. Or…" A mean smile crept over Belkin's face. "Get a confession out of him and make him sign it."

Montgomery got to his feet and took Belkins by the elbow. "Come on out in the hallway and talk to me for a minute."

He turned to me. "I'll be back in a little bit, Jesse. Just wait here."

What else did he think I was going to do?

They left, and the door closed behind them.

Well aware that the wait could stretch into hours, I leaned back in the chair, trying to make myself as comfortable as possible. My hands were still cuffed to the chain. What was it about having such limited use of my hands that made my nose itch? It never did any other time. I closed my eyes and made a conscious effort to relax my muscles.

I must have actually dozed off.

The door opened, and I awoke with a start. A uniformed officer had entered the room.

"Come on," he said to me.

Stiff, I struggled to my feet. "Where're you taking me?"

He shrugged. "Just following orders. Bring you back downstairs."

I expected him to deposit me in a holding cell, but he led me to a bench that extended along a wall with eyebolts set at regular intervals in the wall. Several other men were waiting on the bench, each with his hands raised above his head and chained to an eyebolt. He unlocked the waist chain and indicated an empty space on the bench. "Sit." I did so. Threading the chain through an eyebolt, he locked it again, leaving me with the others.

They were all wearing shoes. My feet felt very naked and vulnerable in nothing but socks. It took an effort not to keep them curled up under the bench where no one could step on them.

The guy next to me was crying. That wasn't going to do much good. His nose started to run. He tried to wipe it on his sleeve, but that wasn't very effective. His breath came in big gulps.

"Waiting to be processed?" I asked him, trying to get him to calm down a bit.

"I guess. They get you looting, too?" he asked, his voice strained.

I considered. "They may think they did. But I doubt that charge would stick."

"What's going to happen to us?" the guy, hardly more than a kid, wailed.

"I dunno. Just got to wait and see. It's not like we got a whole hell of a lot of control over it right now."

He nodded. That couldn't have been much comfort, but it did seem to settle down his panic.

Every once in a while, a uniformed officer would come out, get one of the men off the bench, and they would disappear through the doorway.

My turn would come. Eventually. I shifted on the bench, trying to ease the strain on my arms and shoulders.

"Jesse Damon?"

My turn came sooner than I'd expected. "Yes, sir?"

The officer came over and unlocked the chain. "Come on."

I stood up. He just held onto the chain, not slapping it back around my waist. That made it a bit awkward for me to move ahead of him as he escorted me out the door. It slammed shut behind us, and the lock clicked.

We stood in front of the desk at intake. He unlocked the cuffs. "Go pick up your stuff from the property room," he said.

I stood there stupidly. "What?"

He shook his head. "Get your stuff from the property room and leave."

"I'm free to go?"

Eyeing me, he said, "We sure don't want to keep you if we don't have to. We don't have any beds, the food supply's low, and any staff that lives across the river is having trouble getting to work, so we're shorthanded. Yes, you're free to go."

He didn't have to tell me that another time. I got my stuff—it was all there, minus the cat collar. I hadn't expected that to be there, and I'd be just as happy if I never heard anything about it again.

CHAPTER 19

My boots laced up tight and my possessions back in my pocket, I walked away from the county complex, fighting the urge to break into a run. That was likely to get me back sitting on that bench again.

As I passed by the church that only offered sanctuary to its members, I had to step around some boxes strewn across the sidewalk. Each box was exactly the same, with a picture of a little girl spooning something into her mouth. A box truck with big letters that said "Food Bank—Until Hunger Ends" on its side was parked next to the curb.

A few teenagers were struggling with boxes. One girl had a slipshod pile stacked up on a hand truck and tried to push it over the curb. All the boxes tumbled off.

I went over and took the hand truck. "You can't go frontwards like that," I said, restacking the boxes, this time in a more stable arrangement, on it.

"Watch," I said, as I pushed the hand truck forward a bit, put my foot on the brace, tipped the handles back toward me, and eased it backward up over the curb. "Where do you want these boxes?"

She indicated a side door. "We're setting up an emergency food bank."

Under the circumstances, that was a good idea. I wondered if they'd let me take some for Kelly. They'd be more likely to if I helped out. And I didn't really have anything better to do.

The truck driver was taking pallets off the truck and setting them on the street. A gangly teenage boy was using a box cutter to slice open the shrink wrap.

I stacked another bunch of boxes on the hand truck and took it inside. Since it was obvious to everyone, including the old guy in charge, that I could handle it much more efficiently than anyone else, they set about sorting the boxes and cleaning up the debris.

We hefted the unloaded wooden pallets into the back of the truck. The driver slammed the door shut and drove off.

When the truck was gone, I glanced across the street. There was an all too familiar black Lincoln sitting next to the curb, with Detective Montgomery in the driver's seat, watching me.

My gut clenched into a knot, I loaded up the hand truck one last time and took it inside.

"Look, I got to go," I said to the guy in charge. "Any way I could get some food for my girlfriend and her kids?"

The guy looked at me. "I don't see why not. Each box has a fairly balanced diet for one day for two people. But a lot of it has to be cooked."

"When I was over at her place, her power was on."

"Okay. I do have to get some information from you for the agency." He reached for a clipboard.

My gut twisted further. What kind of information would he need? What would happen if I lied?

"How many in the family?" he asked.

"Three. Four, if you include me."

"How many children under the age of eighteen?"

"Two."

"Anyone over the age of sixty?"

"No."

"Male or female-headed household?"

"Female, I guess."

"Race white?"

That question again. I didn't have any better an answer than I'd had before. So I said, "Yeah."

He nodded. "Standard distribution is four boxes, then. Two days' food for the family."

"Is that all you need to know?" I asked.

"Yes. The agency isn't concerned with individual identities, just the demographics."

One of the girls found a couple of sturdy plastic shopping bags. I put two boxes in each bag and said, "Thanks."

I saw no way to leave that wouldn't send me out on the street in front of where Montgomery was waiting. Taking a deep breath, I picked up the bags and left.

Avoiding looking toward the car, I headed down the street.

The car pulled up next to me. The window rolled down. "Jesse, get in."

What had I expected?

The door lock clicked.

"Put your bags in the back seat and get in."

The passenger seat was empty. At least Belkins wasn't with him.

"Up front?" I asked. Putting a detainee in the front seat wasn't safe. On the other hand, he wasn't searching me and putting me in handcuffs.

He reached over and opened the door. "Yes, up front."

Maybe I wasn't a detainee.

I did as he said. He locked the doors and nosed the car away from the curb.

"So," he said. "What have you got in the bags?"

"Emergency food boxes from that food bank. For Kelly and the kids."

"I thought Kelly was mad at you."

"She is. And she don't like to take help. Charity, she says. But the kids need to eat."

He looked thoughtful. "Suppose we go through the McDonald's drive-through and get some coffee?" he said.

We both knew he didn't have to do that, or ask me if he did want to do it, but I appreciated the gesture. "Okay."

When we had the coffee, he pulled the car into a parking space at the empty back of the lot. "I've got a few things I'd like to ask you," he said.

I took a sip of my coffee.

"You know Aaron's brothers?" he asked.

"His little brother Benji? Yeah. I told you about him. Do you know if he's making out okay?"

"I talked to him. He confirmed pretty much what you told us. He's back with his mother."

I wasn't sure that was "making out okay," but it was the best he was likely to do.

Montgomery hadn't touched his coffee. "What about his older brothers?"

"I might know them a little."

"Do you know their names?"

"Jumbo George and Nick is all I know."

He nodded. "And do you know if they were up to anything with Aaron?"

"Not really."

"Have you heard anything about the father dying and leaving a substantial amount of money?"

"Something about that."

"A lot of it to Aaron?"

"Yeah, well, the old man bought Jumbo George that building he's got his head shop in and Nick his Peterbilt Cabover. So I guess he figured Aaron was due something, too."

"Really? I hadn't known about the building and the truck."

I shrugged.

"Do you know who runs the amphetamine trade around here?" Montgomery asked me.

"Bikers."

"Yep. Predators. Aaron hang around them much?"

I didn't know what to say. I settled on: "Some."

"Truckers use a lot of that, when they're trying to make time. Keeps them awake. Aaron have anything to do with that?"

I considered possible responses and said, "Might have."

"His older brothers?"

"Might have."

Montgomery's hands tightened on the wheel. "Especially the one who's a trucker?"

"Yeah."

He started the car. "Shall I run you over to Kelly's?"

"If you don't mind."

"Just so you know," Montgomery said as he drove, "I don't think you were responsible for Aaron's death. I don't know yet whether it's a coincidence he ended up in your stairwell—that doesn't seem possible— or an attempt to set you up. You got any enemies?"

I chuckled. "Which set?"

"At work, especially."

I thought about Diffy. "You mean like somebody who might be trying to get me in trouble?"

"That, and trying to divert attention from what they're doing."

"Like wrecking the lift that's signed out to me so everybody's paying attention to that?"

"Perfect example."

I slumped in the seat. "So maybe there were a couple of reasons why somebody'd want Aaron dead."

"Who do you have in mind?'

I found it hard to form the words. "Somebody who might inherit more money. And who was getting worried that the CDS distribution system he'd set up for his buddies, other truck drivers, was becoming too big to keep hidden anymore."

I stared miserably at my hands. If I didn't give him something, he'd stop playing the good cop. And I'd be on my way back to prison, maybe with a whole sheaf of serious new charges. Like murder. "Look," I said. "Maybe it's too late. But if I was you, I'd get a warrant to search Jumbo George's place."

"Jumbo George's? Not Nick's?"

"Nick stays there sometimes."

"The head shop?"

"Not the head shop. The apartment upstairs."

"That's rented out."

"There's a front one and a back one. The back one you get to from some stairs inside the shop. That's where Nick stays sometimes."

"Really."

I shrugged again. "Yep."

"I'll do that. You got anything else to tell me?"

I shook my head.

"That's a beginning," he said.

We pulled up in front of Kelly's house. I waited for him to tell me I could get out.

"One more thing," he said.

"Yeah?"

"That cat collar thing?"

I hoped this didn't have anything to do with me. "Yeah?"

"You remember there was a reward?"

"Yeah." Fat chance they'd consider giving it to me.

"I figure you get it."

"You shitting me?"

"No. I filled in the form and put your name in as the one who turned it in to the police. Mind you, I may have been a little less than, shall we say, accurate in just how voluntary the return was, but you did get it back to us."

"Wow. You think I'm gonna get anything?"

"I think you're going to get five thousand dollars."

I felt lightheaded. "Five thousand dollars?" That was an unimaginable sum. I paused. "How much is your cut?"

Montgomery laughed. "You've been hanging around those low-life buddies of yours too long. I don't get a cut."

I sat there. I wasn't going to believe this until I cashed the check.

"Are you going to be where I can find you if I need to talk to you again?"

"I'm not going far."

"You going to stay here at Kelly's?"

"She's probably still pretty mad. I don't think she wants me to stay here."

"So the food's a first-step peace offering?"

"Kind of. She'll take it for the kids."

"So where will you stay?"

I didn't want to let him in on the possible arrangement with Mandy and Nicole. If I did end up staying there, I'd have to tell the parole office, but until then, I wasn't going to say anything. I thought for a minute.

"Well," I said, "I'm not going over to Jumbo George's for a while."

He laughed. "Good plan. You stay there?"

"I did a few nights. But I'll find someplace else for now."

"When do you go back to work?"

"I'm hoping they start up midnight Sunday. For the Monday shift. That's what they were supposed to do."

"Between that and your appointment with Mr. Ramirez, I don't think you'll be too hard to find if I need you."

"No, sir."

"And if you know what's good for you, you'll stay away from the bikers."

"Yes, sir."

"Go ahead and see how mad Kelly is with you."

I took the bags and went up on the front porch.

Before I even got to the door, Chris threw it open. "Jesse!" he shouted.

"Hi, there," I said. "Something wrong?"

"Mom's been trying to figure out how to get in touch with you."

Uh-oh.

I heard Montgomery drive away.

"You know what your mom wants me for?" I asked Chris. I could just drop off the boxes and take off.

"Mom!" he called.

Too late.

Kelly came out of the kitchen. She didn't look me in the face. "Just the person I wanted to see," she said.

I tried to be noncommittal. "Yeah?"

"I wanted to know," she said, "if you'd stay with the kids tonight? I found an AA meeting I'd like to go to."

"Of course." I reached out and gathered her into my arms. "Anytime."

ABOUT THE AUTHOR

KM Rockwood draws on a varied background for stories, among them working as a laborer in a steel fabrication plant, operating glass melters and related equipment in a fiberglass manufacturing facility, and supervising an inmate work crew in a medium security state prison. These jobs, as well as work as a special education teacher in an alternative high school and a GED teacher in county detention facilities, provide most of the background for novels and short stories.

www.kmrockwood.com